I0653695

Angel Ink
Concrete Angels MC, Book 3

Siobhan Muir

DEDICATION

Dedicated to Catharine Lindsey, reader, fan, and lover of
Archangel Michael. Thank you for your encouragement and
patience while waiting for this story. I hope you love Michael's tale.

ACKNOWLEDGMENTS

Writing a book is never really a one-person job, and writing a series is especially difficult alone. Keeping track of details is so much easier when you have help. Not only does it take a great deal of hard work, editing, and research on the part of the author to get things correct, but without help, there'd be a lot more mistakes.

Great thanks to Paige Prince for crossing my Ts and dotting my Is, and for editing this story after the writing spanned a couple of years. Huge thanks to Josh McLees for keeping me on task and helping me show this story off to the best of his abilities. And great thanks to Bianca Sommerland for designing the cover.

Thanks also to the following readers who helped me choose the best tagline for this tale: Denise Callaway, Mary Decker, Patty Dump, Sandie Engle, Tammy Kreis, Emily McCay, Stephany Miller, Becky Parsons, Bianca Sommerland, Jennifer Thibeault, and Diane Nialis Vice.

As always, great thanks to my readers for cheering me on. Y'all make my writing worth the detailed effort.

CHAPTER ONE

Haley

I stood in the art wing of the Denver Museum of Nature & Science and tried to smother a yawn as the curator droned on about the new exhibit featuring rising-star artist Austen Powyrs. *Eye-roll to his name.* Must have been a 90's child. From what I could tell the guy basically used light and dark shapes like Bob Ross with his happy trees and Thomas Kinkaide with his sparkly lights, but not nearly as well.

Dude, my holiday cards were better.

I took a few shots of the curator, the crowd of press, and the art, but my attention wandered. This was a frickin' fluff piece to make the Fort Collins Bugle look good. *And get me off their backs looking into the story I want to write.*

Damn, I was bored with writing fluff pieces. To be honest, I wanted to run through the vaulted rooms of the museum screaming, "Let It Go" at the top of my lungs. *Maybe with a cute, long-haired electric guitarist following along.* It would definitely be more exciting than this story.

A scuffle in one of the side rooms drew my attention and I slipped to the entrance to see what was going on. A tall guy with angelic features around his large nose and wearing a leather cut ran through the room, but paused in front of a painting with light filtering through an autumn forest. For just a moment, I swore I saw huge black wings rising up behind him.

He met my gaze and darted to me before he grabbed me by the strap of my camera bag, pulling me to his chest. He planted a hot and stunning kiss on my lips. I dropped my jaw and his tongue slid along mine, electrifying me more than the long-haired guitarist in my fantasy. I tasted cinnamon rolls and hot coffee before he pulled back with a wild smile.

"I saw wings." Okay, not the best response to a sexy kiss.

"Don't worry, love. It's an illusion."

And then he was gone.

I stood there, completely non-plussed and out of words for the first time in my life, only barely registering the rest of security streaming past me. It took me several minutes to get over the kiss and the scent of the man who'd laid it on me. He'd smelled like freshly baked bread with a hint of rosemary and basil. They reminded me of safe, comfortable places where I'd always had enough.

My cellphone rang, bringing my attention back to the room. The art and people around me came back into focus like hoodoos reappearing as the fog retreats from the lowlands. *Hell, a lot of them look like hoodoos.*

"Haley Michaels."

"Hey Hale, how's it hangin'?"

I sighed. My best friend and co-conspirator Tori Lindhurst did a lot to make me smile, but I didn't need her distraction.

"Hey, Tori. I'm just at the Denver Museum getting the "scoop" on that hot new artist in town."

"Blergh. That sounds as fun as watching paint dry. It's almost over, right?"

"Yeah." I frowned. "Why?"

"Because I got something cookin' that's right up your alley. Remember the story about the dead FBI agent found after the big summer forest fires?"

"Yeah…"

Tori squealed her excitement. "I found out where he'd been working undercover, and who he'd been working for. And it wasn't the FBI."

"What?" I barked the word and winced when people shot looks my way. "Are you going to tell me more? Or just tease me, then let me die of curiosity?"

"Take me out to get a mocha, and I'll dish it up. Soonly!"

I gaped and got my ass moving. None of the other members of the press paid me any mind as the museum curators tried to placate them after security had run through. *After the baked goods guy.* What the heck had he been doing there? Despite his overwhelming presence, he hadn't been carrying any stolen goods that I could tell. Why had security been after him?

I shook my head as I pushed out the front doors into the blustery, frigid February morning. *Fuck, it's cold out here.* We'd had a cold snap so sharp that everyone dressed like marshmallows just to walk to their cars. I sped up my steps so I didn't have to withstand the icy wind shooting down the funnel of the Front Range.

The relative heat of my car's interior made my shoulders loosen as I slammed the door shut and cranked the engine. No matter what people said about those late model Subaru Outbacks, they'd run forever when taken care of. I never missed an oil change or maintenance checkup. I'd drive that baby into the ground before I gave it up.

The wind threatened to push me off the road as I drove north up I-25 toward Fort Collins. All this used to be farm land and ranches, but as Denver grew to engulf Brighton,

Thornton, Longmont, and Loveland, it turned into one long city. It was great for having places to go and things to do, but it made traffic hell. I only came down to Denver when necessary or for the airport. Otherwise, I preferred Fort Collins.

I lived on the west side up against the mountains in what used to be old student housing for Colorado State University. Campus had moved three blocks south of my street and had sold off the old apartments. All the partying had gone with it and my apartment building became secluded and quiet. The offices for the Bugle sat on Harmony Road in downtown Fort Collins and our favorite coffee shop, Jitters, was located just around the corner. I found a place to park and hurried into the heated shop, sighing at the scents of ground coffee and fresh bagels.

Tori sat at a table near the window, her natural golden blonde tresses cascading artfully from beneath her knitted hat around an elegant scarf. She'd draped her fitted winter coat over the chair behind her and I was reminded just how ordinary I was. I was the dark to her light, the woman passed over as forgettable in Tori's brilliance. It was a good thing she had the job of print organization instead of reporting because I'd be out of a job faster than one could say, "pretty."

"Get your coffee and get over here. I have such a scoop for you." She grinned wide and her brown eyes danced with excitement. "Come on. I can't wait to tell you this."

"Okay, okay. Give me a minute to thaw. It's fuckin' freezing out there." I disrobed from my thick coat and draped it over the other chair. "I'll be back."

I headed for the counter and the scents of the baked goods made me think of the hot guy I'd seen in the museum. He'd smelled so good and made me hungry—but not necessarily for food. To make me a liar, my stomach growled and I grimaced. The barista winked at me, the freckles on his nose winking in the overhead lights, his smile warm. He'd been interested in me for a while, flirting when he took my order, but he'd never made the next move. I considered the possibility of asking him out, but the image of the dark-haired guy with the big nose crowded him out of my thoughts and I let the barista go.

I got my coffee and a bagel with garlic cream cheese and headed for Tori's table.

"Okay, I'm ready. What the hell is going on?" I sat down and fixed my gaze on her as I bit into the warm bread.

"So you know about the guy in the wildfires was an FBI agent and according to the ME's report, he died of a gunshot to the head."

I nodded. "Right, executed and left to burn."

"Right. Well, it turns out he was supposed to be undercover in the Concrete Angels Motorcycle Club, getting the dirt on them for the FBI."

I nodded again. The Concrete Angels MC was a club local to the Fort Collins area and were rumored to be into everything from drug and weapons sales to money laundering and racketeering. But no one could ever get any dirt on them because they also donated to charities, paid taxes, and protected the weak.

Good Samaritans with a kick.

A memory surfaced of bikers wearing cuts bringing in a whole bunch of women and kids to the Hopeful Heart Shelter. I don't know why I thought they were bikers— none of them rode Harleys, but their leather jackets all had a gargoyle riding a bike with flaming wheels and they had "rough life" stamped all over them. I'd been there when they'd come in and helped get the kids settled, but didn't pay more attention to them. Turned out the kids had been victims of the sex trade and they all appeared broken and defeated. It had taken a long time for any of them to recover from their ordeal, but I'd volunteered twice a week to help as I could.

For Jeff.

Snapping of fingers in front of my face made me focus on the present with a jerk.

"Earth to Haley, come in, please." Tori waved her hand until I looked her in the eyes. "Jeez, have you heard a word I've said? Where the hell did you go?"

"Sorry, I was thinking about Jeff." I grimaced as her expression softened and waved my hand dismissively. "Don't worry about it. He's doing much better now. What were you saying?"

"Okay, so this FBI Agent, Eisenburg is his name, was supposed to be undercover in the Concrete Angels, but he got his hand caught in the cookie jar for embezzling from them. Rumor has it they killed him for it, but the money didn't go to the FBI."

I blinked. "Wait, Eisenburg was undercover FBI, but he was skimming and not sending the money back to his bosses?" I shrugged. "I assume he was setting up a nest egg for himself. Why is this a big deal?"

Tori shook her head. "Do you think I'd tell you this over a crooked Fed's nest egg? Come on, you know me better than that."

"Kinda. Get to the punch line."

"Okay, okay, keep your bra on. Five months ago there was a big brouhaha over the US Marshal accusing the Fort Collins Police Commissioner of beating him up and taking bribes to destroy evidence." Tori warmed to her subject, her eyes flashing. "He took off and they chased him up into the hills where he drove off a cliff and died in a fiery crash. An investigation was started but the Commissioner, Daniel Ainsworth, had a heart attack and died en route to the hospital."

I frowned. "I remember that, but Ainsworth wasn't very old, was he? Somewhere in his late forties?"

Tori nodded. "Yeah, it was hinky all right, but

everyone passed it off as natural causes due to the stress of his job. They didn't bother with an autopsy and it was swept under the rug."

I tilted my head as I sipped my coffee. "You think someone killed him and made it look like a heart attack."

"No, my source does."

"You're the organizer for print, arranging stories on the page. How do you have sources?"

"Hey, just because I'm not a field reporter doesn't mean I don't have any skills at reporting."

"If you have such skills, why aren't you a reporter?"

Tori grimaced. "Are you kidding? I don't want to be outside if I don't have to. You know how fuckin' cold it is around here in wintertime? Plus, the pay is better as the print organizer and I'm anal-retentive enough to make the Bugle look fabulous every day. Even better than the Denver Post. Our paper is sexy."

I laughed and shook my head. "It is that. So what does a dead marshal and now a dead police commissioner have to do with the executed FBI agent?"

"It all comes back to the money."

I rolled my eyes. "Of course it does. Damn, people are so fuckin' predictable."

"Hey, that's how we have news, right?" Tori winked. "Eisenburg was embezzling but it wasn't going into his own accounts or the FBI's. My source said it was tracked to some offshore and blind accounts that seemed to go nowhere. But they also found a ledger which had a list not only of the accounts and the money, but also of names."

My heart rate went up. "What kinds of names?"

Tori mercifully didn't go for the sarcasm. "Crooked cops, FBI agents and US Marshals."

"Oh my glory. Was the marshal who died in the crash one of them?"

Tori shook her head. "No, he'd been trying to expose them, which is probably why they chased him off a cliff.

But Ainsworth was on the list."

"Holy shit. Where's this list now?"

Tori's lips curled in smug satisfaction. "I happen to have a copy of it, right here, right now."

You ever seen those commercials where the actors get this avaricious look on their faces and make grabby-hands motions? That was me in that moment, desperate for the story that would push me out of fluff pieces and into the world of real journalism. And if I could take down corrupt cops, too, I was all over it like white on rice.

"Are you going to give it to me?" I reached for the piece of paper she held but she pulled it out of my reach.

"I will, on one condition."

I narrowed my eyes. "What condition is that?"

"You have to introduce me to your hot cousin."

I frowned. "Which hot cousin? Jeff?" I shook my head. "He's not ready, Tori."

Her mouth flattened. "You told me he was bi."

"He is. But he was so badly abused, I don't know if he can stand to be around anyone who gives off the sexual vibe." He'd been seduced, held hostage by an abusive sexual predator, and I'd had to kidnap him to safety. He was the whole reason I volunteered at the shelter.

She smiled with satisfaction. "Come on. It's just a tiny meet and greet. Promise me you'll call and set up a time for us to meet him for lunch or something, and the list is yours."

I bit my bottom lip. I *really* wanted that list of names because I could start looking into the backgrounds of the people on it. But could I set my cousin up with Tori? Granted, he felt more comfortable with women after his ordeal, but that didn't mean he was ready for anyone sexually interested in him.

Jeff was beautiful, devastatingly handsome with clear light-brown eyes, golden brown skin, dark hair and a sensual mouth that brought out dimples when he smiled. He stood close to six-five with broad shoulders, narrow waist, and a physique most men paid trainers thousands of dollars for. But he was barely venturing out in public again after his sexual incarceration. I hadn't been able to help him during his ordeal so I put my time in at the shelter for sexual abuse survivors, helping others to make up for it. The shelter had helped rehabilitate him enough to start life over again.

"Tell you what, the best I can do is have you meet us for coffee this coming week. I'll see him Saturday and you can come along." I held up my hand at her enthusiastic look. "Keep in mind he's just now regaining his confidence being in public and you need to be cognizant of that. Don't push him for something he doesn't want, Tori. I mean it."

She gave me a winning smile. "I promise to be on my best behavior."

She handed me the list of names and I wondered if I'd made a huge mistake. Yeah, I wanted this story, but I also wanted to protect my cousin. Jeff had experienced the worst of human behaviors and he didn't need my overenthusiastic best friend pushing him for something he couldn't give. I thanked Tori for the list but kept my worries to myself.

CHAPTER TWO

Michael

"What the hell are you doing, Michael?"

Luke's voice intruded on my thoughts as I viciously scrubbed the kitchenette in my cabin. I resisted the urge to snap at him as I threw down the sponge and turned to face him.

"What the fuck are you doing in my cabin?" Okay, so I sucked at resistance.

"Damn, who pissed in your Cheerios?" My older brother raised a golden blond eyebrow as he tipped his head. "I mean, I'm not expecting rainbows and unicorns, but usually you're usually a lot more mellow. Someone piss you off?"

He could say that. After we took the victims of sexual assault and forced prostitution to the shelter, the fury over their hurts hit me at odd moments. I stared hard at the bubbles in sink, trying to find beauty and peace in their iridescent marbled surfaces as I strove to calm down.

"What do you want, Luke?"

He tried to look innocent. *Heh, the Devil innocent? Not likely.*

"Can't I stop by to see my younger brother?"

"Seriously, I don't need your poking. What do you want?"

Luke sighed as he ran his hand over the angel wing tattoo on the back of his bald head. "I just wanted to check on you. You haven't been yourself since you raided that makeshift brothel. I half expected to come in here and find everything painted black. What's going on?"

I sighed. Anger was exhausting, but I couldn't seem to shake it. "Nothing."

"Come on. We're not teenagers anymore." He smirked. "Come to think of it, we never were teenagers. That would've been fun. Can you imagine cruising the streets, lookin' at hot chicks?"

I snorted. "I suspect you've done that thousands of times already."

"Hey, no one ever told those kids to do shit like that, I just never bothered to rein 'em in."

I rubbed my forehead and reached for what was left of my legendary patience. "Why are you really here, Luke?"

He lost his smirk. "I really am worried about you. I've never seen you like this. You always bounce back. What happened?"

I dropped the sponge and turned on the water to wash my hands and rinse the sink. "I seem to have lost my faith in humanity." As his smirk widened, I held up my hand. "Don't. I don't need to hear it. I just don't understand how humans could do such horrible things to each other for the simple gain of money."

Luke frowned. "Come on. You've seen this for millennia. The powerful hurting and killing others for gold, land, hell, even water. They create wars just to make a buck. What makes this time any different?"

I shook my head. "I dunno. I guess I'm tired. Tired of battling the same shit, different century. Tired of comforting the victims of all these atrocities brought on by their own people. I'm tired of the love of money decimating everything around us."

"Are you listening to yourself, Michael? You're part of the Concrete Angels MC, a group that runs drugs and weapons to make money. Drugs and weapons hurt people every day. Isn't this a bit hypocritical?"

I scowled. "I joined Loki's crew to keep him in balance with you. We're two sides of the same coin and we balance out Loki's chaotic neutral. We balance the scales of action and consequence"

"Right, and without us, Karma wouldn't have anything to do. None of this has changed, but you're still pissed off. What gives?"

I sighed again and slumped into a chair, rubbing my face. "I don't know if I can keep doing this. It's all the same shit, day after day, year after year, without getting any better and nothing to look forward to. I think I'm losing faith in the world. Why defend people who seek destruction, pain, sickness, and the very atrocities they claim to abhor? What the hell am I doing here?"

For the first time, Luke wore real concern on his face. "Michael, you're the one who told me to look for the good things in times of darkness, and glory knows, I'm supposed to be the harbinger of darkness. But one thing my millennia of being the Devil has taught me is people only let the darkness rule for so long, then they rise up with light bright enough to blind. There's an ebb and flow to their love of light or dark. It's a cycle they have to learn from. Without the dark, they can't appreciate the light. And they totally need us both."

He reached out to grip my shoulder. "They need me to be the Dark One, the one they revile and blame for all the wrongs in the world, including their own choices. And they need you to be the bright, shining example of love, compassion, and determination that allows them to swing back the other way. You're not really fighting for them,

Michael. It's more that you're fighting to show them the very best they can be and how to vanquish their own inner demons."

I considered what he'd said, wondering who would fight my inner demons. No one knew my brother very well, though they claimed they had an insight into him. But only myself and a few others knew his secret. He'd been asked to take this role rather than "fell from Heaven" as the humans told it. And he'd accepted, with far greater grace than even I possessed. He'd become the Dark One everyone blamed, because he had the most compassion of all of us.

He tilted his head and narrowed his eyes. "I can't believe I'm asking you this, but isn't there some brightness you've seen that helps you find the good again?"

I opened my mouth to deny it when the face of the woman who'd taken the kids filled my mind. *Her name was Haley.* Like my big brother, she'd shown nothing but compassion to the child victims, listening to them as she led them through the shelter. She had a strength in her kindness and presence that called to me with a yearning I'd forgotten in all my millennia with humans.

"Ah ha, what just went through your mind?"

Damn Luke's sharp perception.

"Nothing."

Luke snorted. "Don't hand me that. I can tell when you're thinking of something good. You actually glow, you know that? Might want to tone down your grace a little when you think of...them. It's a them, isn't it?" He batted his eyes with excited delight. "Oooh, tell me about them. Tell me everything!"

I rolled my eyes and pushed him away. "Sod off, you wanker."

"Oh, no. Not after that reaction. I told you all about Angelina, now you have to tell me who it is that makes you find the light in the dark."

I didn't want to tell him about Haley, not until I knew her better myself. But Luke had a way of pestering people until they either threatened to kill him—which was never a good idea—or they gave in. I was stronger than most, but it was usually easier just to give him what he wanted.

I'd only met her once—and stole a kiss from her—but she'd seen my wings, which weren't normally visible. *Except to those who are our true mates.* True, other angels could see our wings, and sometimes the other Elder Races could see as well, but humans were usually oblivious. I'd originally blamed her momentary vision on my distraction.

I'd only been at the museum because we'd been tracking one of the cops on our erstwhile member Roy's list of Backlog members. He'd quit the Fort Collins PD and hired on as a security guard at the Denver Museum of Nature & Science. I'd managed to get one of Viper's little spy gadgets onto his phone, but he thought I was trying to pickpocket him when I put the phone back and that engendered the chase through the museum.

I don't know what made me kiss her. Maybe it was because I knew the goodness of her heart after I'd seen her take in those kids at the shelter. Whatever the reason, once I'd kissed her, I couldn't get her off my mind, and it worried me. She'd been there with the press, which meant she was a reporter of some kind. Not a good combination with a biker with dubious humanity.

"I don't really have someone." I shook my head and he dropped his chin with a dry look. "Seriously. I've never actually met her."

Luke laughed. "You know, your shoulders twitch when you lie. You should really try to curb that tell."

I scowled. "I'm not lying. I've spoken maybe three words to her."

"And?"

"What and? How do you know there's an and?"

"Because I know you. Have your doubts about your

worthiness of love totally derailed you?"

"What the hell has love got to do with it?"

"Hey, hell is my bailiwick, so let's just leave that out of it." Luke grinned and thumped my shoulder. "Love has *everything* to do with it. Well, at least to do with you."

My scowl deepened. "I'm the Archangel Michael, for glory's sake. I'm a warrior not a lover. The lover is Gabriel's role."

"And I'm known as the Devil in most circles, but we both know the truth. Or at least I do." Luke squeezed my shoulder. "It's okay to fall in love. Anyone would be lucky to win your heart."

I shrugged him off. "She didn't win my heart and I didn't win hers. She doesn't even know me."

"Well then." He gave me his best wicked grin. "That's the first thing we need to change."

I swallowed hard. When Luke wore that look, it usually meant things didn't go as expected or remotely well. At least, not for me, or the person he had in mind. I just hoped the woman I'd kissed wouldn't hate me for it in the end.

****

Haley

Tori had given me the list and I was all set to start researching the backgrounds of the people on it, but Carl had called and reminded me I'd promised to go with him to this Valentine's Day party filled with newsie movers-and-shakers. I hadn't wanted to go and I wasn't sure I wanted to be with Carl anymore, but I'd promised I stood by my word. There wasn't much integrity in journalists these days and I had to find something that made me stand out from my colleagues. *So I picked truth and honesty.* Not exactly the best qualities for a reporter who didn't want to be stuck writing fluff pieces.

So I stood alone at a Valentine's Day party, trying to avoid a predacious drunk guy and wishing I could just get home. At least I had the list of names of the crooked cops in this vast network in law enforcement. I damn near salivated with the idea of being home with my computer and my search engines.

Yeah, while I get to stand here and look like a stupid wallflower.

I stared at Carl, my soon-to-be-ex boyfriend as he cozied up to two women who had bigger boobs and more makeup than I did. He hadn't bothered to introduce me so I wasn't sure if they were the movers and shakers to whom he'd promised to introduce me, or just their main squeezes, but after his hands wandered to their asses, I didn't really want to meet them at all.

They might be high-priced hookers too.

Yeah, that wouldn't surprise me. Inching my way toward the buffet to escape the drunk guy who'd zeroed in on me, I tried to find a quiet corner. Or a phone. Or locate someone who might help my career if I talked to them. I slid past some women who gave me a once-over that said they didn't see much worth value and checked my phone.

Maybe I can call Tori to come pick me up.

Except the phone sat dead in my hand like a little sparkly paperweight. *No, no, no.* My phone couldn't be dead. I'd just charged it that afternoon, and I needed it to get out of this place. Carl was my ride and I couldn't rely on him. I glanced in his direction and grimaced. He was getting handsy with a redhead. I looked around for a phone in the room, but the drunk guy was still lurching after me like a bad B-rate movie zombie and I needed an escape fast.

And that's why they call them 'fire escapes.' I ducked out the emergency exit and closed the door, hoping zombie-guy wouldn't follow. Hopefully, I would be safe to find a quiet and calm place to think. *Since my phone's dead and*

I'm stuck here for a while.

I sat down on the cool concrete steps of the back stairs and rubbed my face with my hands. I swore I'd never put myself in such a position again, but there I was, sitting on some back staircase with nothing but my dress, my high heels, my phone, and what little privacy I'd found. *You're so dumb and trusting, Haley.* Which was pretty stupid considering I was supposed to be an investigative journalist.

Thank glory I didn't have my ID on me. *Of course, when they find your body, that'll make it harder to identify you.* Oh yeah, I was full of those cheerful thoughts. So much for getting into the holiday spirit.

I wrapped my arms around my chest and leaned my elbows on my thighs. I was safe at the moment. Despite the pounding bass coming through the emergency exit doors, the stairwell was relatively quiet. A little light filtered through the dingy windows from the street lights outside, but otherwise, it was dark. So far, no one else had found this little oasis of calm to have a quickie or a good cry. *Although I'm getting close to the second one.*

I'd come here with the guy I'd thought was my boyfriend. Carl had sworn it was going to be a fun holiday party with the YouPros—Young Professionals, the new millennium's Yuppies—of Fort Collins. In Denver. He'd said it was where anyone who was anyone would be at this time of year. *For Valentine's Day?* I hadn't really wanted to go, but he said I'd make contacts with the news corp. *He played you, Haley.* Yeah, it wasn't the first time. Eventually, I'd get wise.

I shoved the unhappy thoughts of the past away and scrubbed my face. I should've known there was something going on. Carl seemed to be getting twitchy, like a guy who'd been using something addictive. He'd also had the look of frenzied desperation, the kind of look on people jonesing for the next best thing, and I totally bought into it.

Right up until he started playing tonsil hockey with not one, not two, but three of the partygoers, one of them a guy. *Yeah, can't compete with that.* I was in the position of no ride, not enough money for a taxi to Fort Collins, and no understanding of where the hell I actually was. Yeah, I had my phone, but I couldn't tell anyone where to come get me. *I'm so fucked.*

I needed to find a way home, but that meant going back through the party to get out of the building. This staircase led to the basement, and there was no way in hell I was going down there. *Hello, serial killerville.* I pulled out my phone to check what time it was and remembered it was deader than a door nail. *Shit.* So much for GPS or calling the cavalry.

I bit my lip and considered the door I'd come through. I might be able to find a phone if I went back to the party. Hell, I could probably lift one off one of the guests and they'd never notice. Those old pickpocketing skills came in handy in the oddest times.

Sighing, I stood up and pulled my skirt back down to the proper length. Yeah, I'd be getting rid of this dress as soon as I got home. I hated when the fitted skirts rode up. *All right, Michaels. Let's do this.* I grasped the door handle and pulled.

Nothing happened.

"Are you fucking kidding me?"

I yanked on the door, but the latch held despite using all of my hundred and sixty-five plus pounds of weight. The door was locked and no one could hear me in the party. And my phone was dead.

"Oh my GLORY!" I slammed my hand against the door, hoping someone might actually hear me over the damn music, but no one came to check it out. "Fuck!"

Biting my bottom lip, I looked up the staircase. Maybe one of the other doors were unlocked and I could at least get back into the building. I memorized the floor number on the party's door and climbed the stairs to the next floor.

I was about to bang on it, but I paused when I heard what sounded like voices coming from the other side. Logically, it would've made sense to thump on the door and have them open it for me. But something made me pause. The voices weren't loud, but they didn't sound happy or particularly friendly. Maybe I didn't want them to know I was there.

This was confirmed a moment later when someone said, "You shoulda thought of that before you went up against Backlog. You was warned. Now you're gonna pay."

What the hell is Backlog?

Before I could peer up the stairs, I heard someone shout what sounded like, "No, wait! Don't!" Just before two gun shots rang out.

I gasped and froze, holding my breath. Not that they knew I was there, but I wasn't about to take any chances they'd notice me.

"All right, come on. Get his legs and throw him in the stairwell. They won't find him until we're long gone. And don't forget to police your brass."

Stairwell? Fuck! Whatever they were planning to do, it involved my stairwell and they were very likely to see me. *And shoot my unlucky ass.* Panic hit me in a wave and I backed away from the door, my shoes clattering loud enough to be heard over the party.

Swearing under my breath, I bent over and yanked off my heels before I padded down several steps and ducked under the curve of the stairs. I flattened myself against the wall as the door above me opened and light spilled into the stairwell. I didn't dare move as two guys dropped something heavy onto the steps, grumbling about the weight.

"Shit, did the guy have to eat all those frozen pizzas? He's fuckin' heavy."

"Shut up, Inky. Just make sure he's got no ID on him."

Inky snorted. "How's that gonna help? His fuckin' face is all over the newspapers and internet. Takin' his ID won't hide who he is."

"Maybe we'll get lucky and get some cops who *don't* know who he is."

"Yeah, right."

"Look, just clear his pockets and let's get outta here. I don't want any of those partiers findin' us here with him. Backlog says we got too much to do in prep for the big boss comin' to town."

"Yeah, yeah. Keep your shirt on." There was some rustling as they rifled through the body's pockets. "Okay, I think I got everything. Keys, phone, wallet, and Chapstick. No wonder his lips looked so soft."

"Eww, Inky, that's nasty."

"No, nasty is your lips, Tinder. There's no excuse for not keeping your lips healthy. You know the skin is the biggest organ on your body, right?"

Their voices faded as the door above started to close. Too late I realized that was my only ticket out of the stairwell with the dead guy. I whimpered with distaste and padded back up the stairs, hoping I'd be able to catch the door before it latched.

Turns out, I needn't have worried. The dead guy's foot had caught in the door, holding it open about an inch. I glanced down at the body's face as I made to pass it and stopped, my stomach dropping into my bare feet.

"Holy shit, that's ADA Patrick O'Donnell."

Inky had been right. Everyone knew Assistant District Attorney O'Donnell and they wouldn't need his ID to identify him. And I'd been present at the scene of his murder. *Without a functioning phone.* This night just kept getting better and better.

I had to find a way to both report on the ADA's death and get home anonymously because I couldn't do a damn thing about a dead guy in the stairwell. Whoever Backlog was, they were powerful enough to take out a famous ADA, and I didn't want them to find out about me. I crept up to the door and peered around the edge. The room beyond looked like a new office space with furniture wrapped in plastic and boxes of office equipment piled around. Nothing remained of the murder except some blood splatter on the floor and plastic wrap.

I reached for the door to pull it open but stopped. *Think forensics.* The last thing I wanted to leave were footprints or fingerprints. I used the heel of my shoe to pull the door open wide enough to slip through, careful not to step in any of the blood. I wanted to bolt toward the elevators, but I forced myself to go slow enough to miss smudging the evidence. *Forensics, forensics, forensics.*

I made it to the elevators and used the heel of my shoes to press the down button. *Take only mental pictures and leave nothing else.* Yeah, didn't have the same ring to it as the usual line, but I didn't want to broadcast my involvement. I put my shoes back on, the heels tight and cold, and stepped into the car. *Shit, how am I gonna press the floor number?*

I stood there a few moments, trying to decide when I remembered the party on the next floor down. Hundreds of people had pressed that floor number to get to it. Mine would be with everyone else's print on the button. Despite that reassurance, I used the hem of my dress to cover my finger as I made my selection.

I could hear the holiday music long before the doors opened and the volume blasted at me as soon as they did. I grimaced and stepped into the room, the party going full swing. *More so if the bra hanging from the overhead light fixture is any indication.* People were "dirty dancing" in the middle of the room where they'd pushed the furniture aside. Some were pretty good at it—*er, correction, those people might actually be having sex*—while others swayed drunkenly along the edges. One woman bent over, her shoulders heaving as she puked. On her knees. In some guy's lap? *Definitely not puking.*

Holy shit, I'd gone away for about an hour, and the party turned into a drunken holiday orgy while the ADA got murdered upstairs. Might as well have been the Nakatomi Plaza. *Yippee-kai-yay, mudfucker.* I spotted my "date" sharing a ménage with the man and women he'd been hanging around earlier and headed for the coat room. Was sex at a holiday party considered prostitution? I didn't really want to know. I had to find a phone.

I threw my coat over my shoulders and shoved my arms through the sleeves just as someone stumbled into me. *Two someones.* I lost my balance and fell into the mass of coats on the hangers, dropping to the floor. A high-pitched giggle was followed by the sound of a belt buckle coming undone and a drunken male grunt.

"Oh, yeah, baby. Whip out that man-meat."

They're not gonna—Never mind.

Another male grunt combined with a matching female grunt and the sound of bodies hitting the wall, rhythmically, filled the coatroom space. The scent of arousal mixed with alcohol perfumed the air and I rubbed my face with my hands. *I so don't need this.*

Gritting my teeth, I stood up and pushed my way through the coats. "Excuse me."

The woman squawked, which was pretty impressive since the guy had her damn near folded in half against the wall as he jack-hammered into her. He didn't even pause as I shoved past. leaving them to their conjugal relations as I returned to the elevators. I needed to get out of here and find a phone.

And a ride. How the hell was I gonna get home? *What I really need is a guardian angel.* I stepped onto the elevator and let it carry me away from the folks getting carried away upstairs. If the lobby didn't have a phone I could use, I'd go to the little convenience store across the street and beg them to call the cops.

When the elevator doors opened, I headed for the security desk as I checked to be sure I had my dead phone and my keys. Yeah, I didn't have a ride home, but I could get in when I got there. *I'm definitely done with Carl.* Maybe I'd break up with him over text message. Nah, that was low even if he deserved it. *I'll send him an email.* I couldn't help the smirk curling my lips as I slipped behind abandoned desk.

Where the hell is the security guard?

I shook my head and built up my gasping breaths as I grabbed the phone and dialed 911.

"Nine-One-One, what's your emergency?"

"Oh my gawd, oh my gawd, there a dead guy. I think he was shot. He's in the stairwell. Oh my gawd." I thought I sounded properly panicked as I turned my face away from the few security cameras I could see from the desk.

"Ma'am, I need you to calm down and tell me where you are."

"I was at a party. On the ninth floor of the Turner Williams Building downtown in Denver. I am calling Denver's emergency line, right? Oh my gawd. I heard him get shot and then they threw him in the stairwell."

"Okay, ma'am, I'm dispatching emergency personnel and police to your location. Just stay on the line while I get your name and number."

Oh hell no. They'd killed the ADA of Denver while mentioning Backlog. There was no way I'd give my name to anyone. But I'd make sure the cops knew all they needed.

"I was just going out for a smoke and I got locked outta the party, but then I heard the shots and the guy was thrown in the stairwell and now he's dead and bleeding and—"

"Ma'am, the police and emergency personnel are on

their way. Let's start with your name."

I had to admit the dispatch operator had a voice full of nothing but serenity and bliss. Or at least Ninja-level calm.

"Oh my gawd, someone's coming. They might see me. I gotta go." And I hung up with a satisfied nod.

I took my scarf and wiped down the phone so I didn't leave fingerprints—*Think forensics*—and slipped from behind the desk. I kept my face averted from the cameras but scanned the area for the security guards. Where had they all gone? Surely, they didn't take this long for a bathroom break.

I zipped up my coat and headed for the doors. I wasn't gonna wait around for the cops to show up and I didn't really need anyone remembering I'd been there. I doubted Carl would remember his first name by the time he was done with those people upstairs. I shook my head and wondered how I'd start the "Dear Carl" email.

Probably with, Dear Carl, it's not me, it's you.

I laughed aloud but cut the sound off the moment I stepped outside. My breath stalled in my chest as I came to an abrupt stop. My gaze landed on the man waiting for me on a black, opalescent Harley.

Holy moly, it's the guy from the Denver Museum.

He wore faded black jeans, a white scarf, and a black leather jacket with a gargoyle riding a motorcycle on it. The patch read SCHNOZ and I remembered those wise eyes and large nose. His eyebrows went up under his black brain bucket as he caught sight of me and my heart pounded for a completely different reason.

"What are you doing here?"

"I was about to ask you the same thing." His voice reminded me of warm fleece blankets and the comforting rumble of a well-kept engine.

How the hell would I answer that? I couldn't tell him it was an accident—hell, I'd been invited to the party upstairs. But it might start to look hinky if I told him about the dead body in the stairwell.

"I was at a Valentine's Day party and my date found someone else to hang with." I shrugged as I mentally broke up with Carl. It would be awkward going to work on Monday, but that was more on him than me. Again, I wished my phone hadn't died. The blackmail photos would've been to die for.

I bit my bottom lip. "Do you think you could let me use your phone to call someone to take me home?"

His dark eyes ran the length of me starting at my head, dropping to my feet and rising to my face. "I could. Or I could just give you a ride since I'm already here and we met at the museum." He winked.

"Where I thought you had wings." Only the Mojave Desert was dryer than my voice.

He shrugged and grinned. "I blame my cut for that. I am part of the Concrete Angels MC after all."

And I wished for a guardian angel to come get me.

His grin faded into surprise as if he heard my thought. "Anyway, I'm here. How 'bout I give you a ride home?"

I tilted my head and narrowed my eyes. "You might have kissed me at the museum, but that doesn't mean I'm gonna tell you where I live." I heard the sirens of the cops and took a couple steps closer to him. "But I will let you take me to a coffee shop or somewhere I can get something warm to drink. What do you say?"

I hoped my voice didn't sound too desperate, but I really wanted to get away from the Turner Williams building before the police showed up. He raised an eyebrow at my bold move and shot a look toward the sirens. My heart rate went up. Did he suspect I knew something about the sirens? Or that I was trying to get away from them?

Hell, he should be wanting to get away from them, too. When anything went wrong, the cops often blamed the dangerous-looking biker dudes first. *And hot damn, is he dangerous-looking.* Which was why my self-preservation mode wasn't sure which was worse for me, the cops or the biker dude.

"I might know a place that has good coffee. But it's Valentine's Day. Shouldn't your boyfriend take you somewhere nice?"

I barely stopped the grimace and shrugged. "What makes you think I have a boyfriend?" Especially since the man-whore upstairs wasn't getting anywhere near me ever again.

He shot me a half-smile. "A beautiful woman like you should be beating men off with a stick."

"Thanks for the compliment. Maybe it's my winning personality. Let's get out of here. I'd rather not be here when the cops arrive." I didn't wait for his invitation as I hiked up my skirt and straddled his bike behind him.

"How do you know the cops are coming here?"

I snorted. "Because I called them. Can we go?"

He laughed and the sound washed over me like springtime sunshine and hot tea. It warmed places that I hadn't realized were cold. I wrapped my arms around his waist and snuggled up to his back, trying not to enjoy the solidness of his body against my chest. *He's just a means to an end.* But that didn't mean I wouldn't enjoy the means.

The rumble of his bike's engine between my legs warmed me in naughty ways as he pulled away from the curb. The sirens and firetrucks rounded the corner behind us as we roared away and I ducked my head out of the wind. I was safe for the moment, even if that was just an illusion.

CHAPTER THREE

Michael

Haley cuddled up to my back and my cock roared to life between my legs. Which was a mean feat given how tight my jeans were when I sat on my bike. But I wouldn't trade her presence for comfort for love or money. I liked her wrapping herself around me, especially in the frigid wind of our ride. She smelled like sunrise and magic, both of which had ambrosia-like scents, and I was determined to enjoy them.

The cops never saw us leave—I made sure of it—but she didn't know that and I liked her closeness. She came out of the building just as I stopped in front and asked me for a ride. I couldn't have timed it better if I tried.

I'm gonna have to thank Luke for making this happen.

I just hoped she wasn't mentally scarred for life by whatever my brother had set in motion.

The snow-filled air whipped past our faces as I headed north on 287. She ducked her head to keep it out of the wind and I tried to hurry to our destination. I really wished I could take her back to the Concrete Angels' compound up above Fort Collins, but I thought it might be better for both

27

of us to talk on neutral ground.

Especially because if she comes in, I might not be able to let her go.

I found my favorite coffee shop and pulled into the parking lot. She didn't look up until I'd shut off the engine and pushed the kickstand down.

"Where are we?"

"One of my favorite coffee shops that's open late. You ever been to Jitters?"

Her eyes widened along with her smile. "That's my favorite coffee shop."

Pleasure bloomed in my chest at that small similarity between us. "Really? Then I guess I'm pretty lucky to have chosen it. Come on. Let's go in where it's warm."

I let her slide off the bike first before swinging my leg over. I offered her my arm to help her walk through the small drifts of snow already accumulating. I glanced down at her feet in elegant heels and wondered if I should carry her.

"Are you going to be okay in those shoes?"

She raised her chin and smirked. "Oh yeah, I'm a professional."

I laughed. "I meant in the snow."

"Yeah, but let's get inside quick."

I didn't have to be told twice. We hustled over the icy parking lot and she grabbed my arm a couple times as her heels slipped. I tried not to enjoy it too much, but her trust and touch made me want to strut, and I usually didn't have so much of an ego. I pulled the door open and helped her through before following. And my gaze slid down to her feet in those heels.

Aw hell, I better carry her back to the bike. And maybe make sure she was covered with my wings on the ride home because the weather promised to shift toward hard wind and heavy snow.

"Welcome to Jitters. What can I get you folks?" The

young man behind the counter smiled at Haley and damn near batted his eyes.

"I want a large coffee, please."

"Want me to leave room for cream?"

"Not this time. Just black, like my soul." She grinned as his eyes widened.

I waved with a grin. "I can vouch for her soul. Not nearly as dark." And I winked. The guy relaxed a little. "I'd like hot jasmine tea with room for cream."

"You take cream in your tea?" She widened her own glorious brown eyes.

"Yeah. Don't you?" I raised my eyebrows in mock amazement. "It's the proper way to drink English tea."

The young guy cleared his throat. "Can I get you anything else, miss?"

"No, that's it."

He nodded with a smile, scrawling her name on the cup in black Sharpie, and I narrowed my eyes. This guy knew Haley pretty well. He set the cup down and grabbed another, filling it with hot water before thrusting it at me along with a teabag. "Your water and tea. Cream is over there."

Nothing like service with a smile. "Thanks." I dug out my wallet but Haley waved her hand.

"I got this. My treat for the assist."

She gave me a grimace. I didn't know if her expression was for the need of rescue or the fawning way barista treated her, but I nodded and found a table near the window where I could keep an eye on my bike and the snow.

The barista took his time getting her black coffee— *how hard is it to fill a cup with coffee?*—and chatted her up until Haley gave him a patently false smile and walked away. I tried not to puff out my chest at her choosing me over him, but it happened anyway. *Dammit, I'm too old to be jealous.* Apparently not.

"Sorry. I've known Earl for a couple of months and he

thinks he needs to defend my honor or some such crap from the badass biker." She rolled her eyes as she gracefully settled into the chair across from me. "I get the impression he thinks I'm not actually here by choice."

"He's right about one thing."

"What's that?" She raised her eyebrows as she cradled the coffee in her hands.

"I am a badass biker."

She laughed, a sound full of delight and warmth, and my wings tingled though not even visible. *How in glory's name can she do that?* I'd never met another person who could literally ruffle my feathers, but Haley did it with just her laugh.

"So, tell me more about why you were out, alone in the snow, on Valentine's Day with a dead phone."

She blinked and sipped her coffee. "Damn, when you put it like that, it really does sound like I needed to be rescued."

I shrugged but my curiosity boiled over to find out what my brother Luke had engineered to get us together. *And on Valentine's Day no less.* Though I'd met St. Valentine and love had been the last thing on his mind when he became a saint.

She sighed and shook her head. "It's a story, but not a very good one. Just one stupid decision after another. You know the drill."

I shrugged. "Enlighten me. You can give me just the facts. Think of it like you're writing a news story."

Haley narrowed her eyes. "Why would you say that?"

I curled my lips into my best half-smile. "After I saw you at the museum, I did a little digging. I figured you were there with the press. Am I close?"

"Do you always research the women you give fly-by kisses?"

I grinned. "Every time. But since I don't give many women fly-by kisses, I made a special effort." I dimmed my grin and tilted my head. "And I wanted to know you a little bit better."

She regarded me with serious eyes for a few moments. "Why?"

What could I tell her? That I'd been hooked on her appearance and scent from the moment I saw her? That the Goddess had chosen her to be my One-and-Only? That I was the Archangel Michael and I'd been looking for her for millennia? That I'd never felt the driving need for connection like I did with her?

Yeah, probably not a good way to start things off.

I rolled my cup in my hands. "The museum wasn't the first time I'd seen you."

She raised her eyebrows. "It wasn't?"

I shook my head. "No. I was part of the crew who dropped off all those victims of the sex trade at the Hopeful Heart Shelter back in the summer. You were there and took the kids in hand. I couldn't keep my eyes off you. Or my mind off you after we left."

"I'm trying to resist the urge to say something like, 'why didn't you look me up?' But then I remember we never actually spoke."

"And do you know how many Haleys there are in Fort Collins alone? It's a very popular woman's name."

"You actually did try to look me up?" She laughed. "Oh, man, I was kidding."

"Yes, I did, and I was halfway through the 1,433 names by the time I saw you at the museum. That helped me narrow the search to Haleys in the press."

"There can't be that many of us." She shook her head. "At least not with the same spelling."

"How was I to know the spelling? I just had to wing it."

Or I could have. Being an archangel had its benefits. If I really needed to know something about someone, I could find out pretty quickly just by visiting where they worked or lived. I was better than the NSA about finding out secrets.

"I couldn't even find you on social media platforms."

She grimaced. "I'll have to be more active than I've been. My last name is Michaels. Haley Michaels." She held out her hand to shake.

My breath left me as I took her hand. *Michaels. Subtle, Mom, real subtle.* But her touch sent reverberations of pleasure and need through me, unlike any I'd felt before. Haley must have felt them too because she shivered before she released my hand.

Or she's just cold, you git.

"It's very nice to meet you, Haley Michaels. I'm Michael." I grinned as her eyes widened.

"That's it? Just Michael?"

I shrugged. "Yeah, unless you'd prefer my road name, Schnoz."

She choked on her coffee and shook her head. "No, I think I'll stick with Michael. It'll be easy to remember." She tilted her head. "How did you come by the road name Schnoz?"

"What, my nose doesn't give it away?" I'd been told enough times by Scott and Attila that I had a big nose but it worked well enough and I didn't see any reason to change it. "Actually, it's because I have an excellent sense of smell. Whenever we take a road trip, I can find the best coffee houses and bakeries along our route."

"Really?" She laughed and my heart expanded. "I might have to come with you some time to enjoy the benefit of such a sense."

"You'd definitely be welcome."

I meant the words from the depths of my soul, and it surprised the daylights out of me. I needed to be around her, and I hardly knew anything about her. *Time to learn.*

"So what happened tonight? You came out of that building like the hounds of hell were after you." I'd seen those hounds when I visited my brother before hell became a little more fluid. Not exactly the cute, cuddly puppies Hollywood often depicted. Yeah, that was sarcasm. They were far worse, and smelled like rotting flesh left out in the sun.

Haley sighed and looked away, licking her lips. "I was at a party with my now ex-boyfriend. My phone died and he decided he'd rather have a ménage with some of the other guests than be with me. But because my phone was dead, I couldn't call for a ride home. It was pretty damn fortuitous that you were outside."

I sensed she wasn't telling me everything, but I didn't expect her to open up to me at the first moment. *Except every other human tends to do that. Why not her?* I could use my grace to settle her mind and make her more amenable to sharing, but I didn't want to do that. I wanted her to trust me without my influence.

"What a stupid git. Was he really having sex with the other guests?"

She grimaced. "I didn't stick around to watch, but clothing was missing and body parts were visible." She finished coffee. "Speaking of which, I should probably get going home. It's late and my day ended on a really shitty note."

I nodded. "Is there any way I can make it better for you? It is Valentine's Day after all."

She gave me a distant smile. "You already have. You rescued me from a long walk home and bought me coffee. I'd call that a win."

Oh, glory, she was telling me she was done for the night, but I didn't want to let her go. Some part of me needed to be with her that night. It was a driving need, an imperative that wouldn't let up and hammered against my logical mind. My instincts screamed a warning I couldn't ignore.

But how to convince her without coming across like a

stalker?

I let a warm smile curl my lips and added just a touch of grace to make it sultry. "How about I take you somewhere warm and safe where you can charge your phone?"

She raised an eyebrow. "You mean where none of my friends know where I am and I don't have the ability to call them without your help?" She shook her head. "Yeah, I've seen that horror flick. It never ends well for the woman."

She wasn't wrong, but the more I thought about her going home to her apartment, the more the warning got louder in the back of my head.

"No, really, I just want to go home, take a shower and relax, and maybe watch some Netflix."

She gathered her purse and coat as she prepared to get up but paused when the chimes over the door rang and someone stepped inside. She glanced over her shoulder and I followed her gaze to the two cops who strode up to the counter. She gave a soft gasp and turned her face away as if she didn't want the officers to notice her.

Curious.

"Are you all right?"

Haley nodded. "Yeah, yeah, I'm fine."

But she didn't look fine. She looked scared and trapped and my gut said more had happened at that party than she'd told me.

"Are you sure?"

"Yeah, I'm good. Look, I'm gonna go. Thanks again for the coffee." Haley stood and zipped up her coat before she headed for the entrance. I tried to follow but my body was much bigger and as strong as I was, I couldn't move as quickly without drawing attention. And for some reason, she didn't want to let the cops see her.

She tossed her cup and pushed open the doors, turning up the collar of her coat as she stepped through. She headed straight out to the parking lot as if headed to a car and I debated staying put or following to make sure she got home okay.

The evening hadn't ended the way I'd hoped. *Luke's gonna give me hell for not getting laid after he set this up for me.* I sighed and shook my head as I dropped my cup in trash and headed for the doors.

Except the cops maneuvered in front of me.

"Sir, can we please have a word?"

I swiveled my head to look at them and narrowed my eyes. "Is there some sort of problem, officers?"

"What's the nature of your relationship with the young woman who just left?"

"Is there some sort of problem, officers?" I repeated my question, gauging their reactions. If there wasn't a problem, I didn't need to talk to them.

"How do you know the young woman who was with you?"

I raised my gaze toward the counter where I found Earl smirking as he wiped down the spotless counter. *Not wise, Earl. Not wise at all.* I cranked up my grace and gave the cops a wide-eyed innocent look.

"She's a friend. We met at the museum a few weeks ago. She was feeling uncomfortable coming into the coffee shop alone because the barista kept hitting on her and cyberstalking her online." I shrugged and let my expression go relaxed and bored. "Apparently, the barista hasn't learned that "no means no" yet. So she asked me to come in with her."

The older cop flinched at my remark about no meaning no and narrowed his eyes. "Then why did she run on out of here so fast?"

I shrugged again. "She said she had to get home and cops make her nervous. Maybe she's had a bad experience with police in the past." I let my gaze rest on the older cop and he looked away.

Being an archangel can have its pluses and minuses.

The cop looked away because he regularly harassed black kids and young women on his beat to show authority. And I knew Earl had cyberstalked Haley. I usually didn't delve into people's secrets—each one would have to face the consequences of their actions with their connection to the divine. *Or with Karma.*

"So, you weren't threatening the young woman?" The younger cop seemed to be looking for confirmation rather than accusing me of anything.

"No, officer. I was just having a cuppa with her." Using my British accent almost always put cops at ease. Mostly because they couldn't imagine a prim Brit being a badass biker. "Did someone report me threatening her?"

The younger cop shot a look toward the barista. "Thanks for answering our questions. You have a good night, now."

"Right, then." I nodded and ambled out the door, shooting a look back at Earl at the last moment. He'd lost his smirk as the cops advanced on him and I suspected his night was going to get much more difficult.

What goes around, comes around, you wanker.

I looked for Haley, but the cops had delayed me long enough that I didn't see her. My gut churned with the same warning about her well-being and I strode to my bike, starting the engine as soon as my arse hit the freezing leather seat. Something told me I needed to find her soon or her night would get a more difficult, too.

CHAPTER FOUR

Haley

My heart pounded in my chest as I walked with determination and purpose away from the coffee shop and the cops. Why the hell were they there? Had they already figured out I'd been in the building when the ADA was murdered? *Oh, that's so not good.*

The snow made the sidewalks slippery, but I kept moving fast. It was freezing outside and my shoes weren't made for the drifts that had already built up. I cursed Carl again and mentally prepared the Dear John email in my head. I kept my hands in the pockets of my coat, but I clutched my keys tightly in my fingers so I could open my door as soon as I got home. *Or use them as claws if anyone comes at me tonight.* I had no illusions about women walking alone in the dark.

I stepped into the street and crossed, making sure to look both ways for cars or other people. But my heel hit a patch of ice under the snow and I slid, wrenching my back and landing on my ass in the middle of the road. I groaned and rolled to my hands and knees, hoping I could get back up without any trouble, but I couldn't find any purchase.

I scrabbled a few moments on the icy pavement just as a car hurtled around the corner, headed my way. I looked up and worked harder, knowing they'd never be able to stop if I couldn't even walk across the street. The world seemed to slow down and I had time for about three thoughts.

Why the hell are they going so damn fast?

I should've taken Michael up on his offer to stay somewhere warm.

Sweet glory, I'm gonna die.

Someone shouted my name and I looked up as the headlights blinded me. Brilliant white light blanked out my vision as someone grabbed me and rolled us both out of the street. I swore I saw silver-black wings and fierce brown eyes as the scent of freshly baked rosemary bread filled my nose. Tires squealed and a heavy crash followed, and I wondered if I was dead for real.

"Haley! Haley, are you all right?"

Wait, I know that voice.

I opened my eyes, but I couldn't see anything. It took me a few moments to realize my face pressed against someone's warm chest with their arms wrapped around me. *And I don't sense any boobs here so it's probably a guy.*

I tilted my head back and looked up to meet his gaze, his eyes full of concern. His scruff looked sexy as hell on him. I idly wondered what it would feel like against my labia and inner thighs as I took in his lovely face. I wanted to reach up and run my fingers over his cheek but my hands remained pinned between our bodies.

"Michael? What are you doing here?"

"Trying to keep you from getting killed. What were you doing in the middle of the street?"

I shook my head. "I slipped and fell. Too much ice."

Relief washed over his features as he cradled me. "I'm so glad I got here in time. Are you all right? Anything broken?"

"I don't think so, though I wrenched my back when I slipped. But I'm not feeling any pain right now." It was true. Somehow all my pain had disappeared the moment he'd touched me. I didn't really want to leave his arms, but I couldn't stay lying on the street.

"Michael?"

"Yes, love?"

"Would you take me somewhere warm and safe where I can charge my phone, please?"

A sweet, gentle smile curled his lips as one hand brushed my hair out of my face. "Of course, love. Are you sure you can trust me to keep you safe?"

I frowned a little. "Are you suggesting I shouldn't?"

"No, just wondering what changed your mind."

I shrugged one shoulder. "This night has been nothing but trouble for me since it started and you're the only one who's been kind. I could use a little more kindness tonight. Plus, we're sitting here on the freezing sidewalk after you rescued me from that car and you haven't copped a feel. My instincts say you're okay."

He laughed and the joyous sound permeated my soul, lightening every stress and worry.

"Right, then. We should get up off the pavement and head to some place warmer, yeah?"

He rolled or moved or sat up enough to help me to my feet. I'd lost one of my shoes and the ice burned through the bottom of my foot. I hissed and hopped a little, but whooped when he bent to pick me up.

"What are you doing?"

"Carrying you. You can't walk without shoes and I won't have you suffering frostbite."

Yeah, I didn't really want to suffer that, either. And I rather liked being cradled in his arms. Yeah, yeah, I know. Very damsel-in-the-distressish, but I felt cherished, protected, and wanted. Three things I'd been missing from the men in my life.

Michael carried me down the sidewalk to his bike where he set me on the seat and knelt at my feet. He flipped open one of the Harley's panniers and pulled out a blanket and rope. Then he whipped out an impressive knife and I jumped. *Holy shit, has he been carrying that thing this whole time?*

But instead of using the knife to carve his initials into my legs or some other scary shit, he sliced through the blanket and cut two lengths of rope.

"What's that for?"

"I'm making you impromptu boots."

He wrapped one piece of the blanket around my right foot and tied the rope to it to keep the blanket in place. Then he folded and wrapped it all the way up to my knee, tying the rope off. He repeated the process on the other leg before stowing the last of the blanket and rope.

"There. That should do it. Here's your shoe."

"Shoe, singular." I held the lonely foot covering and shook my head. "We should throw it in the trash. You couldn't find the other one?"

He shook his head. "I reckon it's under the car that nearly hit you." He frowned and tilted his head. "Do you want me to go back and look?"

I glanced down at my shoe and shook my head. "No. Might as well throw this one away with it. They brought me nothing but trouble." Especially since I'd bought them for the party. *Yeah, don't really want to remember it.* I tossed it toward the nearest trash can on the street and straddled the bike.

"Let's go. I'm cold."

He nodded and sat on the seat in front of me. "Wrap your arms around me and hold on tight. You'll stay warmer on the ride. It's not far from here, but it'll be cold. I'll do my best to get there quickly."

"Okay."

He started the bike and the engine rumbled beneath us,

a comforting sound in the silence of the snowy night. I rested my head against his back and tightened my grip on his waist as he rolled forward off the kickstand. As we started to move, I remembered the car that had nearly hit me. Hadn't it crashed?

"What about the car and the person in it? Are they okay?"

"Don't know, don't care."

When I raised my eyebrow at him, he sighed and closed his eyes a moment—which was freakin' terrifying when he was driving a bike into a snowstorm. I yelped in surprise but he never veered or even shifted, and we stayed on the road until he opened his eyes again.

"They're unharmed and the vehicle isn't badly damaged."

"How the hell do you know that? And what were you doing driving with your eyes closed in a snowstorm?"

"Don't worry. We're perfectly safe and I got this."

I pressed my face against his back and swallowed hard. *We're so gonna die.*

Somehow we made it to wherever he was taking us, but it did take longer than just down the street from the coffee shop. I hadn't turned my face into the wind, but I could sense we'd gone up, like up into the mountains. The snow and wind had gotten worse and I was pretty sure this might have been the stupidest decision I'd ever made in my life. *Including Carl.*

But he turned off the highway and I lifted my head to look around. The snow fell thickly and I could barely see a cute little motel straight out of the 1950's road trip movies. Each cabin had a window box with lights strung over them to give a festive feel, and each door had a pine and cedar wreath hung on it.

"Where are we? This place is cute."

He pulled up in front of cabin number two and let me off the bike before he turned it around.

"Give me a few moments to put the bike in the barn and I'll be back to let you in."

Let me in? I watched him disappear into the whiteout as I stood under the overhang out of the snow. The wind whistled through the buildings around me, but I couldn't see much of anything. I shivered and I rubbed my arms in my coat to stay warm. My feet complained as the snow soaked through the blankets on my feet, but I didn't have much choice.

He came back about five minutes later, looming out of the blizzard like a frost giant. I couldn't hear anything over the wind and I jumped when he appeared.

"Dear glory, you scared the crap out of me."

"Sorry. Let's get you inside before your feet freeze." He produced an old-fashioned skeleton key and fit it into the ornate lock on the door. "Please come in."

I don't know what I was expecting. Maybe shag carpeting, faux wood panels on the walls, and mustard yellow Formica countertops. Instead, I found cream marble tile with colorful and plush rugs, pink and gray granite countertops, and off-white walls with watercolor art hung around. A decent stereo system sat beside the TV, including a real record player, and all the appliances in the kitchenette were brushed steel. Instead of cheap hotel furniture, there were Papasan chairs with taupe cushions, and large throw pillows on the floor.

"Wow."

Michael gave me a half-smile. "Not what you expected?"

"Uh, well, no." I stood in front of the door, afraid of tracking snow into the pristine room. "I expected a dark space with the smells of old wood, damp carpet, and years of grime and cigarette smoke."

He grimaced as he pulled off his boots and set them on a rack beside the door. "It used to be like that before we remodeled it. Took us weeks, but was worth the effort."

"We?"

"The Concrete Angels Motorcycle Club. We bought the property and refurbished it." He headed for the kitchenette to put on a real teal kettle.

I blinked. *The Concrete Angels. Shit-oh-dear, that's right.* That was the group who allegedly killed the crooked FBI agent who'd been undercover. And Michael was a member. Who brought me to their...what was it? Headquarters? Hideout? Compound? I didn't know what it would be called, but this cute, elegant suite didn't fit any of those descriptions.

I bit my lip and wondered if I'd taken a chance on the wrong guy.

"Here, let's get those wet blankets off your feet and warm you up. I've started the tea and I have some biscuits to snack on as well." He appeared beside me and knelt at my feet, reaching for the ropes binding the blanket. "Did they keep you warm enough?"

My mind was still on the possibility that my gut had been wrong about Michael so it surprised me when he reached for the ropes. He rested one hand on my leg to hold me steady while he pulled on the knots. His touch electrified my skin as he gently held me still. I couldn't move, mesmerized by his soft touch and his delicious scent.

When he'd pulled the soaked cloth away he rose with more grace than I had on a good day and held his hand out to me. "Maybe I should run you a bath to keep you warm."

I shook my head. "Only if you're planning to join me in it."

Where the hell had that come from? I'd known this guy for barely two hours and suddenly I'm asking him to join me in the bath? I mentally shook my head and bit my lips as his eyes flared with intensity.

"As tempting as that is, I want to make sure you're warm from the inside out first." He tugged me over to one of the comfortable Papasan chairs. "Let me hang up your coat and get the tea."

I stuffed my gloves and hat into the pockets and he took my long wool coat to hang on a real hat tree near the door. I settled back into the chair as he headed for the kitchenette but my attention snagged on a faded painting on the wall behind the coats. Despite its primitive look, there was magic and emotion in the figure wearing a red hooded coat. *Maybe it's Red Riding Hood and I've just stepped into the wolf's house.*

Michael returned to the living room and handed me a mug of steaming tea. "Thanks." I wrapped my hands around it and nodded toward the painting. "Interesting painting. It's beautiful."

He followed my gaze and raised his eyebrows. "You think so?"

"Yeah. It has real emotion in it. Better than that new artist in the Denver Museum. Did you paint it?"

To my surprise, he blushed. "Yeah. Years ago now. Fancied myself Michelangelo or some nonsense. I entitled it, "I'll Be On My Way." It's just a bit of silly, really." He sipped his tea. "Do you like art? Is that why you were in the museum, for the art?"

I shook my head. "I was there because the Fort Collins Bugle needs someone to do their fluff pieces. Fact or fiction, if it's fluffy, it's me."

"You don't do fluff?"

I shook my head as I held my tea. "I want to report on the real news. Things that make people pay attention and enact change."

He nodded. "Tall order there."

I laughed ruefully. "Yeah, I know. I think my editor put me on fluff pieces because I wouldn't write things just for shock value. It's not about the truth anymore so much as it is about selling papers. There are plenty of true things going on that would shock the readers, but they would expose the investors…" I trailed off with a shrug. Rocks and hard places didn't have anything on this.

"But you're still going to try to be the hard hitting reporter?" His lips curled into a half-smile.

"Bet your ass I am. I just need that one story to get my name out there and I'll be set." I nodded. "And I definitely have something that could develop into the story of a lifetime."

"Yeah?" He raised his eyebrows. "What's it about?"

I shook my head. "Too early to say." And it wouldn't be good if he found out I was investigating the connections to the Concrete Angels. *But isn't it a good thing he brought me here?* Now I could find out stuff first-hand. "I still need to do research before I make any conclusions."

"Won't that put you in danger?" He sounded honestly concerned.

I shrugged. "I think it's worth it. People need to know, and the big entities like government and corporations need to be kept in check."

"So you're an idealist."

I narrowed my eyes but his voice held no disdain or censure. "Maybe I am. Maybe I believe in doing what's right even if it's the harder road. There are certain fights that need to be fought. Change doesn't come by sitting there and watching for danger."

He nodded, his expression thoughtful. "That can be a long and dangerous road."

"Are you telling me I should just tuck tail and stick my head in the sand?"

He shook his head. "No, just pointing out what you might be in for, since you're an idealist."

I frowned. "Does idealist equate to someone who never calculates risk or takes precautions?" I raised my chin. "I'll say it again. Some fights need to be fought." This wasn't a game to me. There were people causing real damage and it needed to be exposed. I wasn't going to sit around and willfully ignore it. Not when I had the power to do something about it.

I set my tea aside and stood but realized I had nowhere to go. The blizzard had ramped up outside and I had no idea where I really was. *Oh, this was a bad idea.* Apparently, I was full of them tonight.

"Fuck."

"What?" Michael eyes widened and his shoulders tensed.

"I'm stuck here, aren't I?" I shot him a look to verify. He didn't nod, but chagrin swept across his expression. "That's what I thought. Got a place I can charge my phone? I need to call my friends to let them know where I am."

"Right. That's easy enough." He set his mug of tea aside and rose. "Do you have a charging cable?"

I shook my head. "Oh, sure, I just happen to carry that around when I figure I'm going to be taken to an undisclosed location in a snowstorm after a party."

He laughed. "Yeah, I can see how that wouldn't figure into your holiday preparations. The charger is over here."

He led me to a real, antique roll-cover secretary with all the little cubbies for pens, paper, envelopes and cards. My grandmother had one in her house when I was a kid and I used to love to poke around and use the random scraps of paper for drawing and writing. This one was much more organized compared to that one, but it also had spaces for the phone to charge, a ceramic change bowl with pennies and nickels in it, and a mug filled with pens.

The mug read, "The Best Place To Light My Fire – Cloudburst, Colorado." The firefighter's emblem emblazoned the side with a pair of crossed axs and Cloudburst Colorado Hot Shots written under it. It sat stuffed with pens and pencils in wild abandon.

"You're a big fan of firefighters?"

Michael snorted. "No. My brother Luke brought that back for me from his trip to the Western Slope. He thought it was cute." He pulled out the charging cable and offered it to me.

I laughed. "Who doesn't like firefighters? I mean, they're the definition of hot." I plugged in my phone and grinned.

He raised an eyebrow as we returned to the living room. "Are they? What do you think about bikers?"

"Mmm, bikers. Let's see..." I trailed off as I tilted my head. "I think bikers are sexy and mysterious. All that leather and hot metal between their legs?" I hissed and shuddered theatrically. "Sexy."

A sultry smile curled his lips and supported my assessment. Michael was definitely sexy and mysterious. And he was damn hot, too. Firefighters had my respect for their work saving people and property, but I'd take a biker every day and twice on Sunday. *Which is probably blasphemous.* I eyed him as he tilted his head. He definitely didn't look like an angel.

"So what do you do for the Concrete Angels? I mean, I know there's an inner circle or whatever, but not much else."

He nodded and sat back in his chair. "I'm the VP."

"Holy shit!" I coughed around the tea. No wonder he had such a nice place to stay. "Vice President? Wow. That's amazing."

He shrugged. "It gives me something to do."

"I'd say it's more than that." I frowned. "What were you doing in a random suburb of Denver tonight, alone? I mean, it's Valentine's Day. Shouldn't you be with your woman or something?"

He shook his head. "No woman. At least, no one permanent who'd be missing me tonight."

I don't know why that made me so happy. I'd just met this guy. I didn't know anything about him other than he was the VP of the Concrete Angels and he was sexy as hell. But that he was unattached just made my night way better.

"Then I'd say someone was missing out, but her loss is

my gain." Damn, when had I become this bold? I shook my head to clear away my inner alley cat, and tried to soften my words with a smile. "So, you just happened to be right outside tonight?"

He dipped his head and shrugged one shoulder. "Actually, my brother told me to be there. He said it would be a good idea. For once he was right."

"Heh, yeah, I guess so."

An awkward silence followed my statement and I saw Michael hesitate. I let my gaze swing away from him and tried to find something to say. *This is a first. A reporter with no words.* Yeah, well, I was stuck in the cabin of a biker club's VP in a snowstorm wearing a little red dress and no idea how I'd get home. *Yeah, this isn't awkward at all.*

CHAPTER FIVE

Michael

Oh good, I'm glad things aren't awkward.

Sarcasm usually cheered me up, but sitting there with Haley and not knowing what to say or do was downright painful. I know what I *wanted* to do. I wanted to take her into the bedroom and give her pleasure. But I wasn't getting the 'get it on' vibe from her, and the last thing I wanted to do was scare her.

Brilliant, what am I going to do now? I was an archangel. Surely I could come up with a way to make us both more comfortable.

"Would you like me to rub your feet?"

Her eyes widened. "What?"

Or I could royally screw things up so she'll panic and hide in the bathroom all night.

"Your feet. I'm sure they're cold from being outside. How 'bout I rub them to get the circulation going and warm them up?" That didn't sound too creepy, did it?

"You want to rub my feet?"

"Yeah. Since I brought you all the way up here to get snowed in, it's the least I can do to make you comfortable."

I hoped. If she told me no, I wasn't sure what I'd do.

Luke had given me the opportunity to get close to Haley. Anything I did to screw it up was all on me.

She tilted her head. "All right. If you want."

Oh, I definitely wanted. I was downright desperate to get my hands on any part of her body that she'd let me touch. I leaned forward and gently grasped one foot, pulling it up into my lap. Her toes were painted an iridescent purple and despite the bluish tinge to her feet, the color made them rather elegant. I rubbed my palms over her foot to get the circulation going.

"Oooooh, your hands are so warm." She flopped back against the chair and closed her eyes. "I didn't realize just how cold my feet were."

I worked my thumbs into her arch, spiraling outward to rub the ball of her foot, her toes, and her heel. She moaned and sank into the chair, her body relaxing into my touches. It had to be the sexiest thing I'd seen in a long time. *And I'm doing it to her.*

My cock pushed against the fly of my jeans again, but I focused on Haley's pleasure and making her feel comfortable. It must have been successful because she brought her other foot up and rested it on my thigh without prompting. I swallowed a chuckle and made sure I'd finished her first foot before moving to the second.

After a while, she stopped making any noises and her breathing evened out. I kept rubbing her foot until her head dropped to the side, her body completely relaxing. She was adorable lying there asleep, but she'd wake with a strained neck if I didn't move her. I set her foot down and rose, trying not to wake her.

Yeah, like she won't wake when I pick her up.

But Haley must have been either a deep sleeper or comfortable enough with me that she didn't do anything other than curl into my chest when I lifted her from the chair. I tried not to read too much into it, but a warm feeling filled my body and my throat closed on me. I damn near choked and dropped her, but my angelic reflexes kept me upright and we made it to the bedroom without mishap.

But when I tried to set her down, she clung to me like a spider monkey and wouldn't let go. *Bloody hell, now what do I do?* I bent down to deposit her in my bed, but her arms tightened and I was forced to lie in the bed with her wrapped around me.

At first, all I could do was lie there stiffly, and not just my body. The last thing I wanted her to feel was my hard-on pressing against the fly of my jeans. But when she didn't stir beyond fitting her leg over mine, I slowly relaxed and so did my cock.

Thank goodness. I closed my eyes and tried not to breathe in her delicious scent. *Sunrise and magic.* Those words seemed the most accurate to describe what my nose picked up while she lay in my arms. *Right, and how are you going to get up now?*

There wasn't a good answer to the question so I lay back and relaxed, enjoying her warm weight against me. Maybe I'd just rest for a few moments before I figured out how to get away from her alluring body and scent.

****

Michael

I woke sometime later to find Haley had rolled off me, her body curled on its side. I gathered my wits after being so deeply asleep, and slid off the bed without disturbing her. Hey, I'd gotten my wish, hadn't I? So why was it so hard to walk away from her all beautiful and relaxed on my bed?

I rolled my head on my shoulders and grabbed the throw blanket off the foot of the bed. I always kept one there for added warmth. I shook it out and snorted at the design as I draped it over her. A pair of red foxes lay curled up together in a meadow of green grasses. I wasn't sure if it was a metaphor for cuteness or a warning about the craftiness of foxes. It could go either way.

I forced myself to walk back out to the living room rather than stare at my guest and wondered if I'd be able to get a few more hours of sleep in my Papasan chairs. They were fairly comfortable and if I used the second one for my feet, I might get some rest. I turned to move one when someone knocked on my door.

What the actual fuck? It was somewhere around three a.m. *Who the hell is up this early in a snowstorm?*

Glancing through the peephole, I groaned. *Hell indeed.* I opened the door to my brother Luke.

"What are you doing here?"

"I might ask you the same thing. Aren't you home a tad early?" Luke strode past me and toed off his boots as if he was getting comfortable. "Damn, it's cold out there. Got any coffee?"

"Seriously, Luke. What are you doing here?" I shut the door on the frozen night and crossed my arms over my chest.

"I saw your lights on and wondered if you'd forgotten to turn them off." Luke settled into the one of the Papasan chairs. "But then I saw your bike in the barn and thought I'd better check on you. What happened with this woman you were so hot for? Did you strike out?"

I narrowed my eyes. "No, I didn't strike out."

"Then what the hell are you doing home so soon?" His eyes widened. "Unless you were more of a sixty-second man. In and out like a thief in the night? Damn, son, I thought you'd have more class than that."

I growled and stomped right up to him. "I *do* have more class than that, you wanker. And keep your bloody voice down. She's sleeping."

"You brought her here?" Luke rolled to his feet and

slid past me. I grabbed for him, but he was more slippery than an eel and I couldn't catch a grip.

He paused at the bedroom door and peeked inside, he gave a low whistle. "I can see why you were all hot to trot over her." He paused and frowned before he backed out of the doorway. "Why is she still dressed? Didn't you get any?"

I growled again and closed the bedroom door. "No, I didn't get any, as you so crudely put it. She was tired, scared, and cold. I couldn't take advantage of her."

"Why not?" Luke shot me a perplexed look.

"Sod off, you prick." I turned my back on him and headed for the kitchenette. "I'm not that kind of bloke." I closed my eyes as I leaned on the counter and sighed. "Haley is...different."

He snorted. "Different? How different? Man, I totally sent you up to get your rocks off and get her out of your system. What the hell went wrong?"

"Nothing went wrong." I raised my gaze to his. "Haley is Angelina different."

His mouth opened into a large O as he lost his smirk. Angelina was Luke's One-and-Only. The one woman he'd damn near given up his job for. No one had seen it coming, especially since she was an angel who'd chosen to stay in this realm and care for the humans in her little town. She ran a shelter in Three Lakes, Michigan, and Luke often traveled up there to see her.

"Seriously?" Luke let his breath out and returned to the chairs. "So, what are you gonna do about that? Are you gonna woo her, ignore her, or let her go?"

"Why in the Goddess's name would I let her go?"

Luke shrugged. "Because you're the Archangel Michael and it's what you do?"

"Fuck off."

His eyebrows went up. "Whoa, okay. I guess you really are more serious about this woman." He shook his head. "If you weren't going to have sex with her, why the hell did you bring her here?"

I frowned and turned on the kettle for tea just to buy myself some time. "I dunno. My gut kept screaming she was in trouble and going home would put her in grave danger. So I brought her here to give her a safe place to sleep."

Luke snorted but his brows creased. "What kind of danger do you think she's in?"

I shook my head as I leaned against the kitchenette counter and crossed my arms over my chest. "Something bigger than just a local rapist or junkie or thug. Turns out she's a reporter. Maybe she's stumbled across something someone else doesn't want broadcasted."

"Wait, she's a reporter and you still brought her here?" Luke gaped at me. "You do remember that a) we're a biker club with less than legal dealings, and b) many of us are the Elder Races, races that humans don't even know exist?"

"So? What's your point?"

"My point is she's a reporter, the nosiest human on the planet, and you brought her into a world full of dangerous secrets. You don't see the problems with that?"

Oh, I'd seen them, all right, and suspected they'd kick my arse. But though I could see and hear the oncoming train, I had my feet planted.

I sighed. "Fuck, yeah, I see the problems. But there's nothing I can do about it. She's the one, Luke. I feel it in my gut like you did with Angelina."

"You never took the easy roads, did you?" Luke shook his head.

"Look who's talking. You're the one who agreed to be reviled for all time."

He snorted. "It seemed like a good idea at the time." He met my gaze. "It's going to be hard. She's a reporter and naturally curious, especially about things people are trying to hide. You better be clear that she's the one you want because there are going to be secrets you either can't tell her or have to ensure she keeps."

I ran my hands over my face. "I'm clear. She smells like sunrise and magic."

Luke hissed. "Shit. That's it, then. You're screwed."

I nodded. "I know."

"When are you gonna tell her? *What* are you gonna tell her?"

"I don't know. I guess I'll take it as it comes and hope inspiration strikes me when the moment's right."

Luke raised his eyebrows. "You're just gonna go with the flow?" He narrowed his eyes. "Who are you, and what have you done with my brother?"

I shook my head but my lips curled into a rueful smile. "I'm not that bad."

"Not that bad?" Luke gaped at me. "To mangle the quote, you don't take a dump, son, without a plan."

"Sod off." The kettle hissed and I took it off the heat before it woke Haley. "But I was serious about the trouble she's facing. I don't know what it is, but I know it's there and something would've gone wrong if I'd let her go home tonight."

Luke nodded slowly. "I got nothing on my schedule, so whoever's planning shit isn't blaming me for it."

I knew Luke often got hints of things before they happened when folks were focused on how 'bad' something was. His position as the Devil often gave him insights on future events. Hell, he'd been busy since the last presidential election.

I nodded. "Whatever it is, it had to do with that party she was at tonight. Something happened there but she wouldn't say what, and I suspect it got her on someone's radar."

"You're sure?"

I shook my head. "Not a hundred percent, but ninety-eight."

He grunted. "I'd take an archangel's ninety-eight percent over a human's hundred."

"Yeah, so that's why she's here. Or in there." I pointed to the bedroom. "Sleeping. Alone."

Luke *tsked* and rolled his eyes. "After everything I did to get you to the right place at the right time? Sometimes you're damn near impossible. What are you gonna tell Loki when he finds out?"

I rubbed the back of my neck. "Do you think we could keep it quiet for a bit? Just until I find out what's wrong?"

Luke raised his eyebrows. "I'm not sure about that. You might have until the end of the snowstorm, but not much after that. He's gonna notice you have a new woman when you go to the clubhouse to eat."

"It's just until I can sort out what she's hiding."

"Why don't you just ask her?"

I rolled my eyes as I sipped my tea. "She's sleeping."

"Not at the moment."

I turned my head toward the bedroom and Haley stood there, sleep-tousled, hesitant and so damn sexy, my heart almost stopped. Glory, I wanted her and I forced myself to swallow my tea and find a smile.

"Haley."

CHAPTER SIX

Haley

I'd been to Thunder From Down Under and Chippendales shows in Vegas with my girlfriends. I'd seen male models do photoshoots for romance novel covers. Hell, I'd even seen the BUD/S classes running on the beaches of California. I'd viewed my share of ripped, sexy men. And none of those experiences even came close to the two men in the living room of that cabin.

They've gotta be brothers.

Michael was dark to his companion's light, they both had strong jaws, broad shoulders, huge biceps and thick thighs. Michael wore surprise and chagrin, while the nearly-bald man's lips curled into an amused smirk.

He rolled to his feet and held out his hand. "When my brother remembers more than your name, I'm sure he'll introduce us. Name's Luke."

His warm hand closed around me and some of my sleepiness faded as I looked into his blue eyes. There was wisdom and weariness in them along with the amusement, and despite his snarky attitude, I liked him.

"Haley Michaels. Nice to meet you."

"Haley *Michaels*?" He shot a look at Michael with raised eyebrows before turning back to me. "The pleasure's mine. I understand you're a reporter."

I shrugged as he released me. "Of fluff pieces mostly, but I won't be doing that forever. What do you do for the Concrete Angels?"

He flopped back into the chair he'd left. "Odd jobs here and there. I'm their nomad and I go all over."

I nodded. Michael still hadn't said anything, but his intensity had ramped up as soon as his brother shook hands with me. When the silence stretched, I cleared my throat and pushed the hair out of my eyes.

"I'm just gonna get my phone and call my friends to let them know I'm okay."

There was a pause as Luke looked at Michael, but my guardian angel seemed to be keeping his silence.

"Uh, yeah, good plan. We'll let you do that." Luke rolled his eyes as Michael just watched me kinda like a deer in headlights.

Great, now I've stupefied him.

I nodded and headed back to the roll-top secretary. The phone sat fully charged and didn't seem to be messed with. Of course it had been dead and he didn't know my passcode to get in. *Not that he couldn't have hacked his way in. Stop living in the 20th Century.*

I snagged the phone and powered it up, trying to ignore the two silent men in the room. Why weren't they speaking? What had they been talking about before I came out? *Why don't you ask her?* That had been the last thing Luke said before Michael turned around. *Ask me what?*

"Looks like it's fully charged." I held up the phone and gave them my patented polite smile. "I'm gonna call from the bedroom."

"Yeah, good." Luke had gotten to his feet again and elbowed Michael.

"Uh, right. Good." His words came out in staccato

bursts and I wondered why he'd suddenly lost his ability to speak.

"Yeah, okay."

I nodded as I hurried back to the bedroom, closing the door behind me. I shook my head and sat down on the bed with a large flower print against a white background. Seemed like an odd choice for the VP of a badass biker club, but somehow it fit Michael's personality as far as I knew him.

Which isn't at all and you need to call Tori or at least Jeff to let them know you're okay.

I'd call them both. I took a deep breath and clicked on Jeff's contact number in my phone, grimacing at how late it was.

The phone rang twice before a groggy voice muttered, "Hello?"

"Jeff? It's Haley."

"Haley? What time is it?"

I shook my head even if he couldn't see it. "I dunno. Some time after three, I guess. I'm sorry to call you so late but I wanted to tell you I'm okay."

"Okay?" His voice sharpened and rustling sounded in the background as he sat up in bed. "Why would you need to tell me that? What happened?"

I didn't want to mention the murder I'd witnessed just in case the killers came looking for me. "Carl went off with someone else—several someone elses—and left me hanging. Then the cops showed up and this guy gave me a ride to his place."

"Are you fuckin' crazy, Haley?" Anger and fear threaded through his voice. "You went home with some random guy?"

When he put it like that, it sounded worse than I'd thought. "Yeah. Uh, he saw me come out of the building and gave me a ride to Jitters. But then I slipped and fell in the street and he saved me from getting hit by a car, and—"

"Holy shit, Haley. You're not hurt, are you?" More rustling came from his side of the phone. It sounded like he'd gotten out of bed.

"No, I'm fine."

"Okay. Hold on just a little longer. I'm on my way."

"No!" I bit my lips, the word coming out far more harshly than I intended. "No, that's okay. I'm fine, really. And there's a raging snowstorm going on out there. No need to get yourself in an accident over this."

"It's barely flaking out there. Tell me where you are and I'll come get you."

"Jeff, seriously, I'm safe where I am and as soon as the storm stops, I'll be able to come home."

"Where are you, Haley?" When Jeff used that tone of voice, it saved a lot of pain and suffering to just answer him.

"I'm at the Concrete Angels' compound in the mountains."

A long ominous pause came from the other side of the phone. I could tell Jeff was still there by his breathing. Thank goodness he was still breathing because I was sure I stopped his heart with that little piece of information.

"Oh my glory, Haley. Those people are criminals! Have you lost your damn mind?"

I wanted to argue the point about the Concrete Angels being criminals, but I didn't have any proof that they weren't. We'd all heard the rumors and seen some of the news reports. And hell, the FBI and Marshals had been investigating them for years. *That can't be good.*

But Michael had done nothing to hurt me and he'd saved me twice that night. Whatever else the Concrete Angels were, they weren't completely evil. *They were the ones to bring in all those kids and women who'd been sexually assaulted like Jeff.*

"I promise I'm safe and I know what I'm doing." I didn't remotely know what I was doing, but I didn't want

Jeff to come up there in the storm. "As soon as the storm is done and the roads are safe, I'll call you to come get me."

"You can't be serious."

"Yeah, I am, Jeff. Trust me, will ya?"

A loud sigh gusted through the phone. "You're the only family I have who cared about what happened to me. Everyone else swept it under the rug and tried to ignore it. I can't lose you, Haley. What if something happens to you and I did nothing?"

"I promise to come back in a dream and tell you it wasn't your fault."

"That's not funny."

"It was kinda funny." Apparently not enough to make him snort. "I'll be fine. The guy who brought me here has treated me well and my gut says he's a man of his word."

Jeff snorted. "That famous gut of yours. You keep telling me about it. Has it ever been wrong?"

"Not as of yet."

He sighed again. "Okay, Haley. But keep your phone charged and handy. And if you need me, I'll be there, snow or no snow."

I smiled at his vehemence. "I know you will, Jeff. Thanks." I took a deep breath. "How are you doing these days? Things starting to improve?"

Yeah, it was three in the morning. Yeah, I asked him these questions every other day. But I wanted to be present when the positive change happened.

"No, not really, and you're not going to distract me from this. I'm serious about coming to get you."

"I'm not trying to distract you."

"Then why do you ask me the same questions over and over?"

I shrugged even if he couldn't see it. "Because I love you and I want to make sure you're okay. And I want you to know I'm thinking about you, sending good thoughts and blessings, and hoping that your breakthrough will be sooner rather than later."

He sighed. "Thanks, Haley. I love you, too. But I don't know if there'll ever be a breakthrough. We might have to concede that this is the new normal and the best it's gonna be."

"I don't believe that." It was a senseless and stubborn thing to say, but despite my jaded reporter's exterior, I was a romantic at heart and believed in happily-ever-after. "I know it won't be like this forever. Of course I don't have the magic bullet to kill your demons, but my gut tells me you're gonna find your balance, Jeff."

"Your famous gut again, huh?" He sounded weary but reluctantly hopeful.

"Damn straight."

He sighed again. "All right, then. Keep yourself safe and watch your back. Lock the bedroom door or something. And call or text me in the normal morning hours so I know you're still fine."

I breathed a sigh of relief. He wasn't going to pull the 'white knight' move and come up to the compound in the storm.

"I will. Get some sleep and sorry I woke you."

"I'm glad you did. Take care of yourself and I talk to you in the morning."

"Okay. Love you, Jeff."

"Love you, too. Good night."

"Night."

I ended the call and sighed. I really needed to get some sleep, but it seemed rude to ignore my host and his brother outside in the living room. I set my phone on the bedside table and headed back out to the main room.

The room sat in darkness and Luke had gone. I found Michael asleep in his papasan chair, his feet propped up on the coffee table with a pillow under his heels. He snored softly, his chest rising and falling at an even rate. His arms lay crossed on his belly as if trying to stay warm.

I found a throw blanket draped on the other chair and picked it up to spread over him. It was the least I could do since he'd given me his bed. I made sure it covered him from neck to knees but paused before I left him. Jeff was right to be suspicious of the Concrete Angels, but my gut said Michael was one of the good guys and I was safe with him.

I made sure the door was locked and the security chain was latched before I headed back to the bedroom. I didn't want anyone surprising him before we were both awake enough to deal with it.

That's ironic. Locking the door to make sure we're safe. I snorted. I wasn't remotely safe from Michael if he wanted to try anything. But I hadn't been lying when I told Jeff I trusted him. I grimaced at my party dress as a nightgown, but I didn't have anything else and there was no way I'd sleep naked. *Now if Michael was in the bed with me...*

I rolled my eyes as I slid under the covers that smelled like him. That would have to do because sleeping with him was out of the question.

****

Haley

Daylight found me crusty-eyed with a good case of cotton-mouth, but I was surprisingly rested. As promised, no one had disturbed me during the night and the bedroom door remained closed. The scents of coffee and food found their way into the room and my stomach rumbled with hunger. I hadn't eaten anything since before the disastrous party and my body reminded me of it in no uncertain terms.

I slid out of the bed and rubbed my eyes, heading for the bathroom. I had no change of clothes for after a shower, but I could at least wash my face and wet back my hair.

The clip I'd worn would keep it out of my eyes. Once I was more or less presentable, I shuffled out to the main room and stopped.

Michael stood in the kitchenette with his back to me. *All* of his back. He wore a pair of sweats and nothing else, showing off the strong lines of his back and shoulders. Tattoos covered both arms and the top of his shoulders. He even had a Tramp Stamp right above his ass.

I'd never thought of myself enamored of ink, but on Michael it made my mouth water. I was so stuck on the beauty of his ink and muscle that I missed when he turned and looked at me.

"Good morning. How'd you sleep?"

I blinked, pulling my attention back to his face rather than his sexy body. "Uh, good. You know, as well as I could in a party dress. How did you sleep? Those chairs can't be that comfortable."

He shrugged and handed me a steaming mug of coffee. The set of angel wings tattoo over his heart flapped with his motion. "It was comfortable enough. I sent my brother over to the clubhouse to deliver us hot breakfast when Grub finishes cooking. I expect him to return with plenty of goodies."

I raised my eyebrows. "Such as?"

"He should be bringing eggs, breakfast sausage, and some sort of pastry." Michael gave me a lazy smile. "I made the coffee and tea, and I have some smoked salmon if that's your preference."

"Actually, my preference would be to get out of this party dress and into something more comfortable and warm."

He nodded and ambled out of the kitchenette to a pile of clothing on one of his bar stools. "Luke dropped these by before getting breakfast. It's just a T-shirt and sweats from Dollhouse, but they should fit well enough." He handed the pile to me.

"Dollhouse?" I set my coffee down before taking the clothing.

"One of our members. She's about your size."

I frowned. "Is she Luke's old lady?"

Michael's eyes widened. "No, definitely not. She's the club's architect and resource manager. She's no one's old lady."

"Do you have an old lady?" I have no idea where the question came from. I mean, I wasn't interviewing for the job. But the words slipped out before I could call them back.

He smiled. "Not yet."

Oh, damn, maybe I was interviewing for the job. Relief cascaded through me with the idea that he was single and I gave myself a mental head-slap. *I am not looking for a bad boy boyfriend.* Even if he was as sexy as sin and yet filled with genuine goodness.

I cleared my throat. "I'm gonna go change into these."

"Right."

I nodded and skittered back to the bedroom. It was a relief to get out of the party dress and I considered just throwing it away. While it had been an expensive purchase, the memories of what happened weren't the best and I'd just as soon not be reminded. *Yeah, that'd be no fun.* I dumped the dress into a pile on the floor as I slipped into the T-shirt and sweats. They settled over my body with a soft caress and I sighed with relief.

I used the bathroom to check out my reflection and hoped Michael was in a charitable mood. I looked like I'd spent some time in a wind-tunnel. I'd heard the "wind blown" look was sexy, but I didn't think I'd qualify for that particular adjective. I appeared more dazed and confused than sexy.

Shaking my head, I returned to the living room. Michael still hadn't gotten dressed, which was a good thing, and Luke had arrived with breakfast, another good thing. The breakfast, not Luke, though he was pretty damn fine to look at, too.

"Good morning, Haley. Sleep well?" Luke raised a suggestive eyebrow but I just shrugged and nodded.

"Need my coffee." I reached for my neglected mug and Michael's hand brushed mine as he handed it to me. "Thanks." I tried to ignore the tingle of excitement from the contact, but his divine beauty rocked my world.

"Luke brought us some of Grub's best crepes." Michael held up a plate full of thin pancakes folded around strawberries and cream, and my mouth watered.

"Seriously? You have a chef in your biker gang?"

"We're not a gang, we're a club, and just because we ride Harleys and dress in denim doesn't mean we don't appreciate fine cooking." He kicked his booted feet up on Michael's coffee table and sipped his coffee with his pinky finger in the air. I couldn't help but laugh.

"Point taken. Note to self: the Concrete Angels eat better than ordinary humans."

I grinned but I caught an odd look shared between the two men and wondered why their shoulders had stiffened. *And what nice shoulders they are.* Still, I filed the reaction away for further consideration and sat down at Michael's small kitchen table to eat.

I took a bite and damn near melted out of my chair. It was a foodgasm on the plate. I moaned as soon as it hit my taste buds and both men's gazes flew to me. Luke wore amusement but Michael's expression turned downright predatory. I shivered, not sure if I felt excitement or unease.

"And that's my cue to head out." Luke rolled to his feet, making me blink in surprise. "I gotta go tune my bike. The snow always makes it bitchy, and nothing's worse than a Harley bitch. I'll catch you later, Michael. Enjoy your breakfast, Haley." He winked and let himself out the door.

I blinked. "What just happened?"

Michael reached out to take my plate from my hands.

"I think he's trying to give me time to do this." He set the plate aside, cupped my face, and kissed the hell out of me.

At first, I froze. Surprise overrode all the other reactions. But as his tongue slid between my gaping lips, I whimpered and wrapped my arms around his chest, pulling him against me.

He tasted like strawberries and cream crepes, and sexy, divine masculinity. The perfect combination to melt my heart and rev my engine. The scrape of his tongue against mine lit my body on fire and I tried to get closer.

One thing stopped me. The hard ridge of erotic muscle pressed against my mound.

Oh sweet glory, I want him.

Hell yeah, I did. And this was my choice. I was going to take what I wanted and he didn't seem inclined to say no. Jeff worried that Michael would take advantage of me, but I was all ready to take advantage of him.

I forced myself to pull back and meet his deep brown eyes.

"Take me to bed, Michael."

"But breakfast—"

"Can wait. This can't." I tugged him toward the bedroom and hoped I hadn't pushed things too far. *Please say yes.*

He tugged backward against my pull and waited until I'd met his gaze.

"Are you sure, Haley?"

I nodded. "I'm sure."

He bit his bottom lip and dipped his head. "It was just one kiss."

I tilted my head and raised an eyebrow. "Was it? Maybe you should try again, just to be sure."

He growled and reeled me into his embrace again, taking my lips greedily. I met his kiss this time with my own desperate need, wanting his flavor flooding my mouth. *There's another way to get his flavor in my mouth.* Oh yeah, my inner alley cat was making a comeback.

He kissed me like he hadn't kissed anyone in way too long and the idea made me unreasonably happy. I wanted him for myself, and that included all his attention. No time for ex-lovers to be making an appearance, even in memory.

When at last he pulled back, we were both out of breath.

"Haley, if we do this, there's something you must know about me."

Oh no, not the 'there's something you must know' excuse.

I placed my hand on his lips to stop his words. "Are you married?"

He shook his head.

"Do you have a long-term girlfriend?"

He shook his head again.

"Some really bad disease?"

He laughed. "No."

"Then there's nothing I need to know. Unless you don't want me."

The look he shot me as he gestured to his tenting pants was drier than the Gobi Desert. "Oh, I definitely want you."

"I thought so. So there's nothing you have to tell me." I dragged him into the bedroom and stopped at the bed. "I just want your full attention and efforts on making love with me. What do you say?"

He growled and the scents of freshly baked bread with rosemary and basil hit my nose just before he grasped the hem of my T-shirt and drew it over my head.

"I say you have all of me, love, and there will never be another for me." Then he buried his face in my boobs.

It was an odd thing to say so early in our relationship, but I wasn't going to argue with him when he'd wrapped his lips around one of my nipples. The wet heat of his mouth on my breast made me moan and drop my head back.

"Oh, glory, Michael. Don't stop."

I wasn't sure he heard me or not, but I was done worrying. *Time to just enjoy.*

CHAPTER SEVEN

Michael

Oh hell no, I wasn't going to stop. Not when she'd begged me to keep going. I'd been dying to touch her since I picked her up on the street the night before. But I wouldn't take advantage of anyone. Until she gave me the go-ahead.

With a mouthful of nipple, I couldn't get enough of her. I didn't think I could become addicted to the scents of sunrise and magic, but when they belonged to her, I was hooked. I ran my tongue over the bumps on her areola and the nipple hardened. She whimpered and thrust her chest against my face with implicit demand for more.

Wish granted.

I slid my hands down her body and grasped her sweet arse to pull her rich heat closer to my body. The scent of her desire filled my nose and my arousal swamped my thoughts. Why the hell did she smell so good? I'd been with enough women to understand what they wanted and how to give it to them, but none of them had made *me* wish to give them more than they asked for.

But Haley tempted me in ways more at home with my

brother Luke. I needed her heart, her mind, and her soul, and that wasn't even my bailiwick. *Luke would be so proud.*

My brother was the last person I wanted in my head with Haley in my arms so I shoved him out of my mind and concentrated on her full breasts under my tongue. I pushed the sweats off her hips and took a step back to take her in completely.

"Sweet Glory, Haley. You're the most beautiful woman I've ever seen." It was true even if it sounded like a cheesy line left over from the chick-flicks I'd caught Viper watching from time to time.

Her full breasts topped a perfect hourglass between her shoulders and hips, and the nest of soft curls at her groin made my mouth water. She dropped a hand beside her hip, palm up and wiggled her fingers to make me raise my gaze. When I did, she gave me a smirk.

"Hey, handsome, my eyes are up here and while you can have what's down there, I want you looking at me when you fuck me."

My cock flexed behind my jeans at her dirty words. "Do you always talk like that to your would-be lovers?"

"Nope." She shook her head as she unbuttoned and unzipped my pants. "Just the really special ones." She pushed the jeans off my hips and stared at my hard cock pointing upwards. "My last "lover" couldn't be bothered to get me wet before he shoved his dick in, rocked a few times, and went off like a bottle rocket. Ooh-ahh-whoosh. That was it."

I scowled. Haley was the kind of woman a lover should savor. She had curves, heat, and fire to play with. Anyone who ignored her wasn't worth the air they used to breathe. She licked her lips and I damn near saw stars, but I grasped her head and lifted her face until she met my gaze.

"Only a wanker would do that to a woman like you, Haley. I'm not a wanker and I like to take my time." I pulled her close and tilted my head, pausing a few millimeters from her lips. "Even when I kiss."

Then I brushed her lips with mine.

It would've been a sweet, sexy, gentle kiss. Until she moaned with a little whimper on the end. That made my cock flex and ignited the desperate need to get closer to her. I groaned into her mouth and tilted my head, deepening the kiss. The slide of her tongue against mine sent erotic sensation straight to my bollocks. They tightened up, crowding against my hard cock with desperate need.

Fuck, I have to slow down. Otherwise I'd shoot off like an untried boy and I'd *never* been one of those.

I pulled back enough to skim kisses down her neck to her collarbones while my hands massaged her full breasts. Each lovely mound supported a dusky rose-colored areola with a perfect bud nipple and I couldn't resist strumming them with my thumbs. Haley arched her back under my hands, thrusting her breasts into my palms as she wriggled her hips.

I hissed as my cock shifted against her thighs, leaving a streak of precum on her silken skin. *Fuck, that's hot.* Hotter than I'd been in a long time. Hell, I hadn't felt this way about anyone in at least a century, and all I'd done was kiss her.

But she tasted like buried dreams and divine light, and I knew a lot about those things. My own hidden dreams had brought me to the Concrete Angels MC in the first place. That, and keeping my brother Luke in balance.

I shoved my brother out of my thoughts and concentrated on licking the delicious curves of Haley's breasts. They quivered with her short breaths and each movement made my cock get impossibly harder.

"Oh glory, Michael." Haley's voice filled with need. "I need you."

"I know you do, my beauty. And I promise to give you exactly what you need."

I'd never heard my voice so rough but it revealed my needs as I kissed my way down her body until I settled between her legs. I met her gaze as I positioned first one leg then the other over my shoulders and dipped my face just enough to kiss her mound. The nest of dark curls already had a glaze of her honey and I licked my lips as I pulled back.

"You're already so wet for me, my beauty. I plan on feasting on your sweet nectar until you scream my name."

She huffed a laugh and tilted her head to give me a smirk. "Come on. That never really happens. But I wish you luck with that."

I laughed, a rough, joyful chuckle from deep in my chest. "Challenge accepted."

She shot me a disbelieving smile until I dropped my chin and licked her sweet pussy from slit to clit. Haley threw her head back and wailed. Her hands tightened in my hair as her divine taste hit my tongue.

It was addictive, sweet and tangy ambrosia and I couldn't get enough. But I forced myself to slow down, savor the cream covering her folds like sugar glaze. I slid my tongue between her labia up to her clit before tugging on it with my lips. She writhed under my touches, whimpering with each brush of my tongue.

Pleasure ramped up in my chest, making me want more. More intimacy, more connection, more of her. I feasted on her pussy, drinking down her cream and her moans as I massaged her soft flesh.

"Oh glory, Michael, please."

I hummed my response as I licked and sucked on her folds, then slowly inserted one finger into her grasping sheath. She gasped and rocked her hips in the rhythm to my finger sliding in and out of her hot body, and my own cock hardened in sympathy.

Sweet Glory I want her.

I added a second finger when her whimpers became

needy and she rocked harder, her juices washing over my hand and tongue. Her flavor filled my mouth and my senses, and her flesh flushed with rosy pleasure. My arousal ramped up and I had to fight the urge to pull my fingers away and thrust my cock in their place.

But Haley made the decision for me. Her hips tightened and her vagina clamped down on my fingers as a flood of nectar filled my mouth.

"Oh my glory, MICHAAEELLLL!"

Her scream hit the ceiling of the room as I drank down her release. The tangy ambrosia flavor damn near intoxicated me and I swallowed all of her cream as she shook under my lips. I pulled back only when her body relaxed and rose over her, desperate to drive her back to the heights of ecstasy with my cock.

She opened her eyes and gave me a languid smile as I fitted the head of my shaft to her pussy's opening. The hot, slickness of her slit made a shiver run through me and I gritted my teeth against shoving straight into her.

"I'm going to make you mine."

I met her gaze with my blood pounding in my ears. This was an important moment, I felt it deep in my gut, and I held her gaze as I slowly pushed my cock into her grasping depths. When I was seated balls-deep I stopped and closed my eyes.

Sweet glory of all.

I'd never felt anything like Haley's heat and slick softness. My heart expanded outward, breaking old restrictions I never knew I had. She fit me perfectly and I didn't want to move.

Until she squeezed me with those internal muscles. My eyes opened just in time to catch her mischievous grin.

"Oh, hell no." I pulled my hips back then pushed slowly back into her seductive grip, watching as pleasure suffused her face. "Two can play that game, my beauty."

But fucking her slowly and watching her arousal build

back up was my own undoing. Hot, relentless pleasure built inexorably from my bollocks, fanning out through my chest and shoulders. I couldn't slow my motions and I rode her hard, slamming my cock into her welcoming embrace.

I meant to go slow, seducing her with the skill of lovemaking honed over centuries, but I was lost in her, feeling more than I had in decades. I rocked my hips and raised my gaze to meet hers. She was there with me, focused on me, her eyes blazing with pleasure, and I couldn't resist pulling her close as I sat up.

"You're mine, Haley." I held her tight against my chest as I rocked my cock into her. "Say you understand. Say you're mine."

"I'm yours, Michael. Oh glory, fuck me." She grasped my shoulders and held on as she rode my cock.

My orgasm wouldn't wait, no matter how much I wished it otherwise and I reached down to strum her clit with my thumb.

"Come for me, my beauty."

Whether it was my words or my thumb, she clamped down on my cock and exploded in pleasure. I followed her over the precipice, my release exploding from my bollocks all the way up my spine to shoot out the top of my head. I let myself go and my wings appeared, closing around the woman in my arms without my say-so.

Warmth, protection, safety, and love hit my system all at once and I never wanted to be without her. She was my one and only, and I'd never be the same again.

I floated in that space of comfort for a long time, my sense of the world outside my cabin fading away to nothing. I had my woman in my arms and my wings protected us both.

Wings...holy shit!

It took some concentration, but I managed to stuff the appendages back under their glamour. Of course that made my dick wilt. I carefully laid Haley back down on the bed and kissed her neck and chest as I backed away.

"Wait, where are you going?"

"Nowhere, love. I'm just going to clean you up before we rest." Yeah, and make sure my bloody wings were back where they were supposed to be. "Sleep now. I'll be back in a bit."

"Okay…" She shot me a languid smile as she closed her eyes and my heart fluttered with exquisite joy.

I made sure to grab a soft washcloth before stumbling into the bathroom. I closed the door behind me and stared at my reflection. My dark hair was mussed and I had an unusual glow to my skin. While angels can glow after they've received grace from some source, usually it didn't show.

I glowed like a bloody spotlight and had to blink at my own reflection. *Thank glory I shut the door.* After my eyes accustomed to the light, I scanned my body to make sure my wings were completely hidden and noticed something on my chest.

A small heart with an old fashioned writing quill stabbed through it sat below the tattoo I'd gotten for being a fighter. Unlike humans, my tattoos arrived after I'd accomplished something. Something important to leave a mark as a memory.

I stared at the heart with the quill and swallowed hard. *Haley truly is my One-and-Only.* Which meant I'd bonded myself to my beloved, and that was great. But I hadn't told her who or what I was, and that wasn't great at all.

How in the Goddess's name am I going to tell her?

I ran the hot water over the wash cloth and returned to the bedroom. Haley lay curled on her side with her hair spread out over my pillows. My heart squeezed with both sexual desire and unbearable tenderness. She'd captured my heart and didn't even know what she had.

I mentally slapped the back of my head and bent to run the cloth over her. Unfortunately, it'd grown cold while I was woolgathering and Haley hissed awake.

"Sweet glory! Did you fill it with ice cubes?"

"I'm so sorry." I skittered back to the bathroom and ran the cloth under the hot tap again. "I didn't mean to wake you, but the cloth got cold and…" I stopped before I dug myself a deeper hole. "I'm sorry. Try this one."

She watched me with suspicion until I slid the hot cloth over her mound. *I'm a sodding wanker.* Nothing like making a post-coital impression with an ice-cold washcloth. I tossed the wet cloth back in the bathroom and crawled into the bed, hoping my body hadn't cooled too much to keep from snuggling up to her.

Because I'd found my mate completely by accident, and there was no way I'd let go of her now.

****

Haley

I sighed with pleasure and snuggled back into the blankets and the man holding me. Normally, I had to be at work at eight, but the snowstorm ensured that wouldn't happen. Hell, I didn't even know what time it was. Not that I was complaining. Michael was a fantastic lover, attentive and responsive. It'd been a long time since I'd been with someone who both gave and received. And damn, he'd received *very* well.

I wanted to stay in the warm cocoon forever, but my body had other needs and wasn't going to wait. I wiggled my way out from under Michael's arm and padded to the bathroom, naked. I snorted. *If this had been a TV show or movie, I would've been tastefully covered in a long T-shirt or nightie.* Thank goodness we weren't on TV.

I finished in the bathroom and took a moment to savor the dim light coming from outside. There was a quality to "snow light" that always made me want to snuggle in bed with a cup of coffee and a good book. *And having a hot man to share the space with wouldn't be bad either.*

Michael was a hot man, but I knew so little about him. Despite that, he made me want to spend as much time with him as possible. *Dangerous addiction, Haley.* Yeah, it was, and I'd have to be careful I didn't imagine stuff that wasn't there. But it felt so good to be wanted instead of needed for a change.

"Are you coming back to bed?" Michael's sleep-roughened voice reached my ears and I turned to meet his slitted gaze.

"Yeah, I was just enjoying the snow light." I drifted back to the bed and crawled in beside his warm body.

"Snow light?"

"Yeah, it's a weird quality that happens when it snows. It's damn near light enough to read outside, even in the dead of night." I scrunched up my face. "It's dark but light, and for just a moment the world feels in balance. I makes me want to snuggle in bed and just rest in the moment."

"I can help with the snuggle in bed part." The amusement and arousal in his voice left no doubt of his interest. "I've never noticed that quality to the light when it snows. I should pay better attention."

I shrugged. "We all have our shortcomings."

"Oy, that's enough of that, you wicked woman." He wrapped his arms around me before he rolled on top of my body. "I'll have to kiss the snark right out of you."

I snorted. "Good luck with that." Although I did enjoy his persistent efforts to do so.

When he rolled off of me again, he pulled me close to his body and we enjoyed the early evening silence. The snow muffled any sounds of people moving around outside and I liked the sense of solitude.

"You know, I wish I could stay here forever."

I meant the words, surprisingly enough, and I loved the idea of always having something like this to come home to.

But I also understood it was a fantasy, the rough edges and misunderstandings of life glossed over and shined up.

"Here at the compound or here in this moment?" Michael didn't pretend to not understand. I liked that about him.

"Here in this moment with the quiet and the snow and the lack of responsibility." I sighed. It was a lovely daydream, but I'd grow bored and have to go find something to do. I wasn't much for sitting around doing nothing.

He snorted. "How long would that last, Haley? You don't strike me as a woman who relaxes much."

It was like he'd read my mind. I laughed. "No, I don't. There's always something to do or something to report on." I turned my head to scan his face. "But I might be convinced to relax if you waited with me. You definitely keep my mind occupied."

He smirked. "I do my best."

I lost my own smile. "But pretty soon here I'm gonna have to go back down to Fort Collins."

Michael shifted beside me and his jaw tightened. "I don't know if that's a good idea. I don't think it's safe."

"Oh come on. The big bad biker can't drive in the snow? How long have you lived in Colorado?"

He didn't take the bait. "It's not the snow, Haley. There's another reason I brought you here."

My gut settled into cold unease. "What are you talking about?"

But he shook his head. "I can't really explain how I knew, but I brought you here because my gut said you wouldn't be safe at home."

I stared at him, trying to figure out if he was joking, but his solemn expression made my unease ramp up. I'd been on my own since I was about sixteen. Or may as well have been. I often walked the train tracks home from my job in the setting sun, balancing on the individual rails, no cares beyond getting home to do the last of my homework and chores.

I'd known a few cops and always felt safe because they protected me. My dad had been the janitor at the police station and had made friends. Most of the cops I'd known had been good people, honest, and hometown heroes who took care of others.

"What, you think my home is compromised?"

Michael raised a challenging eyebrow. "Why were you ducking the cops in the coffeeshop last night?"

I shrugged to try to throw him off his questions. "I dunno. A gut feeling. Those cops made me feel uncomfortable." Yeah, because they might have figured out I was the one to call in the murder. "It's not like I thought I'd be stuck in some cop hell and wouldn't be safe at home."

"Cop hell doesn't exist. Believe me. I know from first-hand experience." Michael rolled his eyes. "But I also know when to trust my gut and when it's just a feeling. Last night was a big-time gut check. Sounds like it was for you, too. Want to tell me why?"

No, I didn't, but I had to tell him something because he struck me as a man who intuitively knew when something was wrong and wouldn't rest until he understood what it was. Oh, I could work on him and divert him for a while, but I suspected it wouldn't be worth the effort.

I sighed and snuggled closer to him, listening to his heartbeat. "My cousin Jeff is the only family I have who really gives a shit about me, and vice versa. Recently, he got involved with some bad people, and when I say bad, I mean so bad they make mob bosses look like saints."

Just thinking about Jeff's appearance after his ordeal was enough to make me roll out of bed and look around for the t-shirt and sweats Michael had given me. I threw them on and rubbed my arms, wondering what time it was. Midafternoon? Evening? Whichever, I was hungry and needed some tea to get through this story.

"Do you think we can get something to eat? I'm starving."

Michael nodded slowly and rolled out of the bed. I couldn't help but enjoy his magnificent body. It was damn near angelic the way he moved. The muscles slid over the bones in perfect rhythm and ease, and I shamelessly watched him until he threw on a shirt and another pair of sweats.

"I think there's some food left in the kitchen. We'll make a carpet picnic and settle on the couch."

I nodded, glad for a short break. I followed his sexy ass into the kitchenette and helped him put together a meal before we sat down in the living room. He even started the kettle so we could have tea.

"Eat a little before you finish your story."

I piled things on my plate before I found my seat on the couch with one foot curled under me. He sat down beside me and leaned back with an expectant look on his face while he waited for me to stuff my face. I put some cheese and crackers together with tomato and tried to ignore my stomach growling. Yeah, I'd worked up a bit of an appetite fucking him.

We ate in silence for a few moments until the kettle whistled. He rose and headed for the kitchenette while I gathered my thoughts. This was the first time I'd told this story to anyone other than Tori, and I'd even left out details with her. But I wanted to tell it to Michael. Some inner voice suggested he might understand better than anyone else.

He returned with two cups of tea. It smelled like green tea. I took the cup and sipped as he settled on the couch.

"Good?" He raised an eyebrow. I nodded. "Continue when you're ready."

I held the tea and tried to remember where I'd left off. "Jeff met a guy who seemed really into him. We'll call him

Dick, because he turned out to be a huge one and I don't mean what he carried around in his pants."

Michael snorted but didn't interrupt.

"Dick was rich, or at least had more money than Jeff, and seemed really sweet at first. He paid Jeff lots of compliments, bought him clothes and gifts, took him out to clubs, etc." I let my lips curl in a smile, even as sorrow tugged at my heart. "Jeff didn't get that kind of attention from family much. Being bisexual made my aunt and uncle very uncomfortable, and they made it pretty clear they were a "don't ask don't tell" family. So Dick's attention and apparent kindness were a temptation Jeff couldn't walk away from."

I took a fortifying sip of tea, shivering. Michael tugged a fleece blanket off the back of the couch and wrapped it over us.

"Thanks. Jeff told me all about this guy and how happy he made him. We really thought there was something real there. But Jeff didn't realize until it was too late that Dick was actually grooming him to be a pretty boy sex slave."

Michael didn't move or say anything, but his expression filled with sorrow and compassion.

I nodded. "Yeah. I won't disgust you with the details, but it was a couple of months before I realized he'd stopped communicating with me regularly and that it was strange. Finally, I tracked him down at his job in California just to find out he was quitting. Packing up his stuff and leaving. A job he loved."

The sick feeling I'd had then returned to the pit of my stomach and I gripped tea mug in both hands.

"When I cornered him, he said his boyfriend was going to take care of him now and he wouldn't have to work." I grimaced. "Normally, when someone tells me that, they're excited to have a Sugar Daddy who gives them a luxurious lifestyle. But Jeff only looked panicked and haunted while talking to me, like he was afraid Dick would see him talking to anyone."

"What did you do?"

I rubbed the back of my neck. "I strong-armed him into coming to my hotel so we could talk. When he told me everything, I realized I had to get him help. It took a long time, a lot of counseling, and cutting him off from all his social media, phone, email, and moving him out here to Colorado." I sighed. "He wanted to escape but he was too afraid to go against Dick, who was rich, powerful, and a "pillar of the community," especially in the L.A. LGBTQ crowd. But he was just a rich predator and a creep. I essentially kidnapped Jeff and brought him to the Hopeful Heart Shelter for sexual abuse survivors."

Michael nodded and laid a warm hand over mine. "You did the right thing."

I nodded. "I know. He hated me for a short time because he was always afraid Dick would come for him. And he still has a tough time being around men, even if he's attracted to them. But I couldn't let him think no one cared. I'm the only family he has. And now we watch out for each other."

"Does he know where you are right now?" A curiously tenseness filled Michael's voice.

I narrowed my eyes. "Yeah. I called him to let him know so he wouldn't worry. Why?"

Michael grunted and his eyes took on a faraway look. "He's still worried about you."

That was an odd thing to say. He was right, no question, but how would Michael know that Jeff was worried? *Because family always worries.* I nodded and shrugged.

"Yeah. He wanted to drive up here and rescue me from the 'bad bikers of the Concrete Angels,' but I told him I was safe and I didn't want him driving in the snow."

"Wise of him." Michael gave a self-deprecating chuckle, almost as if he'd been found out. "But you're right about being safe here. When the snow lets up, I'll make sure to get you back to Fort Collins tomorrow."

Now why did that make me sad? I'd known this guy, what, a handful of hours? It wasn't like some paranormal romance novel where he was my One-and-Only after one bout of sex. I mentally snorted. *Real world love doesn't happen that way.* Despite my love of angel and demon romance, my life never moved along romantic lines, and I doubted it would start anytime soon.

"Great." I tried to sound happy. It was what I wanted, to get back to my job and my life. This had just been a minor aberration. Right?

"Come, let's get a little more sleep before we tackle driving down the mountain in the snow." He rose and held his hand out to me.

I took it as I smirked. "Sleep, huh?"

He grinned. "That's right. Something tells me you're far more energetic when you're on the go and we'll need all the rest we can get." He tugged me into the bedroom and undressed while I crawled back into the bed.

"You sure you don't want to do anything other than sleep?" I tilted my head and gave him a sly smile.

He chuckled. "For now, yes." His smile warmed me in places I didn't even know were cold as he gathered me into his arms. "Rest. You can tackle the world tomorrow."

"Sounds like a plan." I closed my eyes and snuggled back against him, glad of his warmth, and if I was honest, his protection.

CHAPTER EIGHT

Michael

We slept in later than I expected but the dim snowy light made moving out of the warm bed damn near impossible. I still chewed over the discovery I'd made the day before and hadn't figured out how to tell Haley. I'd learned a lot about her and her love of her cousin, but there was something else she was holding back.

By the time the snow stopped and Flint had marshaled the Scooters to plow the yard, Haley was champing at the bit to head back into town. The woman was a powerhouse of energy and she'd made coffee, tea, and checked her social media accounts while peering out my front windows more times than I could count.

"Fuck."

I raised my eyebrows at her soft exclamation and she grimaced.

"Something wrong?"

"Yeah, the Denver Tribune reported on the death of ADA O'Donnell before our affiliate did. Dammit." She shook her head. "I wish my phone hadn't been dead."

"What are you talking about?"

She blinked and looked up at me as if remembering where she was. "Oh, nothing. It's a big story and it sucks that our competitors got to it before we did." She dropped her gaze back to the phone. "And they didn't even get the details right. Jeez. I really gotta get to work." She shot a look out the window again.

Her anxiousness sparked my own and I shoved my feet into boots to go start my bike. But her words on the death of O'Donnell sounded like first-hand experience rather than professional disdain. I zipped up my vest over my thick flannel shirt and headed out into the snowy day. Flint nodded to me as I passed and raised an eyebrow, tilting his head toward my place. I didn't bother to respond but more than likely our security expert knew about Haley.

I'll tell Loki soon enough.

I made it to the Barn and found my bike in its allotted spot. No one else was around beyond the Scooters who shoveled the yard. I thanked all the saints for this brief respite from the other senior members of the club, but I knew the questions would come soon. Of course, given who I was, I could pull off the Inscrutable Serenity(tm) look pretty well and very few people would push for answers.

Unfortunately, Loki's rarely impressed with my skills.

All I had to do was get Haley out of the compound before anyone noticed and we'd be golden. Easy, right? Until the entire bloody club decided that's when they needed to check their bikes too. Scott came in with Torch to work on their respective bikes. I nodded to them as I headed toward the door but didn't stop to talk.

Then Attila stopped me halfway across the yard and inhaled deeply. Normally, this wouldn't have been a problem except Attila was a Moonsinger, what werewolves called themselves, and his nose told him more about people than body language. I'd showered but that wouldn't stop Attila's nose unless I'd doused myself with cologne.

Bloody hell.

"Where're ye off to in such a hurry, Michael? We just got the yard cleared."

"Yeah, I know. Good thing. I have to run an errand down in Fort Collins. I've been waiting for the storm to clear." I straddled my bike and cranked the engine. It fired up with a gratifying rumble.

Attila narrowed his eyes. "What is that scent yer wearin' now? Ye didn't get some stink pretty, did ye?"

Despite my unease, I laughed. "No."

"Are ye sure? Yer scent's different. Kinda girly." His eyes opened wide. "Have ye been visitin' a brothel finally?"

I had nothing against sex workers, but Haley wouldn't appreciate being thought of as a prostitute. I shook my head and moved the bike toward my cabin.

"Weel, I know ye've been shaggin' some sort of woman."

He'd followed me closer to the door and I hoped Haley would have the sense not to come out where he could see her. Not that I had much hope of hiding her for long. I just needed to get her back to Fort Collins before I showed everyone that she'd be visiting more often. What kind of a role model was I to the other members if I just hauled off and deposited a woman in my cabin? Yeah, being the VP offered a few perks, but I preferred to lead by example.

Ever the rule follower. Luke's sarcastic voice came through load and clear. I ignored him.

"Some sort of woman?" I snorted. "I'm sure she'd appreciate your observation, Attila. Now, bugger off. I gotta get down to Fort Collins."

"Why are ye stoppin' at yer cabin, then?"

"To pick up something I forgot while the bike warms up. I don't feel like freezin' my bollocks off on the ride down. You want a rundown of what I ate this morning?"

"Only if it's pussy." He smirked.

I gave him my best enigmatic smiles. I had enjoyed Haley's pussy, several times, but that was my treasure to keep.

"Och, ye sly dog."

"Dogs more your skill set." I winked at his scowl as I dismounted and strode to the door. "But if you're looking for pussy, I think there are a few honeys still in the clubhouse."

"Kiss me arse."

I pointed at the clubhouse. "Like I said, there's probably a honey or two to do that for you."

He flipped me off, but stomped toward the clubhouse with my laughter following him. *Maybe I aroused more than just his suspicions.* I took one more glance about before I opened my cabin door and looked for Haley. I found her at the window.

"Damn, how can that guy be wearing a kilt? It's freezing out there. I'm sure his balls are the size of marbles by now."

I laughed. "Attila would be terribly offended and required to lift his kilt just to prove you wrong." I scanned the yard to make sure no one was around. "The yard and road are clear. I can take you to Fort Collins now."

"Great." She gathered up her dress and purse as she headed for the door, but she stopped and looked up at me with a smile. "And no, I don't want to see under his kilt. Well, not much, anyway." Then she winked and darted out the door.

I slammed the door of the cabin as hard as I did the one on my jealousy and tried to school my expression. But the idea of Haley being anywhere near Attila's dick sent a spike of discomfort through me.

What the hell is wrong with me? I was older than time and had never suffered such petty emotions as jealousy. And the Goddess had chosen Haley for me. What did I have to be jealous about?

Maybe that you haven't told her and she could pick someone else before you do?

I told my inner voice to piss off as I handed her the extra helmet. Haley pulled it on over her head and sat on the back seat, waiting for me without a word. I settled in front of her and rolled the bike off its stand, steering toward the gate as my gut churned.

Fortunately, no one stopped us getting out of the gate, though I did catch some raised eyebrows from Quan-Yin as I passed her. I didn't often take honeys on my bike with me and since they could see Haley's face, they must have found it odd. I nodded as we slid through and hoped I wouldn't catch the first degree when I got back.

I didn't have Blutooth speakers in the helmets so it was a silent ride down the mountain. Despite the cold, the trip was beautiful with the hills and trees glowing brightly in the morning sunshine.

She directed me to an apartment complex with external entrances in covered walkways. Covered parking lined the sidewalks out front and Haley had me pull up behind a sage green Subaru. She tapped my shoulder and slid off the bike before doffing the helmet.

"Thank you for the ride and...and everything." She handed me the brain bucket and I traded it for the bag of clothes. "Thanks. I'll get Dollhouse's sweats back to you after I wash them."

I nodded, the words of who she was to me beating against my lips, but I swallowed them down. "I took the liberty of adding my mobile number to your phone. Call if you need anything, Haley. I'll be there."

"Oh, I couldn't ask you to do that."

"You didn't ask. I offered. And I'm serious. I'll be there." I met her gaze and tried to convey my sincerity. "It's no trouble."

She bit her lip and I wanted to crush her into a hug, but she stepped back and nodded. "Okay, I'll keep that in mind.

Thanks again for the ride."

She turned and hurried up the steps to the second floor landing then waved before she disappeared into the covered walkway. I made note which building and which staircase before I threw the bike into gear and headed back up toward the compound.

Though I'd been tempted when I added my phone number, I hadn't checked anything else in her phone. But something bothered Haley about the night I'd found her in Denver and I suspected it had something to do with the murder of the ADA.

My next move was to ask Neo to look into it, and research who the ADA had hacked off. My gut told me it was more than the usual organized crime or disgruntled common criminals.

And I needed to talk to my brother about Haley and who she was to me. Because I'd need him to back me up when I faced Loki. The Concrete Angels MC was generally fearless when it came to the press or the authorities. But Haley was a truthseeker and that could make things very uncomfortable with the Elder Races among the membership.

****

Haley

"You have to get out of here, Haley."

That's never a good thing to hear the moment I step into the office. I'd been floating through my morning after I called to tell my boss I'd be late. Having Michael take such good care of me, along with his divine sexiness, was enough to derail my usually frenetic mind. But Tori's efforts to turn me bodily toward the door and shove me ahead of her brought the holiday to an end.

Holiday? Jeez, Michael's British accent is totally

getting to me.

"What? Why? What the hell is going on?" I tried not to trip over my own feet as she propelled me down the hallway away from the glassed in newsroom.

"Some detectives came in looking for you and went directly to Hank." She hustled me back out to the elevators in the lobby.

"Wait, what detectives? What are you talking about?"

She grimaced and shook her head. "I didn't catch everything, but it sounds like they think you saw a murder last weekend."

"What?" I swallowed hard and hoped my face didn't reflect my unease. "I didn't see a murder, I heard it and reported it anonymously. How the hell did they know to come here?"

"Carl must have sold you out." Tori scowled. "I told you that guy was lower than pond scum. And why didn't you tell me about this murder you witnessed?"

"Keep your voice down." I glanced around then dragged her toward the windows overlooking the street, conveniently next to the door to the stairs. "I didn't tell you because my phone was dead. And it was the fuckin' ADA who was murdered, Tori. I didn't really want to let them know who saw it."

"Why not?"

"Because it was a hit and if they're willing to take out the ADA, they're not gonna think twice about a fluff reporter for the Fort Collins Bugle."

Raised voices came out of the office. "You couldn't keep your mouth shut, could you, Carl?"

"Hank—"

"Tell us where we can find her, Mr. Cortland." The detective sounded frustrated.

"I'm outta here." I headed for the door.

"Just don't go home. And call or text me when you get somewhere safe."

Right. Where was I supposed to go?

I swallowed hard and ran down the stairs. The stairwell was empty so I didn't have to hide my hurry, but once I hit the ground floor, I took a moment to settle myself so I didn't look panicked to everyone.

I inhaled a deep breath and stepped through the door, trying to look at ease. Just a fluff reporter headed out on a regular ole assignment. I kept my head turned from the most obvious cameras, wishing I had my winter hat to hide my hair. I really needed to get back to my apartment, but Tori told me not to go there. Where the hell could I go?

Think, Haley!

I nodded to a few people I passed as I headed for the front doors of the Bugle. I didn't want anyone to really notice me, but if I acted like I didn't see them, they'd know something was up and would tell anyone who asked. And for some reason my gut told me I didn't want the cops catching up with me.

Maybe I've been spending too much time with the Concrete Angels.

Yeah, well, I trusted my gut more than I trusted people, and if it said keep my head down, I'd do it. I had to find a place to hunker down until I could figure out what was going on and who was really looking for me. I knew the cops wanted to talk to me about the ADA's death, but I didn't know which of them were part of this weird group of crooked law enforcement officials. I thought of Tori's list and blinked. *Was that the Backlog the killers had been talking about?* I had Tori's list, but I didn't know if the two detectives in Hank's office were on it.

Shit, who the hell can I trust?

I could trust Jeff. He'd do anything for me, but I didn't want to lead any crooked cops to him. I looked both ways before I crossed the street, trying to think of somewhere I could go and someone I could call. I couldn't visit Jitters because that was my favorite place to go, and the first place they'd look. I tried to think of what Jason Bourne would do. I didn't have any special training, but I had some idea on how to avoid people from all the romantic suspense books I'd read. First step was to avoid all my usual places. Which is why I couldn't call Jeff. Or go home. Or hang out at Jitters.

I kept walking past the coffee shop and headed toward the open-air mall two blocks down. I could lose myself in a couple of those stores while I figured out what to do. I kept an eye open for police officers. No doubt they'd report my whereabouts to the detectives if they saw me. I kept my strides purposeful but unhurried even though my heart thundered in my chest.

Just as I reached the first shop in the mall, a pair of cops riding those Segway things rolled around the corner. I took an immediate left and found myself in a novelty shop with items like boob mugs and rubber dog shit. I hid behind a rack of naughty card games and whoopee cushions until the cops passed by. I pretended to browse the t-shirts with images of comic book characters as I waited to be sure they'd gone, wracking my brain to figure out what to do.

Who could I call for help?

One name shot to the forefront of my mind and the faux leather vests hanging on another rack against the wall seemed to cheer me on. *Michael.* Right. If I needed to avoid the cops, who better to call than the VP of a notorious biker club?

I exited the novelty shop and headed deeper into the mall, hoping to lose myself in the crowd. I stopped with my back to a shop's wall and pulled out my phone to text Michael. I didn't need anyone listening in to what I said. I hit send and bit my lip as I let my gaze rang around me.

Come on, Michael. Check your damn phone.

Two or three minutes passed before I swore and glanced at my phone. Where the hell was he? I scowled and debated making an actual call. But the longer I stood still, the easier it would be for the cops to find me.

I swallowed hard and brought up his number. *Just do it, Haley.* My hands shook as I dialed Michael's number, but whether in excitement or nervousness, I didn't know.

"This is Michael."

The deep voice on the other end of the call made my heartbeat slow in relief and my knees go weak in delight. *What's wrong with me?* Every time I heard his voice, the world seemed brighter and sweeter, while I just wanted to melt into a puddle of pleasure.

"Michael, it's Haley. Have you, uh, got a minute?"

He chuckled and I wanted to wrap myself up in the sound. "For you, I have all the time in the world."

I couldn't help my smile. "Thanks. I kinda need your help. I got to work today and there were people there looking for me. I got the hell out before they saw me, but my friend suggested I not go home."

Michael's voice grew sharp. "Are you all right? Where are you now?"

"I'm in the Mountain Shadow Mall on 28th street."

I shot a look around. A mall cop wandered between the bath store and the lingerie shop. I shifted my path into a clothing store for hipsters, figuring a person on the phone wouldn't be that out of place.

"Hang tight. I can be there in ten minutes. I'll meet you outside the burger place on the corner. You know the one I mean?"

I nodded and peered out the store windows for the cop. "Yeah, I know it. The one with the name of a Rolling Stones song. I'll be there."

"Right. I'm on my way. See you soon."

Michael ended the call and I shoved my phone in my purse before I wrinkled my nose at the clothes and headed out the door. What the hell was I going to do for ten minutes? I considering buying a cup of coffee at the Dunkin' Donuts, but I didn't have any cash on me and I was pretty sure the cops would be tracking my credit cards when they couldn't locate me. I'd watched enough CSI and cop TV shows to know how they tracked people.

Which meant it was going to be hard to get money without them noticing. Maybe there'd be a way to get to my account and empty it before anyone caught on. My mind worked over and threw out possibilities as I meandered down the mall, pretending to browse. I looked enough like a regular shopper that when a cop did spot me she didn't even blink or look twice. My heart tried to beat its way out of my chest, but I kept walking and she didn't stop me.

Sweet glory, I gotta get out of here. Had it been ten minutes yet?

CHAPTER NINE

Michael

"Neo, I need you to look up Assistant District Attorney Patrick O'Donnell."

"Any reason you wanna look into an ADA?" Neo's voice held reserve but I could hear his fingers on the keyboard.

"I have myriad reasons, but suffice it to say it has to do with a woman." While I wasn't into airing my personal affairs, I knew that would catch his attention and make him work harder.

"Would that be the woman you had on the back of your bike when you hightailed it outta here this morning?"

I grimaced as I put up the gas nozzle and tightened the cap on my bike. So much for leaving under the radar. "It might."

"She got a name?"

"As it happens, she does, but right now I'm more interested in ADA O'Donnell, what happened to him, when and where." I had the sneaking suspicion I already knew.

Neo snorted. "All right, Schnoz. I'll have something for you when you get back."

"Right." I ended the call and shoved the phone in my pocket as I started the bike.

The sun played hide-n-seek with the clouds as I continued my ride back home. Something Haley had said kept my mind going over the time we'd spent together. *I wish my phone hadn't been dead.* She'd been talking about the night I brought her up to the compound, when she'd been spooked of the cops and running from something. My gut told me it had something to do with the ADA.

I returned to the compound in record time but it might have been because my grace tended to bend time a bit when I worried. Haley was my bonded mate, though she didn't know it yet, so whatever affected her affected me. I needed to know what in glory's name I was going to face when the shit hit the fan.

By the time I parked my bike in the Barn, I had several messages on my phone from both Neo and Luke. I ignored all of them and headed straight for Neo's Black Room, the hub of our communication and observation network. I didn't often use my angelic powers on my fellow club members, but I didn't have time for casual chitchat.

I made it to the Black Room and knocked. The camera positioned outside the door focused on my face before the door unlatched, and I pushed inside.

"I got your message but didn't have time to read it. What have you got, Neo?"

Neo didn't bother with pleasantries either. "Assistant District Attorney Patrick O'Donnell is dead. His body was found in the Turner Williams Building in downtown Denver last Friday night by police after an anonymous caller gave them a tip. Police also managed to break up a drunken orgy of some of the city's biggest media movers and shakers."

"Media. As in newspaper, TV, and internet?"

Neo nodded. "Yeah. Apparently, the ADA had been at the party to get some backing for his new honesty and integrity push in local law enforcement, but most people interviewed couldn't remember seeing him after he arrived."

I narrowed my eyes. "You said he was killed in Friday night?"

"Yeah, Valentine's Day. Why?"

That's when I'd picked up Haley in front of the Turner Williams building. Had she been at the party? She'd been dressed to the nines and hurrying out alone. Had she seen the ADA get killed? Was she the anonymous caller who'd tipped off the police? And if she was, why wouldn't she want to be acknowledged for that? She'd told me she wanted to be more than just a fluff reporter. That would've been her moment to shine.

Unless something else made her choose to hide her identity.

I thought back to what we'd learned from US Marshal Cooper DeVille before he was "killed" by his own. He'd been investigating a shadow group in law enforcement called Backlog and they'd come for him with a vengeance. *Which technically is Karma's bailiwick.* He'd said that Backlog had infiltrated all levels of law enforcement and possibly into members of the local government. He hadn't known how high it reached, but I suspected it went to the highest levels.

"The woman who was here. I picked her up in front of the Turner Williams building that night. She looked spooked so I brought her here to keep her safe."

Neo snorted. "Safe. Riiiiggghht. Did you keep her safe from the monster under your bed, too?"

"Kiss my arse, you tosser. I slept on one of my chairs while she took the bed." At least the first night. "But we went to a café and she was nervous when the coppers came in. What if she witnessed the murder?"

Neo frowned. "If she did, wouldn't she have been screaming it to the rooftops? I mean, she'd have to be press to be at the party. I'm pretty sure that would be a career-making story. Why would she tip off the cops anonymously?"

"I don't know. Her phone was dead so she couldn't get the word out or pics of it, but maybe there's another reason." I studied the information Neo had displayed on the monitors. "Do you think she was worried about something else, something bigger?"

"Bigger? Like what?"

"Like Backlog. If she announced anonymously, could it be because she didn't know which cops to trust? According to Eric, Backlog goes high up in law enforcement."

Neo rubbed his chin as he sat back in his chair. "That could be. From what I found on O'Donnell, he was doing this 'integrity and honesty' thing in an effort to clean up corruption not only in the judicial branches but in law enforcement. That would definitely cramp Backlog's style."

"And mark him for death." I nodded as my phone buzzed. I figured it was another message from Luke and ignored it. "No way to prove it was them, of course, but if they figure out who was the anonymous caller, my woman could be in danger."

"Your woman?" Neo tilted his head up and raised his eyebrows.

Fortunately, my phone rang at that moment and I excused myself to go back to the main room of the clubhouse.

"This is Michael."

"Michael, it's Haley. Have you, uh, got a minute?"

I chuckled, but the fear in her voice made it strained. "For you, I have all the time in the world."

"Thanks. I kinda need your help. I got to work today and there were people there looking for me. I got the hell out before they saw me, but my friend suggested I not go home."

"Are you all right? Where are you now?" I'd already headed back out the doors to the Barn.

"I'm in the Mountain Shadow Mall on 28th street."

"Hang tight. I can be there in ten minutes. I'll meet you outside the burger place on the corner. You know the one I mean?" I ignored anyone trying to catch my gaze and settled on my bike's seat, turning the key.

"Yeah, I know it. The one with the name of a Rolling Stones song. I'll be there."

"Right. I'm on my way. See you soon." *I'd better see her soon.* I wasn't taking any chances.

****

Haley

Shit, I so don't blend. This undercover stuff was way harder than I'd thought it would be. How did I walk around like I wasn't up to something when I was totally up to something?

I paused in a Hallmark shop, studying the boxes of stationary mixed with yard schlock and wind chimes at the front of the store. I drew out my phone to check the time and almost slapped my forehead with it. Phones had GPS chips in them. It might take a bit to get a warrant to track them, but they could. I sighed and turned my cell off. If I was going to do this for long, I'd need a new phone.

After pretending to debate between the cutsie panda stationary and the knock-off of Thomas Kinkade—*Austen Powyrs, I presume*—I resumed my trek to the burger place. I hoped Michael would be there. Standing on the corner out where anyone could see me made me nervous.

Hell, who am I kidding? I'm already nervous.

I stopped beside the entrance doors and peered outside, waiting for Michael to arrive. I didn't have to wait long. I made one last look around to be sure cops weren't skulking before I stepped out the doors and waved to him. He pulled over to the curb without a smile, his expression full of intense focus.

"Are you all right?"

"Yeah. Good. Let's go. The cops are looking for me."

"Why are the cops looking for you?" He handed me a helmet and I slipped it over my head.

"I'll tell you later. I really just need to get out of sight and I didn't know who else to call." I bit my lip. What if he got pissed about it? This whole situation made it look like I was using him. And I was, except I really liked him and felt I could trust him.

I hoped like hell I could trust him because there weren't many people left I could.

"Right then. Hold on."

I straddled the bike and settled in behind him, trying to be all relaxed like I wasn't running from the authorities. *Just fake it till you make it.* Yeah, sounded easy, but the actual application of it when my heart pounded like a snare drum made it a challenge. I wrapped my arms around his waist and my fear deflated, draining out of me.

What the hell? Something about Michael's energy settled my heart and my mind all at once and I let my breath, and tension, out on a long sigh. It wasn't the first time I'd felt it. I'd gone from being in an action-adventure suspense show to a cute, mellow romantic drama just by wrapping my arms around him.

To my surprise, he jumped on 287 and headed north to I-25 and into Cheyenne, Wyoming. It had been forever since I'd visited the state's capital city, and that had been for the rodeo. He parked his bike in front of a little funky coffee shop called The Tilted Teacup in downtown. There was one of those shops in Fort Collins, but we'd be less noticeable there. He helped me off the bike and led me inside to defrost with a hot cup of flavored tea. We found a table in the back and settled in with our drinks before he fixed me with his unnervingly direct stare.

"Now, tell me why the cops are after you."

I glanced around for local officers. "It's a long story."

"I have time, and so do you, even if I have to tie you to a bamboo post with a barge hawser."

"A what?"

He sighed. "Just tell me what's going on, Haley."

I wrapped my hands around the paper cup holding my tea, letting the heat seep into my hands as I gathered my thoughts. I didn't want to tell him but I'd called him for a rescue. *Kinda ungrateful to ask him to be a knight in shining armor with only half the information.*

I licked my lips and sat up, straightening my shoulders. He probably knew about the murder of the ADA because the Denver Trib had run the story. But what would I tell him if the murder had something to do with the crooked cops, the dead US Marshal, and the missing FBI agent who'd been embezzling from his club?

I took a deep breath, scrambling to answer his question before meeting his gaze. "Remember the night you found me coming out of that building in Denver? I was at a Valentine's Day party up on the ninth floor. My date abandoned me and some creeper was following me around, so I ducked into the emergency exit stairwell for some peace." I shook my head and ran a hand over my face. "The problem was the door to the party locked and my phone died, so I was stuck out there until someone found me."

"And did someone find you?"

"Not exactly. I headed up to the next floor in hopes the door up there was unlocked when I caught people talking on the other side. I was going to call out to them but then I heard gunshots. I didn't have a lot of time but I ran down the stairs and hid while they threw the body in the stairwell." I rubbed my face and glanced around, making sure no one was paying attention to us. "I really like this tea. I'm going to remember this place after we head home."

Michael tilted his head and narrowed his eyes. It took me a minute to realize I'd used "we" and "home" in the same sentence. *Since when does it feel like I share a home with him?* I mentally shook my head and sipped more of my tasty tea.

"So what happened after they left the body?"

"I waited a little bit for them to go and then followed them out."

"Did you report the murder?"

"My phone was dead, remember?" I shook my head and rubbed my arms, suddenly cold despite the tea. "I went back to the party to find my coat and my ride, but it had become an orgy and I'd already had a rough enough night. So I went down to the lobby and called the cops to come investigate. That's when I left and found you on the street."

He nodded with a frown. "Why didn't you stay around to talk to the cops?"

I raised an eyebrow. "Aren't you the VP of the Concrete Angels Motorcycle Club? Would you have stayed around to talk to cops?"

"This isn't about me, Haley. Why didn't you stay?"

I grimaced when he wouldn't be diverted. "Because I couldn't do anything for the dead guy and I didn't want anyone to know it was me who'd heard the murder. I might be a lowly Fort Collins Bugle reporter, but I'm high profile enough. I didn't want them to find me and put me down, too."

Michael grunted as some folks came in the coffee shop. I scanned them to make sure they weren't cops as I weighed the information I'd refused to mention while I'd stayed with him. I'd have to tell him something about the story I was working on, but I didn't want to muck up the relationship we'd built. *How the hell am I gonna tell him this?*

When I didn't continue my story, his eyes narrowed.

"That can't be everything. What aren't you telling me?"

Frankly? I wasn't telling him lots of things. Like just seeing him made my world brighter. And I couldn't stop thinking about him when we were apart. And that he made me feel safe even though he was a member one of the most notorious biker clubs in Colorado.

I looked around the room, taking in the few people nearby before taking a fortifying sip of my tea. *We're in Wyoming. They won't think to look for me in Wyoming, right?* I lowered my voice.

"The dead guy? It was the assistant district attorney of Denver, Patrick O'Donnell."

I waited for him to react but he only nodded.

"Don't you get it? O'Donnell is high up in the justice department of Denver. And they killed him, which either means he was crooked as a bendy straw or he found out something that made them silence him. Either way, I'm not a difficult target to remove."

"Was that why the cops in the coffee shop made you run?"

I grimaced, trying to explain my gut feelings. "Sort of. I've been working on this story about…"

I trailed off and glanced away. I had a damn good source in front of me, but it was his club, and he was the fucking VP. Before I'd met him and had sex with him, they were just another fun thing to report on. Now I faced a person I liked. His club meant a lot to him and I doubted he'd be thrilled with me poking into their business.

"What, Haley? What are you working on?"

"Here's the thing." I set my tea down and rubbed my hands on my thighs. "I told you I'm a fluff reporter right now, but I don't want to do that forever. I want to report on real events. Things that matter to people."

"Hence our conversation in Jitters that night."

I grimaced. "Yeah. That's right, I mentioned that, didn't I?"

He tilted his head, but didn't look away. Damn, why was he so determined to get this out of me?

"I stumbled across some information about a dead FBI agent who'd been embezzling your club while undercover and a dead US Marshal—"

He hissed and looked away, his expression stoic. "You need to let that one go, Haley."

"What? Are you kidding me? This is a huge story. I'm not interested in your club, only the crooked law enforcement officers who got into illegal stuff—"

"No, it's too dangerous. This is bigger than you know."

"That's what I'm trying to understand." I balled my hands into fists under the table and lowered my voice again. "I can't trust the cops, which is why I anonymously reported the murder. I don't know who's involved with the murder of the ADA or if it's tied to this group of dirty law enforcement. But I wasn't going to take my chances with them finding me before I'm prepared."

Michael shot me a sharp look. "Prepared for what?"

"To bring them all down and expose them." I spread my hands. "Don't you see? This is a career-making story that could get me onto the front page. I don't have to mention the connection to your club. I want to make sure the crooked cops are taken down."

He shook his head, his lips tightening in to a flat line. I was pretty sure I could convince him to help me if I played my cards right.

"Come on, Michael. You know I'm right."

He made a noncommittal noise and sipped his tea. "Why were the cops looking for you today?"

"I don't know. I went to work and they were there. My friend Tori suggested that my date sold me out and said it was me who reported the murder." I shrugged as my lips turned down. "It wouldn't surprise me. That guy's all about himself and he wouldn't know a real story if it landed on him." I shook my head. "The thing is, the crooked cops don't wear their sponsors on their jackets so I don't know who I can trust with this. Hell, they took out a US Marshal. I'd be easy pickin's."

"This is a dangerous road you're walking, Haley." Michael's face had gone stoic. "There are secrets you might not like to know. Secrets that can hurt those you care about. Secrets that are meant to stay secret for the safety of many."

I drew myself up to my full seated height. "I can be discreet. I always protect my sources."

Michael chuckled and shook his head. "You know you sound like every reporter on every TV show on the networks. And how does it work out for the sources on those shows?"

I scowled. "Shut up. I'm not like that. I have ethics and integrity. The story's important, but I'm doing this for people. People are the reason and who are most valuable. I have principles, and not just when they're convenient."

He nodded. "Just remember that when the story is as tempting as forbidden fruit. Most reporters don't care whom they hurt as long as they get their explosive story out. Don't let the ends justify the means, eh?"

I wanted to tell him off, but some cops came in the coffee shop and I ducked my head and sank into my thoughts. Hadn't I always upheld my ethics? I thought so, but I'd always been a fluff reporter and the details of the latest duck-feeding at the park weren't dangerous to anyone. Would I have enough ethics to walk away from a story when it would make my name in professional circles? *Better reporters than I have sold their souls to the Devil for such stories.* Was I as Machiavellian, justifying hurting the few to inform the many?

I let those thoughts chase themselves around in my head as I finished my tea until I noticed the cops eyeing Michael's cut with curiosity.

"I think we should go." I bent my head and kept my hair in front of my face as I rifled through my purse.

"I'm serious, Haley."

"I know. So am I." I nodded toward the cops, one of which spoke on his shoulder radio. "They're pretty interested in you and me."

He nodded and rose. "Don't worry. They'll forget about us as soon as we step out the door."

I snorted. Sure they would. Just like I'd forget about the dead body I saw in the stairwell on Valentine's day. A line from a recent song came to me: *You know that somethin' ain't right.* Yeah, I knew deep in my gut a lot of shit was wrong and going down, but proving it and not getting caught in the process were my top priorities.

I felt like an old dirty SUV parked in the parking lot of a mall after going mud-hopping. I was out of place and distinctive without trying. We gathered up our cups and tossed them in the trash as we made our exit, the cops watching us the whole way.

"So where to now?"

Michael handed me my helmet and shrugged. "Back to your apartment."

"Tori said I shouldn't go home."

"We're just going to pick up a few things before I take you to my place."

I settled on the bike. "Is that a good idea? They'll be looking for me. It could bring heat to your club if I just disappear with you."

"Haley, if you don't find a safe place, you'll disappear permanently."

That shut me up and I wrapped my arms around his waist as I swallowed hard. Had it really come to that? He started the bike and we wound our way through the quaint downtown streets of Cheyenne before heading for the freeway. My mind spun along with the wheels.

I needed to be somewhere safe, sure, but it was my job

to get in people's faces and expose the truth. *Which is what I wanted, right?* The traitorous voice wasn't pulling any punches. But I'd already gone through one crisis. *And I don't know if I can handle two.* Not that the cops or the murderers were giving me much choice in the matter.

So what're you gonna do about it, Hale?

Tori's voice echoed in my ears as the miles sped by and I didn't know the answer. Normally, my mind worked great under pressure, but that's when I had a clear picture of what I was doing. Or where I was going. At the moment, I sat on the back of Michael's bike and let him take the lead.

We parked in my reserved space in front of my apartment building. Snow remained piled up against the foundation and in the places that didn't get sun, but the walkways were clear and the steps had been salted. I headed up the stairs to the covered hallway and walked along it until I got to my door.

And my instincts screamed a warning.

The door stood ajar and my gut froze, which was a trick considering the snow melted outside in the sunshine. I never left my apartment door unlocked since the covered walkway between the apartments was open to anyone walking by, and I definitely hadn't when I'd left that morning. Someone had been in my place.

"What's wrong, Haley?" Michael paused, his bulk filling the passthrough behind me.

"The door's open."

He frowned. "Did you leave your door unlocked?"

I shot him a scowl. "Never." I wanted to step in to see what all had happened, but I couldn't make my feet move.

"Let me go inside and check first." He slid past me and I'd never be sure how he fit between me and the door jamb as big as he was.

I swallowed back fear and nodded, but I didn't want to stay outside alone. So I followed him and closed the door behind me, locking the deadbolt. I let my gaze skim the room and all my breath left my chest in a hurry.

"Good glory."

The room didn't look much different than when I'd left, but my laptop, the external hard drive that had been on the desk, and my Kindle was missing. *What the hell do they need the Kindle for?* I shook my head. *I hope they like spicy romance with angels and demons.*

"Someone's been in here." Michael reappeared in my living room, his expression verging on angry. "They've gone through your bedroom and kitchen drawers. Now do you understand why I said you should pack some things and come back with me to the compound?"

"I get it. But what were they looking for in the drawers? Contraband cutlery?" But my usual snark didn't hide my unease. "Do you think this's more than just a random break-in?"

"Someone's very interested in your communication devices, including any flash drives you might have had stored in odd place. And now, they're looking for you, that's what I think."

"Maybe you're right." I bit my lip. Good thing I'd saved all my files onto a cloud server and had my tablet with me. They could get copies of my work, but they couldn't delete it once I changed my password. I hoped. "Help me pack."

CHAPTER TEN

Michael

We didn't speak much as we packed what Haley thought she'd need to survive an extended stay away from her flat. She wore a tight expression that told me she was scared but determined, and I couldn't blame her. We couldn't know for sure who'd been in her place, but she said her laptop, external hard drive and e-reader were missing. Someone definitely wanted to find out what she knew.

"Why the hell would they take the Kindle?"

Though I didn't have an e-reader myself, I knew from Viper that if anyone had access to the account, they could see what books the owner had downloaded. And most of the electronic devices had GPS and location capabilities.

It was unusual to find myself in a woman's intimate space—okay, maybe not *that* unusual as I did most of my itch-scratching trysts at my partners' places—but I took my time to enjoy Haley's personal environment.

While her flat didn't scream utilitarian, there weren't many knickknacks I expected to see on every surface. The lines of her home were clean and uncluttered, like a photoshoot for a house magazine. Throw pillows and a fuzzy blanket rested on her small couch. A basket with papers in it sat on a small entryway table by the door. The TV hung on the wall above the "mantle" and tasteful art had been spaced around the room, but it all appeared to be museum clean.

The only place with any personality was the little office space she'd created in the dining area across from the kitchen. She'd pushed her desk against the wall with her printer on one side and a charging station on the other. Neatly stacked papers sat beside a small keyboard and mouse, and the desk's surface held a small globe made out of semi precious stones and a picture frame with an image of Haley with a handsome black man with the physique of a Greek god. Irrational jealousy roared to the fore and I damn near swallowed my tongue.

I'm the Goddess-blessed Archangel Michael. What do I have to be jealous of?

I must have scowled because Haley hurried to my side. "What is it? Did they deface something? Don't touch anything. We might be able to figure out who was in here."

I shook my head. "No, I haven't found anything. Who's this?" I didn't mean the question to come out quite so demanding and harsh, but I still wrestled with my puzzling emotions.

Haley's face softened as she picked up the picture, making my gut tighten.

"That's me and Jeff last Thanksgiving. He'd been avoiding me for months when he suddenly asked me if he could come over to share the meal. It was a huge breakthrough for our relationship after I made him go to the shelter." She shot me a rueful smile. "I was so scared we'd never be friends again, but the months of therapy really helped him. As well as seeing me at the shelter, volunteering. We're now closer than ever."

She tucked the frame into her duffel bag along with her

keyboard and mouse before scanning the room. "I think that's everything I need. Well, other than my laptop, hard drive, and Kindle. Still can't fathom why they'd take that."

"Maybe they're hoping to see which reference books you accessed." That sounded plausible, right?

She snorted. "Ain't none of them on there. It was all hot and sexy romance books about angels and demons."

It was a good thing she turned away because I froze solid enough to become a still-life.

"You read romances about angels and demons?"

"Yeah." She shot me a puzzled smile. "Angels and demons are sexy. Angels in particular. There's something illicit about the idea of getting together with one. I mean, you gotta know he probably has a lot of experience." She hissed and shivered theatrically and my cock rose in salute.

She didn't notice my stillness and went back to packing up the things she needed to take with her. I was still stuck on her comments about angels and experience. *Not that she's wrong.* I couldn't wait to get her back to my place to show her just how much experience I had.

But first we had to get her safe. My attention sharpened with a snap as a warning sizzled up my spine.

"Are you almost ready to go?" My voice came out much harsher than I intended and Haley looked up with a frown.

"Yeah, I think so. Why?"

The sound of a car braking outside made me hold up a finger to my lips. I stepped out the door and moved closer to the stairs to check the parking lot. Nothing moved on the side with my bike. I turned my head to glance at the back stairs. *Sneaky wankers.* I reversed my direction and headed to the other end as Haley stepped out her door, locking it behind her.

"What's going on?" She hitched her bags higher on her shoulder as she gazed after me.

I kept my body in the shadows enough to get a good

look without showing myself. Two men got out of an
unmarked sedan. The first buttoned his suit jacket and tied
his trench coat closed as he glanced around the parking lot.
The other headed straight for the stairs, his sunglasses
reflecting the weak sunlight.

"Time to go." I spun and grasped Haley's arm as I
passed her, hustling her down to the other set of stairs.

"What's happening?"

"Someone showed up looking for you. They must have
left cameras in your place."

I sent out a little magical energy to corrupt the feeds.
Tech and magic didn't often get along, which worked great
if I knew about the cameras in the first place. They'd have
our images but get nothing more. It still felt too little, too
late as we strode over to my bike and got on.

"Someone's here? Right now?" She set her bags on her
lap and wrapped her arms around my waist as I kickstarted
the bike.

Adrenaline made me want to peel out of the parking
lot, but that would give the guys in suits a clue to who we
were. *And they'll get enough of that on the camera feeds.* I
took a deep breath and waited for her to settle before we
rolled out of the parking lot like we were headed to the
market. Hopefully the men wouldn't notice us and we'd get
a head start on them.

****

Haley

My heart pounded in my chest and I leaned against
Michael's body to get comfort as much as hold on. When
he'd told me I was in danger, I hadn't believed him. But
when the detectives showed up to the news station and then
my place had been tossed—he had a point about the danger
factor.

And you knew he was right anyway.

Yeah, I'd known at the gut level that something was off the minute I saw the dead ADA. I didn't have proof, but I didn't trust the cops to have my back. I wasn't sure I could trust the Concrete Angels any better, but so far Michael had rescued my ass enough times to give him the benefit of the doubt.

I closed my eyes and snuggled closer, wondering what the hell I was going to do. How did I fight someone I couldn't see? If the cops were looking for me, that was far larger than I could take on. Plus, they'd taken my laptop and external hard drive. I still had my tablet, thank goodness, but they also had my Kindle.

Michael had seemed surprised and bemused when I'd told him about my preferred genre of reading. Not that most guys thought about a woman's reading preference, but it seemed to catch him off guard a lot more than usual.

I snorted. Didn't he think angels could be hot and sensual? Little did he know.

I could definitely use a guardian angel right about now.

The trip back up into the mountains took far less time than I expected but I looked up when we slowed to take a turn through the Concrete Angels compound's gates. Thank goodness for the helmet, but I still met the cold, implacable gaze of the two security guards. The bald white guy in only a vest and jeans made me nervous, but not as much as the regal Asian woman in a red tunic under her vest. She turned to watch us drive into the barn-like structure and I hoped they wouldn't throw me out.

Michael parked the bike and helped me off before taking the helmet from me. "I need to go talk to the president of the club about having you here."

I swallowed hard. "Uh, are they gonna kick me out? You know, I could just go stay with my cousin Jeff for a bit. I don't mean to cause trouble for you, too."

"Haley, don't worry. It's going to be fine. I just need you to stay in my cabin until I get everything sorted. All right?"

I swallowed hard and bit my lip, scanning the few faces in the barn with us. None of them seemed particularly welcoming. There was the big white guy with long hair and the kilt who smirked and winked at me, and a white woman with long black hair and a leather corset with more knives on her than a cutlery shop. She narrowed her eyes and tipped her head as she scanned me from head to toe.

"Haley?"

I came back to Michael's questioning gaze. "Yeah, yeah, that sounds fine. I have some calls I need to make to let my friends know I'm okay."

"Are you all right? Do you need some tea?"

Tea, the quintessential British cure-all. "I can make some. I'm just shaken up by the cops showing up at work and my place being ransacked."

"It's going to be all right. I promise." He took my hand and led me out of the barn under the curious gazes of his fellow club members. "Let me get you inside and settled with a cuppa before I go."

He sounded so sincere and I had no reason to doubt him. Except for the distrustful looks from the other CA members and the feeling of having their gazes burning into my back and ass. *Well, the ass part is from the guy in the kilt.*

Michael let me into his cabin and closed the door before striding to the kitchenette and kettle. I set my bags down on the chair in the living room and checked my phone. I'd missed a couple of texts from Tori and a call from my boss, and it reminded me that I needed to get another phone to stay off the radar.

"Hey, would you all have a burner phone I could have? Or help me get one? I don't think I want my current phone on much."

Without missing a beat, Michael nodded. "Yeah, that would be a smart move. I'll ask Neo if he has any lying around. And you'll need to remove the battery out of that one."

"Remove the battery, why?"

"Because the cops can get the phone company to turn the phone back on remotely."

"Oh, yeah, that would be bad." I stared at the small black rectangle in my hand like it would come alive and bite me. "How do I get the battery out?"

"Here. I'll take it out. Use this one."

Michael handed me an old flip phone and took my smartphone. I stared at it a moment. It was in pristine condition despite its age. "Is this a museum piece?"

He laughed and shook his head. "Bite your tongue. That's vintage. But it works and doesn't have a GPS chip in it."

I nodded, impressed. Maybe I should have considered going old school. "Thanks."

The kettle whistled and he went to pour the tea as I opened up my phone to search the contacts. I'd memorized the numbers I sought, but I was so shaken up I wanted to make sure I had them right. I wrote them down on a sticky note on his desk and turned off my phone just as be brought me a steaming cup of tea.

"Here now, this will make things better. I won't be long, just need to clear some things with the boss man. You'll be okay?" Michael paused at the door.

"Yeah, go. I'll be fine. I'm just gonna call Tori and Jeff and let them know I'm okay." And I'd email my boss because I wasn't about to call his phone.

"Right." He opened his mouth to say something more but apparently thought better of it and opened the door. "I'll be back soon."

I nodded and he stepped out, leaving me to my tea and my thoughts. The first thing I needed to do was change all my passwords for my cloud server and the connection to the Kindle. I needed someone to get into things they shouldn't like another hole in the head. It took me a few minutes, but I finally got everything reset so the laptop wouldn't connect to them anymore. I sat back and sipped my tea, wondering what I was facing.

Use the phone. Tori might have some information.

I punched her number into the keypad and lifted the flip phone to my ear. It seemed so strange to be holding a device I could fold in half to end the call, snapping it closed in a fit of anger straight out of the 1990s. The idea made me giggle just as Tori answered.

"Tori Lindhurst." Her voice sounded wary.

"Tori, it's me."

"Yes, just a moment." I heard her get up and walk a short time until a door closed. "Haley, oh my glory, what number are you calling from? Are you okay?"

"Yeah, Tori. I'm fine and I'm safe, but I had to get a burner phone so no one can track me." I bit my lip, wanting to tell her about Michael rescuing me, but I realized I hadn't gushed to my best friend despite having done the horizontal mambo with him.

I hadn't exactly had time.

"Look, I don't want to take much of your time and I can't tell you where I am, but you were right to suggest I not go home."

She hissed into the phone. "What happened?"

"Someone ransacked my apartment. They took my laptop, my external hard drive, and my Kindle."

"Kindle? Why the hell would they want that?"

I shrugged. "I dunno. Maybe they needed the latest hot romance books?" I snorted but sobered when I thought of the guys coming after me. "But I've packed a few things and managed to get away without getting caught. I know the cops are looking for me, but they wouldn't ransack my place without a warrant, right?"

"Maybe they ransacked it to get you to call them. Then they'd find you without having to work for it."

That was a frightening thought. The problem was this story I was working on made it difficult to trust any cops. I didn't know who was clean and who worked with the dead guy Commissioner Ainsworth. I reached into my little wallet and pulled out the list of names Tori had given me a couple weeks earlier. It was creased like an old receipt, but it made it easier to hide. I thanked my lucky stars I hadn't put it on my computer or my hard drive.

Yeah, Michael was right. Sometimes old school was the best way to go.

"Haley, are you still there?"

"Yeah, yeah, sorry. I was just thinking of the list of names that you gave me. What if they're not just random guys in a crooked cop's ring? What if there's a larger problem, like a shadow group made of all levels of law enforcement? Do you think that group could've been responsible for ADA O'Donnell's murder?"

Tori hissed into the phone as she took a breath. Her voice dropped. "You mean like Backlog?"

Immediately, my mind filled with the voices from the stairwell at the party. *You shoulda thought of that before you went up against Backlog. You was warned. Now you're gonna pay.*

"How do you know about that, Tori?"

"I overheard the detectives who were here talking about Backlog not liking any loose ends. I can only assume it's more of an organization than just a random reference." She took a deep breath. "I did some digging just to see if there's anything in any records about Backlog and came up with zilch. Literally nothing, which makes me think there's a whole lotta something somewhere."

"You know, if this is a real thing and a real shadow group, you have to be careful, Tori." I bit my lip. "Hell, I'm calling you on a burner phone because someone is seriously looking for me. Don't make them look for you, too."

"I'm being careful. I'm not leaving electronic footprints or paper trails." She sounded confident and I hoped she was right. "Here's the thing. My source says the new ADA of Denver is Antoine Mitchem, handsome and slick, and shit don't stick to him. O'Donnell wasn't cold in his grave before Mitchem stepped in. It was like they'd paved the way for him."

"Why are you telling me this?"

"Because, silly, you want to be an investigative reporter and there's a huge story here. It goes much further and deeper than just the death of Denver's ADA. This is your chance, Hale."

A combination of panic and excitement hit me and my breath shuddered in my chest. She was right, but digging into this was becoming far more dangerous than I'd originally expected.

So, are you just gonna curl up and forget about it? You'll be running for the rest of your life.

I'd be running if I broke the story wide open, too.

Yes, but at least there'd be legitimate reasons for looking over your shoulder.

Another scary thought.

"So, you think Backlog set up Mitchem to step in because they were planning to take out O'Donnell and I just happened to be there when it happened?"

"Yup, you got it, sister."

"Shit, you're right. I gotta get on this, but I don't have a car. I left mine at work and I'm sure those looking for me know what I drive." I wracked my brain to figure out how to get some wheels.

"Can you get a ride from wherever you are to the airport shuttle depot off on I-25?"

I thought about it, wondering if I could convince Michael to give me a ride. "Probably. Why?"

"Because I can leave my old Datsun pickup truck in

the parking lot there and no one will notice it."

"Aw, I love that little old truck. It's been running forever."

Tori snorted. "That's because I'm an ace mechanic. I'll leave a hide-a-key in the right front wheel well." Suddenly she hissed. "Shit, I gotta go. I'll leave the truck there when I got to lunch in a half hour. Take care of yourself and be careful who you trust."

"Right. Bye, Tori—" But she'd already disconnected.

I stared at the phone and let the emotions rattle around in my chest a bit. Excitement and dread from the thoughts of investigating the new ADA. Gratitude and love for Tori leaving me some wheels. Worry at what Michael would say when I told him I had to leave.

I grimaced. I'd known him a week and already I was concerned with what he wanted.

Jeez, Michaels, get a grip.

I blinked. Damn, even my surname gave me a weird connection to the hot guy on the Harley. He'd never told me his last name, but then I supposed in his line of work he wouldn't necessarily need one. *Maybe his last name is Schnoz.*

I snorted a burble of laughter before I shot a guilty look toward the front door of the cabin. Michael Schnoz was the silliest name and he was anything but silly. *Sexy, hot, badass, powerful, but not silly.*

I shook my head and scrolled through my contacts to find Jeff's number. He picked up on the fourth ring.

"This is Jeff."

"Hey, Jeff. It's me, Haley."

"Haley? Are you all right? Where are you?"

"Yes, yes, and take a breath, Jeff."

"Sorry, I've been so worried about you, what with the weather and you not being at work."

I blinked. "Whoa, wait. How do you know I'm not at work?"

"Because I went by to see if you wanted to get coffee and bagels, and ran into Tori. She said you weren't there and the cops were looking for you. What the hell is going on, Haley?"

I opened my mouth to tell him what I knew, but the words stuck in my throat. I'd seen enough cop shows to know if the cops just wanted to talk to me, they wouldn't hunt me down, trash my home, or track my phone. But they would keep an eye on my friends and family, and watch my vehicle. The problem was, I didn't know which law enforcement officers I could trust.

"I'm okay, Jeff. I'm not at work because I'm on another story." Or I would be soon. "It's out of town and that means I have to be away from home for a bit."

"Sweet glory, Haley. What have you gotten yourself into? Does this have to do with the biker?"

"No." Well, not directly. "No, but he's the one giving me a place to lay low after my apartment got trashed." I squinched up my face and gritted my teeth. I hadn't meant to tell him that.

"Wait, your place got trashed? Good glory, Haley. Is that why I don't recognize this number? What aren't you telling me?"

Lots of things. "Nothing you need to know, Jeff. Calm down a little and listen to me. I'm safe and I'm using a different phone. The story's big and I needed a place to lay low while I research. I'm fine."

He was quiet a few moments. "You're there, aren't you? With the Concrete Angels."

"Shhh! Don't say anything aloud. Those looking for me will be looking at my friends and family, too. The less you know the better. This story is worth the effort, but we have to take extra precautions."

"You should call the cops. Right now."

I sighed. "I can't. Look, I don't want to involve you. This is my story and it's dangerous enough. I need you to know as little as possible so if anyone asks you, you can give them a straight answer without lying. Because I know you're not good at it."

Jeff's voice changed. "I never said I wasn't good at it. I said I refused to do it."

The hard, cold certainty sent chills up my back. Granted, I didn't know everything that had happened to him while involved with "Dick", but I thought I knew enough. *Apparently not.*

"Okay, well, I don't want you to have to make that choice, then."

"Fuck that. I'm a big boy and I can make my own decisions. You're my family and you need my help."

"Yeah, but Jeff—"

"I'm coming up there and they better let me in because I won't take no for an answer. I'll be there in thirty minutes."

"No, wait. You don't have to—"

But I was talking to dead air. That was the second time I'd been hung up on and I worried it was becoming a pattern. I stared at the phone in my hand, debating if I should call him back and get him to listen to me. But knowing Jeff, once he made his mind up, he didn't back down.

I bit my bottom lip and shot a look out the cabin's front window toward the gate.

This is going to be really interesting.

CHAPTER ELEVEN

Michael

I headed to the clubhouse ostensibly to talk to Loki, but first I needed to talk to my brother. Luke had been blowing up my phone with texts and missed calls, but I hadn't been in the position to answer them.

Or I just didn't know what the fuck to say.

I shot a look around the clubhouse main room, but Luke wasn't at the bar or the pool tables. Someone watched a cooking show on the big screen TV. I almost stopped to see how they made the perfect chocolate ganache, but I needed to talk to my brother about Haley more.

Where the hell is he? Not in Hell, obviously, but not in the kitchen, Neo's Black Room, the offices in the back or the bathroom. I headed out to the pool, covered for winter, and found him standing at the far west end, leaning against the fence. He'd once told me he sometimes got "hot flashes" and needed to be outside away from people and heat. Given the cleared space in the snow around him, I'd say he'd had one.

"You all right, Luke?" I made sure to let him know I was coming. Sneaking up on Luke wasn't advisable.

"Hey, it's my little brother. Where the hell you been? Neo said you lit outta here like your ass was on fire." Despite his jovial response, the twinkle was gone from his eyes.

"Yeah, I got to talk to you about that, but first tell me what's going on. You look like the world is ending and you had no hand in it."

Luke snorted, but his lips didn't curl into a smile. "It's Angelina."

My gut sank. Angelina was the love of Luke's life. She was a "fallen" angel, one of the Goddess's messengers who'd chosen to live among the humans to do her part to make their existence better. But she'd settled in a little town in northern Michigan called Three Lakes and wouldn't leave.

"What's going on with her?" I settled against the top rail of the chain link fence.

"She told me my minions have overrun the world and she can't keep up with it, and I need to do something about it." He shook his head and scowled. "I don't have minions. I work with Karma. What can I do about humans being awful to each other? They blame me, but I have no control over them."

I frowned and rubbed the back of my head. "Have you told her about the real reason you became the Devil?"

He shook his head. "No."

"Whyever not? She's your lady, your partner. Why haven't you told her?"

"Because no one is supposed to know. That was the deal."

"Except you told me."

"You're my brother and you're here with me doing what we're supposed to do."

I clapped a hand to his shoulder. "So is she. You might try offering her that little tidbit about your past. She deserves to know about you."

"Yeah." Luke took a deep breath and shoved his emotions aside. "You figure your shit out about that woman you had hidden in your cabin?"

"About that." I let my gaze slide over the snowcapped hills above us and tried to figure out how to tell my brother I'd found my One-and-Only when he was struggling with his own love. "I found a new tattoo."

He narrowed his eyes. "A new tattoo? Of what?"

"A writing quill stabbed through a heart."

"Where?"

"On my chest, under my warrior's tattoo." I tried to say more but the words wouldn't come.

"What does it mean?" He met my gaze and held it, his expression stoic.

I shrugged, trying to downplay its significance.

"Come on, Michael. I know that look. You only get tattoos when it's something significant that has either happened to you or you've done." Luke narrowed his eyes. "What does it mean?"

I shifted my gaze away up the snowy mountainside. Karma had once told me Eric sat up there and watched the pool when he was trying to figure out how to talk to her. It could've been romantic or creepy, depending on which way he meant. I just wished there was a neon sign up there telling me what was coming because it felt like I'd stepped in some deep doo-doo and it wasn't just gonna wash off my boots.

"I'm reasonably sure it means that Haley Michaels is truly my One-and-Only. She's a journalist after all."

"Fuuuuucccckkk." Luke's expletive came out on a long sigh. "Guess you were right about her scent. And she even has your name as a surname." He shook his head. "You've known her, what, maybe fifty-four hours? When did the tattoo show up?"

"Early this morning."

"After you did the bedroom rodeo with her, I bet." He

smirked.

I nodded, not wanting to encourage him. "Yes."

He sobered when I didn't rise to the bait. "Have you told her who you really are?"

I sighed. "No. She's not ready for that. She's not even ready for the knowledge that we're now bound for eternity, not just her lifespan."

"You stupid tosser. She's not going to like that the decision was taken out of her hands."

I nodded again. "I know."

"Have you talked to Loki?"

I shot him a dry look.

"Bloody hell." He shook his head with a rueful laugh. "I'm not really surprised, you know. I figured she was someone special when you asked for my help getting connected with her."

"You mean when you manipulated your way into "helping" me."

He shrugged. "Hey, whatever works."

"There's another thing. People are after her because she witnessed a murder. One I reckon was perpetrated by Backlog."

"Oh, good, I thought this was going to be easy." He threw his hands out. "Now you *gotta* tell Loki."

"What am I going to say? No worries, mate, it'll be fine since she's a reporter and we're Elder Races, but she'll keep the secret? Oh right, that'll go over well."

"Man, you done fucked up real good this time."

"Thanks for the support, Luke."

"Anytime, little brother." He grinned and thumped me on the back before he sobered. "You know he'll make her sign one of his creepy contracts."

I nodded. That was what I was afraid of. The problem with Loki's contracts was he always managed to find a way to weasel out of them. Or rather, uphold them his way, which didn't benefit the signer at all. Haley was human and she wouldn't understand what it meant to sign it.

Not unless I tell her who I am.

"So it seems to me you have a choice to make." Luke shot me a sharp look. "You can either tell her who you are and all that entails, especially if Loki gets wind of it. Or you can let Haley go and walk away forever."

I barked a disbelieving laugh and pointed to my left pec. "Did I mention the tattoo? There is no sodding walking away. She's my One-and-Only, Luke."

He nodded. "Then the choice is easy. You're gonna have to tell her who you really are."

"How in the bloody hell am I going to do that? It's not like archangels are everywhere."

Luke snorted. "Actually, they are. People pray to you all the time, don't they?"

"Yeah, but they don't actually believe we're there, standing next to them. She's not going to believe me."

"Would you rather Loki told her?"

"Sweet glory, no. That would be a disaster."

"Right, so when are you going to tell her?"

My phone buzzed in my pocket and I pulled it out to find a text from Haley. "Bloody hell. Haley's cousin Jeff is coming here to 'rescue' her from us."

"That'll be entertaining." Luke's countenance had lightened and while I was glad he was feeling better, I wasn't thrilled with his amusement. "Sounds like he's got a white-knight complex for her."

"I suspect it's our reputation that calls for this kind of heroism." I rubbed my hand over my face. "I gotta got talk to Loki."

"You definitely need to talk to Loki. This shit's only gonna get more complex if you don't." Luke clapped me on the shoulder. "I'll let Flint and Quan-Yin know that a guy's coming who's gonna make a stink at the gate and to let him in to talk to you."

"Thanks." We both headed back toward the clubhouse.

"Oh, don't thank me. I'm gonna make popcorn 'cause this is gonna be good." He grinned and ducked as I swiped at him.

Once inside the doors, we split ways and I looked for Loki. Normally, I had no problems dealing with the President of our club. Yes, I knew he was the true Norse God of Mischief, but he and I shared a level of understanding. He'd always be chaotic neutral and I'd always be lawful good with Luke being lawful evil. We balanced Loki out and made sure the system didn't tilt one way or the other.

But I'd never had to face him with this kind of request on my own behalf before. The humans had relationships left and right, some settling for a quick shag and moving on while others settled with one or two others and stuck with them. But I'd never found anyone who captured my attention like Haley, and I had no earthly idea how Loki would react.

I found the prez in the kitchen poking at Grub's cooking and irritating the daylights out of him. The chef stood back with his jaw tight and his beefy arms crossed over his chest, his eyes narrowed as he watched Loki stir something on the stove.

"Loki, might I have a word?"

The prez glanced up at me with his mixed color eyes and raised his russet eyebrows before lifting the spoon and tasting whatever bubbled in the pot. He grimaced and shot a look at Grub.

"Too much salt."

Grub snarled. "Yeah, I know this. Because you added it. Get out of my kitchen."

Loki grinned and sauntered out the door, nodding to me. As I drew abreast of him, he winked his pale green eye and shot me a secret smile. "He will now improve on the recipe. I just hope he remembers to write it down, *ja*?"

I snorted. If there was anything Grub didn't joke about

or mess up, it was cooking.

"So, what do you need to talk to me about, Michael? Might it have something to do with the pretty brown haired woman shacking up with you in your cabin?"

I shouldn't have been surprised he knew about Haley already, but I thought I'd been discreet. The last thing I wanted was for him to take the piss out of me so I nodded.

"Yeah, Haley Michaels. She's a reporter from the Fort Collin's Bugle and I believe she's gotten tangled in one of Backlog's schemes." I tried to keep my voice even, betraying none of the emotion underlying my interest in her.

"So, you're providing her with a safe haven because of Backlog only?" Those heterochromatic eyes bored into mine as he settled behind the desk in his office. A half smile curled his lips and I started to sweat.

What could I say? If told him the truth that Haley was my One-and-Only, there'd be a contract in the offing. But if I lied to him, he'd make my life a living hell for a few months, and more than likely drag Haley down with me.

"Yes, and no. There's something about Ms. Michaels that I need to explore. It's not something I'm familiar with, but I'm unable to walk away." I rubbed the back of my neck, playing up the uncertainty aspect. "The problem is she's human and a reporter. I'm aware of the dangers of having an overly curious human amongst the Elder Races, but she's too addictive to me to ignore."

He narrowed his eyes, studying me down to the minute detail. I forced myself to stand still and relaxed, hoping my body language would hide my nervousness.

"This is unusual for you, Michael, *ja*? I expect this kind of distraction from Scott or Viper, but not an angel. Why is this human woman so important?"

And here's where we enter the mine field.

I shrugged with a grimace. "I don't know yet, but I need more time to find out. And I can't do that if Backlog hunts her down. I'd hoped to give her sanctuary here in the meantime, allowing me to ferret out why she's been put in my path by the Goddess."

That sounded plausible, didn't it? It also gave me more time to tell Haley who I was and impress upon her why we were connected. Because no matter what, I was connected to her irrevocably. She just didn't know it yet.

"Also, her cousin thinks we've kidnapped her and should be arriving any minute to storm our gates." I rolled my eyes as his russet eyebrows climbed to his hairline. "I've asked Luke to let Flint and Quan-Yin know to let him in so we can sort out his misunderstandings."

"Perhaps we should let him stew and worry outside for just a bit. It might be more entertaining."

I repressed my grimace. Only Loki would find drama entertaining.

I shrugged again. "Better to let him in and deal with his own insecurity in the face of our members. We are a fearsome lot."

"Ach, you're no fun, Michael." Loki rolled his eyes but he nodded. "Okay, let the fool in to deal with us. We'll see how he does. In the meantime, you must determine why this woman is so important, *ja*? It's most unusual."

He had no idea.

But before I could say anything more, Gopher, one of our newest members crashed into the doorjamb of Loki's office, out of breath and red-faced.

"Like, there's this dude out front who says we have to let him in, but Flint's got him all trussed up like a turkey at Thanksgiving and Luke is just grinning like a fool."

"Bloody hell!" I shoved past Gopher and strode for the front doors. "I'm gonna kill him."

Loki's laughter followed me out into the yard.

****

Haley

Raised voices and swearing filtered through the window and door of Michael's cabin as I poured myself some tea. I set the mug down and peered out the window, wondering what was going on.

At first, I couldn't see anything through the mass of bikers all wearing their leather cuts with the gargoyle against a flaming wheel emblem. But they finally parted and my gut froze so hard I could barely breathe.

A tall black man stood between the woman with Asian features and the bald white man with tattoos all the way down one arm. They held him steady despite his struggles and shouting. It took me a moment to realize the man in the middle was Jeff and he looked ready to tear someone apart.

Sweet glory!

I didn't want to get Michael in trouble, but I couldn't have the members of the Concrete Angels kick Jeff's ass on my watch. I threw my coat over my shoulders and headed back out into the yard.

"Let him go!" Normally I didn't roar at people, even when I needed their immediate attention. But this was my family they were manhandling and I didn't want Jeff to retreat back into his protective shell. "Let him go. He's here for me."

"Haley!" Jeff's struggles renewed and he actually dragged the two guards ahead a few steps before they subdued him again.

"Who the hell are you?" A curvy elegant woman with skin almost the same color as Jeff's rounded on me and measured me with her deep brown eyes. "Someone bring in a honey who thinks she's more than just a good romp?"

"I'm not your honey and I don't require nicknames, but he is here for me so let him go." I raised my chin and met her gaze without flinching.

A collective gasp and a few surprised chuckles went

through the crowd of bikers as I stared the woman down, but some of my initial courage failed. I couldn't tell if they were impressed or excited to see an ass-whoopin', but I held my ground even though my heart stuttered.

"Haley!"

Another, deeper, more-commanding voice made me want to run into his arms, but I stiffened my spine and planted my feet. I couldn't depend on Michael rescuing me for every little thing. Respect was earned not handed out like a booby prize.

The woman's gaze lifted to look over my shoulder and she tipped her head. "This honey belong to you, Michael?"

I ground my teeth and shifted my body so I could see both the woman and Michael as I tilted my head to look at him from under my brows. I didn't know what a "honey" was, but I could tell it wasn't anything good. Apparently I needed to work on my Death Stare because he didn't even flinch. He wore calm serenity with a steel core like nothing could shake him. I wished I could feel the same as anger coursed through my chest, raising my heartbeat.

"This is Haley Michaels, investigative reporter with the Fort Collins Bugle. She's come to do a piece on the Concrete Angels MC in light of how law enforcement sees us and the rumors of our involvement with the death of a US Marshal."

Michael's voice was unruffled and matter-of-fact while my eyes widened and my jaw damn near dropped. We'd never discussed me doing a piece on the club. He'd specifically told me to drop the issue and I'd promised to leave them mostly out of it. What the hell was he trying to pull now?

The woman's gaze returned to mine. "You're a reporter?"

Time to reach for the job I wanted. "Yup, and the guy you're holding is my assistant, so could you kindly let him go?"

She stared me down and I resisted the urge to blink, look away, or swallow. I figured any sign of unease wouldn't go well for me or Jeff. I had no illusions about what the Concrete Angels would do to either of us, but Michael had made it clear what I did for a living, and they seemed okay with that.

Yeah, well, I don't do it yet, but he might have given me my big break.

At the last moment, she nodded and Jeff damn near fell out of the guards' hands. He staggered to his feet and gave them all the evil eye before he jerked his clothes straight and scuttled to my side.

"Thanks. Next time I'll have him come with me so you'll know to expect us both."

"You're really investigatin' the Concrete Angels?" A tall, white man with a dark beard and a cowboy hat sauntered over to stand in front of me. So close I could smell his aftershave.

I was tempted to take a step back, but I'd played the intimidation game enough times to know this was one where either I had to move away like his crowding didn't matter or hold my ground. Snarky, hardboiled reporter wouldn't help.

I looked up at him and let the silence last just long enough for him to lose some of his bravado. "Yup. You wanna be my first interview?"

He shot a look over my shoulder and blanched whiter than his normal skin tone.

"No, ma'am. I don't know nothin' of importance. I, uh, reckon you'll get all you need from Michael." He nervously tipped his hat to me and backed away, never turning his back. I almost looked over my shoulder to see the expression on Michael's face, but I didn't want to let my guard down.

"Right, so anyone else want to be my first interview?" I pulled out my little notebook that I used for show and looked around expectantly.

Immediately, the club members dispersed like smoke in the wind until just Jeff, Michael, me and Luke were left in the yard. Luke grinned and winked at Michael before he hightailed it out of there as well.

Jeff let out his breath in a sigh. "Holy shit, Haley. Those people could've killed someone. I've only seen one time when the notebook trick worked and that was it." He shook his head and fixed me with a sharp gaze. "What the hell have you gotten yourself into?"

My own heartbeat was finally getting down to normal but anger flared in its absence. "Let me make something clear, Jeff. You're family and I love you, but you don't get to ignore my warnings. These people aren't swayed by charm and good looks. And most of them didn't know I was here. You put us both in danger and my story in jeopardy. Don't ever do that again."

He opened his mouth to protest, but I shot him a narrow look, daring him to dig himself deeper, and he paused to think his response through.

"I'm sorry, Haley. I didn't realize this was for your job." He bit his lip. "Are you really an investigative reporter for the Bugle now?"

Now wasn't the time to gainsay Michael. Not when there were hundreds of listening ears around us. "Yeah, it's one of the reasons I'm here. Now come on. I'll fill you in somewhere less public, okay?"

"Yeah, yeah, okay." Jeff turned to follow me but stopped when Michael planted himself in front of him. "Whoa. Who the f—I mean, hi, I'm Jeff and you are?"

"Wondering why you're really here, Jeff." Michael crossed his arms over his burly chest and I swallowed hard, from both attraction and unease.

Jeff's chin came up. "I'm here to protect my cousin and to make sure she's okay."

"Oh yes, I see how you protected her. You've

endangered her person and her project. Well done."

Jeff's expression flattened and anger bloomed across his cheeks. "Look, buddy—"

"Guys, now is not the time to get into a pissing contest. You want to do that, let's take this inside. I feel really exposed out here." I gestured back to Michael's room. "I'll explain what's going on and why you're both being jackasses there."

Jeff grimaced as Michael shot me a look of surprise. I didn't know how long I had until he refused to listen to me, so catching him off guard seemed to be the best policy until we got inside. I started walking back to his place and the men couldn't help but follow me. *Maybe that's the reason I have a sexy ass.* Though I doubted Jeff noticed. But he followed along.

Once we got inside the cabin and the door shut tight, I rounded on both of them.

"Okay, listen up. I don't need stupid from either of you. I'm perfectly capable of making dangerous mistakes on my own. I don't need help." I pointed at Jeff. "You're here because you wouldn't listen to me, but that's as far as it goes. You'll behave yourself and pay attention because we could both end up worse than dead. And you." I rounded on Michael who stood up straighter as he blinked at my pointed finger. "This behavior smacks of ridiculous jealousy and considering he's my first cousin, you don't have to worry about that. Also: ew."

I strode into the kitchenette to pick up my discarded tea. "You wanted me here, Michael. You said I wasn't safe at home so your brought me here. Fine. You were right, but this isn't the only place I can go. I can stay with Jeff. But if not, you have to allow me access to my family. He's all I have and he actually is a really good assistant when I need one, so keep that in mind."

Michael growled but nodded. "Fine."

I grunted with my own dubious belief.

"You said you're in danger and you can't go home. In danger from whom and was he part of it?" Jeff pointed at Michael.

I sipped my tea and gripped the cup hard to keep from throwing it at Jeff. "There's a big story I'm working on and it requires me to learn more about the Concrete Angels, spend time here, and keep my head down a little. When I went home today, there were guys looking for me and some of my stuff had been stolen."

Jeff gaped. "Like what?"

"My laptop, my external hard drive, and my Kindle."

He frowned. "Your Kindle? Where you read all those romance novels? Why would they want that?"

I debated arguing why anyone would want to get their hands on a Kindle full of romance, but in this case, his surprise was warranted. I couldn't imagine the thugs coming after me to be all that interested in hot sexy intimacies, at least not on pixels. *Who knows? Maybe they're looking for tips on being better boyfriends.* Glory knew most men could use the practice.

"I don't know. Maybe they thought I'd kept files on it. It's still a tablet that connects to the internet."

"Maybe they thought it was your tablet and didn't recognize it for an e-reader until they took it." Michael shrugged. "I doubt they stayed long enough to investigate, the tossers."

"Yeah, well, they might have gotten my external, but they didn't get my notes on this story. I hope they enjoy my notes on the latest celebrity dog wedding, the botanical gardens upcoming spring show, and the Valentine's Day special at Elitch Gardens."

Jeff choked a laugh. "Celebrity dog wedding, seriously?"

"Oh yeah. They did a New Year's 2020 theme, but the animals hated the fireworks. The dogs, too." I winked and he laughed. "But the notes on this story I've kept on the

Cloud server and this tablet." I held up my work tablet. "Nobody's getting this baby."

"Tell me what's really going on, Haley." Jeff set his hands on his hips. "Why is this so important to these people? And who are they?"

I shook my head. "I don't know and that's the problem. I thought this story was just about the Concrete Angels MC and the missing FBI agents, but I think it has more to do with law enforcement than the motorcycle club." I paused as I considered how much to tell him. If he knew very little, he might be safer. "I said you were my assistant outside so you'd be allowed through the gates without trouble, but do you really want to assist me or just get the flock outta here?"

He rolled his eyes. "If you need help, just ask, Haley."

"Fine. I need two things. I need you to run down a list of names I'm going to give you. I want as much public and background information on them that you can find. If anyone asks you why you're looking into these people, tell them you're doing an exposé on law enforcement to show how the city has improved after the recent scandals."

"The list is of law enforcement people?"

"Yup, and a couple of lawyers high up in the judicial system."

"Glory." Jeff swallowed hard. "What's the second thing?"

"I need a ride."

Michael's head snapped up. "I can give you a ride."

"No, you're too visible and the corrupt officials looking for me would recognize you in a heartbeat. I mean, you're VP of the Concrete Angels, and if I'm right about who's looking for me, they'll know you."

"You're the VP? Holy shit, Haley, you couldn't just pick a regular biker for a boyfriend?" Jeff gaped at Michael.

"He's not my boyfriend." I rolled my eyes, but

Michael had stilled with an uneasy look etched on his face. "What? You're not. Having sex doesn't mean we're bound for life."

If anything he looked even more uncomfortable and my gut tingled. He wasn't telling me something important, I could read it in the stillness of his body and the unease in his face. *What the hell isn't he telling me?* But it wasn't the time to get into it.

"You had sex with him?" Jeff gaped.

"Isn't that what you do when you're with someone you're attracted to?"

"Yeah, but, you're…"

"I'm what? A woman? We do have sexual urges and can enjoy sex. Who do you think a lot of men have one-night-stands with? Antelope?"

Jeff had the grace to blush in chagrin, caught in exactly what he'd thought. "I was gonna say you're so reserved."

"Sure you were. Look, I need to get some unrecognizable wheels and you need to get started on my list."

"Do I have a say in what happens here?" Michael raised an eyebrow as his arms settled over his chest.

"No." I shook my head. "This is my job. You can take me from my home to protect me, but this is a story I have to write."

"I told you it was dangerous and you should let it go." His brows lowered.

"Yup, I remember." I turned my attention to Jeff. "You ready to go?"

He shot an uneasy look at Michael. "Maybe you should listen to him, Haley."

"Listen close because I'm only gonna say this once and I want it real clear." Taking a deep breath, I lifted my chin and stared them both down. "Either give me your keys while you stay here and do research, or give me a ride because, and this is important so pay attention: I rescucd your ass and protected you long before you thought to do the same for me, so don't tell me what I can and can't do. I'm an adult and I'm doing this story." I held out my hand for his keys.

"Haley—"

I nodded sharply and grabbed my purse. "Fine. I'll ask Luke for a ride."

"Haley, wait!"

But I was out the door before either of them could move, hurt and angry that both the men in my life didn't have enough faith to believe I knew what I was doing.

CHAPTER TWELVE

Haley

I held back the tears of frustration as I scanned the yard outside. Most of the bikers had dispersed but I figured they were either in the clubhouse or the Barn where they kept their bikes. I headed for the Barn because I wasn't confident enough in my welcome to enter the clubhouse without Michael's approval.

I wasn't sure I wanted to speak to Michael or Jeff at the moment, but Luke had been friendly enough and I needed to get to him before Michael told him what I bitch I seemed to be. I reined in my furious vibe and scoped out the large room. Sure enough, Luke stood in the back talking to the big guy with long curly hair wearing the kilt.

"Hey Luke, could I talk to you?" Both of the bikers turned their attention to me and my neck prickled. Damn, they were intense and there was something otherworldly about them, but Luke nodded and headed my way.

"Sure, Haley. What's up?" His response was affable enough but I caught him glancing over my shoulder as if looking for someone.

"Could I get a ride down to the warehouse store off I-

25? If I'm going to be visiting for a while, I need some stuff."

His brow wrinkled. "I'm sure we have plenty of items around here. What do you need?"

I sighed. He was going to be difficult. "Honestly, I need some feminine hygiene products that are kinda specific and I just need a ride down to the warehouse store."

"What about Michael or your 'assistant'?" Luke wore a dry look.

"My assistant is actually doing work for me for the story I'm working on and Michael is too visible as the VP of the Concrete Angels for me to move around unnoticed. I just want to shop in peace." Okay, that wasn't true, but he hadn't seemed too keen to let me go on my own and I didn't need a babysitter. "Besides, the last thing a guy wants to do is take his woman shopping for tampons and pads. I just need a ride down there. My girlfriend will give me a ride back." That was one way to term it.

He cocked his head and I started to sweat. Would he help me get out of the compound when Jeff and Michael wouldn't?

"You're not running from him, are you?" Luke's voice had grown cautious.

"What? No, I'll be back this afternoon. I just need some stuff. Why?" That prickling sensation I'd gotten when I talked about being bound to Michael came back with a vengeance. Did Luke know something I didn't?

He shrugged with apparent indifference, but my gut tightened. "No, reason. It's just when a woman who's come in with a biker wants to leave but not with him, I start to wonder if the biker has been a shit and a half."

I barked a surprised laugh. "No, Michael hasn't been a shit. Well, not completely. But he *is* high profile and I'm trying to keep a low one with this story brewing."

Luke nodded. "Okay. I'll take you down to warehouse

store. You sure you don't need a ride back?"

I shook my head as I followed him to his bike. "I'm sure. I'll have too many large items to bring back on a bike. As I said, my friend has a car."

"Yeah, okay. And Michael knows about this?"

"Yup." He knew I wanted to go, at least. I was surprised and sad he hadn't followed me, but I'd moved pretty fast and he might have checked in the clubhouse first.

He handed me a helmet as he strapped on his brain bucket and straddled his bike. I settled behind him and it immediately felt different than riding with Michael. I had no urge to cuddle up to him and kept my hands lightly on his waist as he eased the bike out of the Barn.

There were a couple of raised eyebrows as we sailed through the gates, but no one stopped us and we headed down the hill toward Fort Collins without issues. It was weird to ride on the back of a bike with someone else. But what was even weirder was that I had gotten used to riding behind Michael and I'd only ridden with him a few times.

It didn't take long to make it to the warehouse store despite the crazy drivers and the impatient shoppers. Luke pulled up to the front to drop me off and I thanked him as I handed him the helmet.

"Are you sure you don't want me to stick around?" He raised his eyebrows.

I shook my head. "Nope, I'm good. I'll text my friend while I'm doing my shopping. Thanks for bringing me here."

He nodded, his eyes narrow. "Do me a favor and text Michael, too, okay? More than likely he's gonna be worried out of his gourd and need to know you're all right."

I bit my lip and nodded. "I will."

"I'm serious, Haley. It's important." Luke's usually jovial face had lost its humor.

"Okay, Luke. I promise. I'll do it while I'm in the

store." I meant it and he nodded.

"All right, then. I'll see you when I see you."

"See you when I see you." I waved and dug out my wallet to show the door attendants my card as he pulled away.

I stepped inside the store and headed toward the pharmacy portion. I really did need some feminine hygiene products to take back with me and it would give me time to figure out what to say to Michael so he wouldn't worry.

I found the product I was looking for and grimaced at the amount. But hey, I'd never run out of them. Maybe I'd donate half of them to the shelter when I next volunteered. I headed for the check stands, still chewing over what I'd type when my burner phone chirped with an incoming text. I held my breath and opened the phone.

Truck left at the park-n-ride. Key under the right back fender.

Relief cascaded through me as I handed my store card to the checker. I typed out a quick thank you and shoved the phone into my pocket. I smiled at the cashier and paid for my item before I headed toward the door. I kept my gaze moving as I pulled out my phone and texted Michael.

I'm safe. Doing some shopping. Will be back in time for dinner if you still want me there.

I closed the phone as the greeter checked my receipt and let my gaze slide out the open door. I didn't think anyone had followed me but someone could be keeping an eye out for me. Who knew if they had cameras with facial recognition. I didn't see anyone I recognized and stepped out into the sunny day. The wind made it too cold to go without a jacket but the sun warmed me enough to make my walk comfortable.

I set off across the huge parking lot toward the bridge over the freeway. I was sure I cut quite a sight. Nothing says sexy like a woman carrying a big ass package of menstrual pads under her arm as she hoofed it across the freeway. The wind made things exciting for a few minutes, but I felt the phone vibrate in my pocket with an incoming text.

I waited to get across the bridge before I pulled the little gadget out and flipped it open. Michael's number flashed on the screen.

Where are you? I'll come get you. Of course I want you here.

I shook my head and grimaced.

Don't worry about it. I got a ride. I'll see you tonight.

I was pretty sure he wouldn't be satisfied with that answer but it was all I'd give him. I tucked the package of pads tighter under my arm and leaned into the wind as I headed to the park-n-ride on the west side of the freeway. It had been built for smaller communities to catch a shuttle to the Denver airport, but it worked to hide a random truck in amongst the travelers' vehicles.

I found the truck and searched out the key, keeping my motions confident so no one questioned why I was taking the vehicle. Most of the people in the parking lot were either waiting for arrivals or hoping to board a shuttle south. I found the key and opened the passenger side door to deposit both my jacket and the pads.

I strode around the little blue and white truck and slid into the driver's side. The inside smelled like stale air and old cloth and foam, but the engine turned over without a complaint. I manually rolled down the window just as the phone rang. I dug it out of my jacket pocket and looked at the number.

"Tori? What's up? I got in the truck. Is everything okay?"

"Haley, you gotta get moving." Tori's voice held excitement.

"What? What are you talking about?"

"My source just told me the new ADA is taking a

meeting somewhere in the south end of Fort Collins. He just ordered a car to drive himself and he never drives."

I frowned. "What does this have to do with anything?"

"Pay attention, lady. This guy was appointed to ADA by the powers-that-be and you know who that is."

"Backlog." I whispered the word as I looked around to make sure no one stood near the truck.

"Yeah, exactly."

"What kind of car?"

"Crown Vic, silver, with Colorado tags, November Juliet Foxtrot double zero forty-seven."

"Damn, y'all are specific. But if he's leaving for Fort Collins, how the heck am I going to spot him? It's not like he's driving around with a sign saying "I'm the Denver ADA" on the car."

"After the last guy got killed, they installed tracking software in the work phones." Tori snorted. "I guess they wanted to find the bodies sooner or something. In any case, ADA Mitchem didn't turn his phone off so my source will let me know where he stops and I'll text you."

I huffed a laugh. "You're sneaky and diabolical. Tell me, why is your source helping us about this? If they work in the ADA's office, shouldn't they want to keep his private life private?"

There was a pause on the other end of the phone. "The source hasn't told me anything specific, but I get the impression they lost someone pretty close to them because of Backlog. I don't know if it was to prison or death, but some of the things they've said lead me to believe they want to take this group down a notch or two."

"Shit." I threw the truck into reverse and backed out of the parking stall. "Okay, I'll head south down 287, but I need to have some sort of clue. And here's the thing. Even if we find out that Mitchem is Backlog, we have no idea how deep this goes or which judges will stand up to them. Hell, they killed an FBI agent and a US Marshal."

"Are you getting cold feet?" Tori's voice had grown cautious.

"No, but I don't know what I'll do with the information once I have it. Will the Bugle even have the guts to publish it?"

That was my concern. If Backlog was as powerful as we thought, it was going to be difficult to get anyone to talk about them and bring them into the light. I might be sitting on a nuclear bomb of info with no one who'd accept it.

And if they kill me, no one else will know and they can continue with business as usual.

I pulled out of the parking lot and chewed my bottom lip. What was I really getting into and was it worth it?

"You have a good point. I don't know if the Bugle is big enough to make a dent." Tori sounded thoughtful, and not the good kind that sends get-well cards when someone's sick. "What about that guy you know?"

I blinked. "Guy I know? That really narrows it down, Tori. Granted, I'm not a mover-and-shaker by any means, but I know a few guys. Who are you talking about?"

"The one at the big parent of our TV affiliate. You said you met him at a news conference in Denver two years ago?"

My mind immediately filled with an image of Ryan Sutton, investigative reporter, mentor, and middle-aged Asian guy too married to his work to have a family. I suspected he was Ace, but he'd generously taken me under his wing and taught me a few reporting tricks because he'd 'liked my tenacity and style.' *Well, duh. I totally should've remembered him.*

"Oh shit, the boss is coming. I'll text you when I get the info on the Crown Vic."

The click of a dropped call sounded in my ear and I closed the phone. I hadn't thought of Ryan in a long time, but he'd made a big name for himself in the western news community.

He'll definitely have all the contacts and reach.

I drove out to the main road and headed toward the mountains watching out for cops or motorcycles. Luke and Michael were definitely crafty enough to try to follow me, especially when I hadn't agreed to their oversight. But the regular traffic on a weekday flowed around me and nothing seemed out of place.

I reached the 287 turn off when my phone buzzed twice. The first text was from Michael and he didn't sound pleased with my decision to do things on my own. I sighed and clicked on the next message.

Crown Vic NJF0047 has GPS and the guy plugged in his destination. Not sure how soon he'll get there, but it's an old rail yard in south Fort Collins. Kinda out of the way for the ADA of Denver, yeah?

I snorted. Maybe a little out of the way, yeah. I made the turn onto 287 and pulled over to the side of the road. This little truck always had a city map of Fort Collins in the glovebox and I pulled it out to look at the locations of the railways. I missed my smart phone with its satellite map access, but I really didn't want anyone else finding where I was going.

The train yard sat just east of the warehouse distract so I was able to park the truck next to a building without any external cameras and walk the rest of the way. I had no idea where to find the luxury sedan in the maze of abandoned train cars, but I had to hope I'd get lucky.

Turned out, I got more than lucky. I wore a sweatshirt I'd found stuffed behind the seat of the truck, a dark brown thing with the University of Wyoming's bucking bronco on the breast in gold. I threw up the hood to cover my face and hair as I walked in the gravel through the train cars. I almost walked around an older, more ornate carriage when I saw movement.

Oh shit, it's another car.

Panic gripped me and I darted through the gaping

doors with scrollwork along the windows. I froze in the space between the seating compartment and storage area, a sort of wood paneled pantry at the end, my heart in my throat.

The crunch of tires over gravel reached my ears before the engine shut off and car doors slammed. I held my breath as I pressed my back against the storage compartment, but I kept my eyes open despite the urge to close them. I possessed a form of eidetic memory where I could remember every word spoken if I concentrated on it enough. I hoped I'd be able to do it despite my hammering heart and the fear of discovery.

Taking a deep breath, I crept through the old train coach, the ancient velvet seats faded and torn, and tried to find the best position to hear any conversation going on outside. Most of the windows had been blown out, either from gun shots or weather, and glass littered the floor and seats. If I wasn't careful, they'd hear my footsteps through crunching shards.

Just a little closer.

I peeked over the edge of one of the windows and found the new ADA standing in front of his car, waiting for someone at the other end. *Good place to meet out here in this abandoned yard where the old coaches sit derelict.* He looked out of place in his crisp, clean charcoal suit and blood-red tie. *If he's going for subtle, he totally missed the mark.* But if he was being courted by Backlog, he had to look the part of an ordinary ADA, powerful and untouchable. I mentally snorted and sank back out of sight to listen. *The guy takes more bribes than a Mafioso if that suit's anything to judge by.*

I settled on my belly in a dusty seat and positioned the phone camera and microphone just over the lip of the broken window just as the men approaching ADA Mitchem stopped. Two guys who looked like the Mafioso thugs I'd been thinking about waited several feet in front of a

Lincoln Town car. After a few moments, someone got out and sauntered ahead of the thugs.

"Why did you have me come all the way out here to meet you, Mr. Butler? Why couldn't we do this by phone or email?"

Butler shrugged, but his face never moved at all below the dark sunglasses. "I find it both expedient and prudent to find places where there aren't any witnesses. Emails and phone calls leave a trail. This way protects all of us. And I prefer to see the faces of my employees when I give them instructions."

Employee? I thought the ADA worked for the public and the DA.

This just confirmed what Tori and I suspected about Backlog. They were a private entity manipulating the system for their benefit, and apparently it included the ADA of Denver. *I'm gonna roast your asses when I get my chance.*

"So, what do you want from me now?"

Uh-oh, trouble in paradise already?

"I want you to bring charges against Mayor Rothschild for corruption and embezzlement of public funds."

Mitchem gaped. "Rothschild? There's no evidence of that. If anything, the man's cleaner than an unused diaper."

"There will be evidence when you get back to your office. It'll be waiting for you on your desk."

"Then why are we meeting like this? Face-to-face meetings are dangerous. Someone might see us." Mitchem looked over his shoulder toward the Crown Vic behind him and his nervousness showed through.

Made me wonder if Mitchem was totally into working with Butler. The other man closed his mouth and icy silence fell over the conversation. *Maybe Butler's wondering the same thing.* He stayed silent long enough to make Mitchem fidget.

"I'm well aware of the risks of meeting in person, Mr.

Mitchem. But Rothschild is getting too close like O'Donnell. O'Donnell exposed you indirectly and you don't need that attention from Rothschild. The consequences can be deadly, as is questioning the instructions. Are you prepared to follow O'Donnell's footsteps?"

To my surprise, Mitchem swallowed hard as his gaze skirted over the other men standing behind Butler. Apparently, this guy was a scary mudfucker and the new ADA knew it.

"No, Mr. Butler, but I'm concerned there'll be too many questions about why the evidence just suddenly shows up." Mitchem backpedaled pretty quick, but he made his reasons sound plausible.

"Don't worry about questions, Mr. Mitchem. They won't matter in the long run. Just make sure he's charged with corruption and embezzling. We'll do the rest."

I gritted my teeth and hoped my phone caught all that. I'd need it as proof when I took on these guys because if they could kill an ADA, manufacture evidence against the mayor of Denver, and threaten the new ADA without breaking a sweat, I'd be dead faster than one could spell the word on the evening news.

It took every bit of willpower I possessed to remain where I was when the meeting broke up. Did I want to run like hell to get away? Fuck yeah, but they'd see me and the last thing I needed was their attention. I'd get plenty of that once this information got out.

I heard footsteps and a car's door slammed. An engine turned over and the crunch of tires on gravel suggested ADA Mitchem had left the area. I didn't need to follow him, nor did I need to follow Mr. Butler or whomever he reported to, but I really wanted to leave. I tightened my hands on my phone and flattened my body against the dusty seat, trying to slow my breathing. I didn't want them to hear me panting in panic.

Calm down, Haley. They don't know you're here and won't if you just stay still.

Yeah, easier said than done when some really bad dudes stood no more than fifteen feet from where I lay.

"Do you think Mitchem will play ball?" That was Butler's voice. I didn't dare look to verify.

"I think he will. He's too power-hungry and ambitious to buck the system. And he knows we'll replace him without a thought if he doesn't follow our directions."

I recognized the second voice, but couldn't place where I'd heard it. But it was someone I'd heard speaking before. My curiosity urged me to look, but prudence kept my head down. *But I know that voice. I've heard it before.* Where the hell had I heard it?

"Do we have another replacement if he gets a conscience?" Butler again.

"Nothing concrete yet, but there are others being groomed should the need arise." Their voices started to fade as they retreated from the meeting place. "Get McMasters on the phone and tell him to keep an eye on his people in the Marshal Service. I'm pretty sure there's still someone actively working against us..."

Wait, is Butler talking to one of the thugs? No one else had joined the little *tête-à-tête* so it had to be one of the other men standing around. *Damn, is the big boss a thug-looking dude?* I hoped my phone had caught them all on camera and I could figure out who it was.

Their footsteps sounded on the gravel outside the train coach before car doors opened and closed. I breathed easier as the car backed out from between the coaches expanding the distance between us, but I didn't move. I had to wait them out. If anyone caught me here, not only would the information disappear, but I had a feeling I would, too.

I slowly lowered the phone and shoved it into the inner pocket of the hooded sweatshirt. I needed it to be safe when moving around. The problem was, I also needed to let someone know where I was in case Butler's thugs found me first.

Shit. How long should I wait for them to leave?

I'd parked the truck far enough away that it shouldn't expose my presence, but creepy dudes always seemed to find the good guys no matter what precautions they took. At least, that's the way it worked in movies and on TV. Holy shit, lying there, waiting for the ax to fall or the shoe to drop damn near killed me, but I forced myself to stay still. I didn't even retrieve the phone to text anyone.

After twenty minutes of silence, I finally allowed myself to roll off the dusty seat onto my hands and knees. I grimaced at the broken glass and wood debris littering the cracked floor, but I picked my way slowly toward the back of the train carriage, crawling as quietly as possible until I reached the door to the coupler.

I stopped and listened, holding my breath so it wouldn't fill the space with sound.

Nothing. No voices. No footsteps. No car engines.

I bit my lip and took my time rising to my feet. I kept my body behind the wall of the car, hoping no one could see through the windows to where I stood, then peered around the edge to make sure nobody stayed behind.

The area around the coach appeared empty and quiet. I pulled the hood of the sweatshirt forward on my head, took a deep breath, and climbed down steps to the ground. My heart pounded in my chest as panic roiled in my stomach, but I kept moving with deliberate slowness. If anyone caught sight of me, I wanted to portray unconcerned innocence.

It was a mystery how I managed to walk away from the train coach when I wanted to run like the hounds of hell were after me, but I acted like I was unconcerned with being in the abandoned train yard. I was just there to have a leisurely stroll. In the late afternoon during work hours. In a place no one worked. *Right. Completely innocent here.*

Despite my efforts to look nonchalant, I still paused at each railcar before stepping into the open. Innocent or not, I didn't want anyone to notice me. I hadn't had time to scope out the yard to see if there were any security cameras in the area, but from what I could see, they had the minimal ones to keep out the riffraff. It didn't stop people from tagging the abandoned cars given the brightly colored art around me. I kept my path between the ranges of the cameras and when I had to step into their field of view, I made sure the hood covered my face.

It took me about fifteen minutes to reach the truck from the yard, but no one saw me and Mr. Butler and his thugs were long gone. The problem was I didn't know his real identity or who I could trust with the video to find out. If Butler and his mysterious friend with the familiar voice had people in the Marshal Service, the ADA's office, and any other law enforcement agency, what was to stop them having moles in the newspaper or media offices?

Unease and panic built in my gut again, making me pant. I had to expose these assholes, but I kinda wanted to live through the experience.

One face filled my mind as the most trustworthy, dark brown eyes and even darker scruff.

Michael.

I nodded as I slid into the truck. Yeah, he'd help if he wasn't mad at me. Jeff and Tori, too. But the man I needed to call was Ryan Sutton. I couldn't see him allowing any kind of tomfoolery when it came to exposing corruption. But I wouldn't expect it of the ADA either.

The question is, can I trust him from what I only remember about him?

I started the truck and eased it away from the warehouse as I thought about my next move. Reconcile with Michael if I could, then consider calling Ryan.

CHAPTER THIRTEEN

Michael

You better fucking call me, you sodding bastard.

Okay, it might not have been the most cordial text to my older brother, but my fury had boiled over when I got Luke's text that he'd taken Haley down to the warehouse store near the freeway. But the phone remained stubbornly silent as I stood in the yard and scowled. Jeff stood beside me, his expression full of guilt and fear.

"We should've just listened to her." He rubbed the back of her neck.

"Sorry?" I raised my eyebrow.

"We should've just taken her where she wanted to go. Then at least one of us would've been with her to keep her safe." He shook his head with a muttered expletive. "I should've known she'd go on her own whether I helped her or not."

"She's not safe."

Jeff snorted. "One thing you need to learn about Haley. Once she sets her mind on something, she does it, come hell or high water. Did she tell you about how she rescued me?"

I nodded.

He grimaced. "Right, well, I told her not to come. I was too afraid she'd get hurt. And I think our families told her not to do anything about it either. But Haley doesn't give up, especially when it's important to her. She'll do everything she can to protect or rescue family and friends."

"She's not doing that here." I threw my hands out. "This is taking on something far bigger than her to save...what? Strangers? Cities and towns that don't care if she lives or dies?"

Jeff shrugged. "She took on one of the wealthiest sex predators in L.A. to rescue me. She'd make a good secret agent if she trained for it. We should've had a little more faith in her."

I scowled. "So what are we supposed to do now?" I wasn't used to doing nothing. I was a Goddess-blessed archangel. I was the fighter and defender. I didn't sit around waiting.

"I'm going to go back to your room and start the research she asked of me. What's the WiFi password?"

I barked a laugh. "Let me talk to our IT man and get you access. He's rather territorial."

To his credit, Jeff didn't roll his eyes. "Yeah, given your...profession, you wouldn't want just anyone having access."

That was an understatement. Before I could respond, my phone rang with a call from Neo. "Speaking of IT..." I pulled the phone to my ear. "Michael."

"So I did some more digging. Your girl was right. O'Donnell and his replacement are eyeballs-deep in Backlog."

"She's not my 'girl'. She's a woman."

Neo snorted. "She's the one who came earlier, right?"

"Yes, what's your point?"

"She stayed with you and returned with you, she's your woman. Unless you'd like me to tell Loki everything

I've found on this random reporter you've invited onto the compound."

Sodding tosser. Yeah, that was the last thing I wanted.

"What do you really want to tell me, Neo?"

"Right to the point. Okay then. She may be kicking over a hornet's nest with this one, but if she can expose these guys, it'll probably put a big dent in Backlog's operations at least in the Denver area."

Glory, what had Haley stumbled across?

"The problem is I wasn't the only one poking around. Seems like someone is flagging all of Haley Michaels' social media accounts, her bank accounts, her phone. They're actively looking for her."

I frowned. "How would you know that?"

"Because I've been doing the same thing when researching whether she's a danger to the club, Michael. It's one of the first things Loki has me do."

"Loki put you up to that?"

"Nope, it's just one of the services I provide."

"And is she? A danger to the club?" My gut cramped. What would I do if the answer was yes?

"That depends on who targets her and if they think we're a threat."

I snorted. "I'm pretty sure we're already a threat given Loki's interest in why they chose to blame us for their underhanded dealings."

"We're not exactly saints, here, Michael."

"No, but we only take credit where credit is due and to quote Scott, that ain't us." I rubbed the back of my neck and shot a look at Jeff. "Oh, since I have you on the phone, Haley's assistant needs limited WiFi access to do some research for her."

Neo went silent a moment. "I'm not sure that's wise. What's he researching?"

"A list of names. I suspect they're either Backlog or at least sympathizers. She wants background and connections on them."

"Damn, she had a list of these people? Why didn't you tell me that first?" He sighed. "Tell you what, I'll give her assistant access through Nightingale's terminal—it has internet access without compromising my system—in exchange for that list."

"You want to take a look at Haley's list?"

"What?" Jeff's eyes widened. "That's confidential information. I can't give you the list."

"Oh yeah, I definitely want that list. Bring me that with her assistant and I'll get him set up."

"Will do." I ended the call and fixed Jeff with my best warrior stare. "Now you listen to me, Jefferson Holliday, if you want access to a computer to do your research, you're going to hand over that list so the IT guy can do his own research on it. That's the deal. Take it or leave it."

Jeff narrowed his eyes. "How do you know my full name?"

I shrugged. "We know all about the people who show up at our gates. What's it going to be?"

I watched frustration light his eyes and tighten his mouth just as my phone buzzed with a text. As I waited for his answer, I checked the phone.

I'm safe. Doing some shopping. Will be back in time for dinner if you still want me there.

Haley's text simultaneously frustrated me and let relief skip through my chest. I immediately texted back.

Where are you? I'll come get you. Of course I want you here.

Actually, I wanted her here where I could protect her from the gathering Backlog storm.

Don't worry about it. I got a ride. I'll see you tonight.

Bloody hell in a tight woven basket, the woman would send me over the edge. I was going to thump her. No, first I'd thump Luke for having given her a ride out of here.

Whenever Luke gets back to the compound. I noticed he'd made himself scarce.

"Fine, I'll give you a copy of the list."

For a moment I had no idea what Jeff was talking about and stared at him hard as a scrambled to catch up. But it finally dawned on me what he'd said and I nodded sharply.

"Good. List first, computer after."

Jeff scowled. "This is betraying Haley's trust, you know."

I raised my chin. "I can't help her fight what I don't know. If this list of names are suspected Backlog members, the more we know will help keep her safe."

"Yeah, good luck with that." He shook his head but handed me a small piece of paper torn from a notepad. "Take a picture of it. I'm keeping the original to give back to Haley."

I did as he asked and sent it to Neo. He immediately responded that the computer would work for Jeff with a specific username and password. I handed my phone to Jeff while I led him to the infirmary in the clubhouse. Nightingale, our resident physician and *Morukai* healer, glanced up with a smile when she saw me.

"Good afternoon, Michael. It's nice to see you. You aren't hurt, are you?" She tilted her silver-crowned head and her eyes took on a faraway look as if she read more than our outer shells.

Not physically, but possibly emotionally.

"No, madam. We've come to use your computer for some research." I stepped aside to introduce Jeff. "This is Jeff Holliday and he'll need the computer for a bit."

Her unnerving brown gaze hit Jeff and her eyebrows went up. "Oh, my." She took two steps around me and placed her hand on Jeff's chest. "It's a good thing you came, Jeff. The computer is right through here."

Nightingale turned and motioned Jeff to follow her

into the office connected to the infirmary. I shifted my attention around the room and found Samurai resting on one of the beds in the room, his golden gaze focused on the door to the office.

"What are you doing in here, Sam?"

The kitsune shifter turned his gaze back to me with visible effort. "Took a fall and dislocated my shoulder. Hurts like a mudfucker." He blinked slowly. "Who's in the office with Nightingale?"

"Guy by the name of Jeff Holliday. Haley Michaels' assistant. Neo's letting him use Nightingale's computer to do research."

"Hmm." Sam's gaze returned to the doorway and I recognized I'd been dismissed.

Shaking my head, I headed back out to the main room of the clubhouse. Given the temperatures outside being mild, most of the club members had taken advantage of the warmth to work on their bikes or help with clearing the excess snow. I could hear voices coming from the offices, and the kitchen where Grub orchestrated the evening meal prep, and Chemistry worked behind the bar. She'd taken over from Karma when the parties got too complex. She was a master mixologist and I'd grown fond of her Ambrosia mixture. She said the recipe came from Mt. Olympus.

"Michael." Her voice flowed over me and tugged me closer. "I've a message for you."

I raised my eyebrows. Chem didn't often expose her connection to the Goddess, but I'd gained her trust since she arrived to join the Concrete Angels.

"From Her?"

Chem nodded. "She said you need to go back to your cabin and make some tea. She'll be waiting."

Sweet glory, She must really need to tell me something.

I nodded. "Thanks, Chem." I paused as she handed me a plate of biscuits. "What's this?"

"She requested English biscuits with her tea. Thought you could use them."

I swallowed hard and nodded again. *Bloody hell, She wants biscuits? This is going to be a rough conversation.* I took the plate and headed out of the clubhouse for my cabin. The sunlight on the cleared snow blinded me, so I keep my gaze on my boots until I reached my door. Taking a deep breath, I paused to calm my energy. One didn't storm into a room with the Goddess. I held my breath for a count of five before letting it out and opening the door.

At first, I didn't see Her, but it took my eyes a few moments to adjust. When they did, I found Her seated on the chair Haley had used, one jean-clad leg crossed over the other. Tea already filled my living room with a fragrant scent of Jasmine and honey, and the creamer and sugar bowl sat beside the teapot.

I drew myself up to my full height and bowed at the waist, my hand extended with the plate of biscuits.

"My Lady."

The Goddess snorted, uncrossed Her legs, and leaned forward to tap my shoulder. "Let's forego the formalities today, okay, Michael? I just wanted to talk to my warrior son a little."

I rose and my cheeks suffused with heat and love and warmth. "Okay, Mom. Why did you make the trip? You could've called or emailed."

I settled into my chair beside Her and She poured me some tea. I ignored the urge to do that for Her, since She was the Holy Goddess of All, but She was also mom, and I rarely stopped Mom from doing what She wanted to do.

"Ugh, I'm still not thrilled with this electronic communication the humans have developed. It's quick, yes, but you miss so much nuance with it." She waved her hand and offered me the teacup. "Do you want milk today?"

"Please." I tried to shake off the mundanity of Her serving me tea, but couldn't quite avoid it. "Why are you really here, Mom? Am I in trouble?"

"Not yet," She remarked before She laughed at my uneasy expression. "I came to talk to you about Haley Michaels."

I swallowed my tea hard and hoped something hadn't gone wrong. What if I'd chosen unwisely and the Goddess wasn't pleased with my connection? *But that doesn't make sense, I have the tattoo.* Except, the tattoos didn't only come for things I was supposed to do, but also as lessons I had to learn. *Sweet glory, Haley's not a lesson, is she?*

I cleared my throat. "What about her?"

Mom met my gaze and studied me for an eternity of moments, Her starry eyes at once filling me with peace and dread. Wisdom saturated the air around Her and peace knocked at the door of my mind. But fear and unease danced around the edges as I waited for Her to speak.

"You love her with all your heart, don't you, Michael?"

The very American response of "duh" came to mind, but I'd learned long ago that snark wasn't the best approach with Mom. She usually did things like smite someone with that kind of attitude. It made mothers with wooden spoons look tame.

"Yes. She's my One-and-Only. I told Luke about her, too."

The Goddess nodded. "I know. I spoke to him earlier. He's going to need your help and understanding in the coming months."

I blinked. Luke would need my help, but not Mom's? Or maybe She'd already given him the tools to deal with whatever was coming. Mom was frustrating like that. She'd give us everything we needed to figure shit out and wait for us to see it clearly. Sometimes She'd laugh when we took our time and made ourselves miserable over it, but mostly She did a lot of face-palming until we got it.

"Does this have to do with Angelina?"

Mom gave me a look that said She was done speaking about Luke. I sighed and nodded. "Okay, I'll do what I can."

"Good, your brother's very intuitive when it comes to the hearts of others, but his own remains a mystery to him." She shook Her head. "Perhaps it's because he has the greatest heart and he's yet to explore all of it. I'm glad you'll help him, Michael. You're far more experienced in love and intimacy. So let's talk about Haley."

"All right. What do you want to know?" *What doesn't She already know?*

"It's not what I need to know, Michael, but what you're willing to do if you choose to be with Haley long term."

My gut froze. "What do you mean, choose to be with her? The tattoo showed up on my skin. Doesn't that mean she's my heartmate?"

Mom nodded slowly. "Yes, Dear One, but like the humans, you're given free will as well. If you choose to stay with her, you'll have many difficult trials. But if you choose to walk away, the pain will be immense. The choice is yours and no path is easier than any other."

I sat back in my chair, my tea forgotten. No one liked to hear when their choices would kick their own asses, but having my Mother lay it out for me dampened my mood.

I raised my gaze to meet Hers. "I can't walk away, Mom. She's too important to me."

The Goddess nodded, an approving smile curling her lips. "And can you let her do her job as an investigative reporter even if she puts herself into dangerous situations?"

I gasped as the fear stabbed me in the gut like a sword. I groaned and leaned forward, bracing my elbows on my knees. The idea stole my breath and I closed my eyes against the tears. I'd always been the warrior, the one fighting and protecting. I thought that was what it had meant to be strong. But trusting Haley to keep herself safe while courting danger made me weak in the knees.

"I don't know."

Mom sighed and patted my bowed head. "I know it's hard, Michael. I know you're used to being the one in charge. Even Loki, bless his heart, sees you as someone who has leadership qualities. But you must learn to trust Haley to know what she has to do and to ask for help when she needs it. You can't control her every movement."

"But she's putting herself into a situation that is more dangerous than anything she's done before." I raised my head to plead with my Mother. "Backlog isn't some art opening at the Denver museum or the latest celebrity's fashion choices for the Met Gala. This organization kills to keep its secrets. It's dangerous."

"How do you think she'd feel when you go into dangerous battles?"

I sat up and scoffed. "But that's my job. I have the skills for it."

"And you need to trust that she has the skills for her job, too."

"And if I don't?" I couldn't stop myself from asking the question.

Mom sighed again. "Then you'll lose her in ways you can't fix. You expect everyone to have faith in you. It's who you are as the Archangel Michael. But now, you must have faith in the one person you care about most. And if you can't, she'll be lost to you forever."

The news rocked me to my core as my Mom set aside Her teacup and rose. She patted my face and I wanted to crawl into Her lap like a little boy seeking comfort.

"I told you it was your choice, and none of the paths would be easy, but you have to decide what's most important to you and what's a dealbreaker. She loves you, Michael, but you have to have faith in her for it to last. And part of that faith is telling her who you really are."

I reared back and swallowed hard. "How can I do that,

Mom? She's human and absolutely convinced that only humans live in this world. She'll laugh at the thought that there's more."

"What's wrong with her laughing?" The Goddess tilted Her head with a half-smile curling Her lips. "People only laugh until they believe. It doesn't change the truth. You are who you are and nothing she says or does will change that. If you're confident in yourself, she'll understand once she's had time to absorb the information. You want her in your life, don't you?"

"Yes, of course."

"Then you must have patience and faith, Michael. Both are things you're known for. This is the first real trial of the heart you've ever faced. Don't run away now."

She leaned forward and kissed my brow, Her smile gentle. "Be clear in what you want and believe in achieving it. Have as much faith in Haley as you do in yourself. It'll all work out, you'll see."

I nodded and in a flash, She was gone, leaving the scent of spring hyacinth in Her wake. I sighed and retrieved my tea, magically still hot despite my neglect. I let the heat from the tea and my Mother's words seep into me, trying to sift through all the emotions when it came to Haley. Fear roared to the fore, but was it the fear of what would happen to Haley or the fear of what she'd do when she realized I wasn't as human as she thought? I didn't want to lose her, but I realized the situation had brought the true meaning to the humans' phrase, "damned if you do, damned if you don't." I had to pick the choice that would hurt less.

The question is, which one?

CHAPTER FOURTEEN

Haley

I arrived at the compound gates around six that
evening, wondering if they'd even let me in. Michael had
gone silent since before I learned what Mitchem was up to,
and I hadn't had the courage to text him to renew the
conversation. I didn't see any friendly faces when I rolled
up to the gate, but I figured the bikers of the Concrete
Angels MC had their reputation to uphold. No one ever
expected bikers to be anything but scary.

Thanks, Hell's Angels.

Once they figured out it was me, the stoic bald white
guy nodded and motioned for the gates to be opened. I
drove the little Datsun truck through and someone directed
me to park behind the Barn next to a hot little sports car
from the 1960s. Peacock green showed in the light
gleaming from the edge of the Barn and I took a few
moments to admire the little vehicle.

Or that was what I told myself. In reality, I was trying
to figure out how to approach Michael after my dramatic
disappearance earlier that day. I was still mad at him for
doubting my ability to do my job and for having a pissing

contest with Jeff over who needed to be more protective. Sweet glory, they were as bad a mother hens.

After I'd gotten away from Mr. Butler and the Thug-in-Charge, I'd driven around for a bit, trying to think about everything I'd learned and to whom I could entrust the information. But it wasn't really Mitchem and Butler who worried me. It was Michael. Was I making a big mistake getting involved with him?

I'd wanted to talk to Tori about him, but we both agreed she was probably being watched by the people looking for me and it was best to minimize our communication. But I missed having a girlfriend to vent to. In the end, I texted Tori to meet me at the bakery in Loveland. She hadn't received any new information from her source so the meeting was necessarily brief, but before she went back to the office she peered at me from behind her chic cat's eye glasses and frowned.

"Are you okay, Hale?"

"Yeah, yeah, I'm good. Just running on adrenaline and caffeine. Breakfast of champions, right?"

She hadn't looked convinced, but I promised to text her later when she got home so she wouldn't be missed at the office. She still hesitated, her mouth tightening into a flat line until someone she knew called her name. I took advantage of her momentary distraction to slip out the service entrance in the rear of the bakery and hoof it back to the truck.

But standing in the overhead lights outside the Concrete Angels' Barn, I wished I'd asked her to stick around longer to talk. I wanted her insight on what the hell to do about a hot biker dude who made my heart soar but didn't trust me to be the person I wanted to be.

The scuff of boots on frozen gravel made me look up and I met the gaze of a wiry white woman with shoulder-length brown hair pulled back into a severe ponytail. Her startling gray eyes focused on me with razor-sharpness, but while the intensity rivaled that of the bald white guy at the gate, she wore calculation along with her camouflage cargo pants and military grade black sweater.

"So you're the reporter." The soft English accent thumped against my chest. Or maybe that was my heart from the woman appearing out of nowhere.

I cleared my throat. "That's right. Who are you?"

She tilted her head. "Calhoun. I'm the Fixer."

I swallowed hard but hid it by opening the truck's door and manually locking it. The old Datsun didn't have electric anything.

"What does the Fixer do?" I closed the door and resettled my purse over my shoulder.

"Fix things."

I didn't crack a smile though the answer was obvious. "Excellent. Totally clears up your role in the club."

"Why are you here?"

I raised my eyebrows. "I came back for dinner."

"Why are you really here?" Calhoun crossed her arms over her chest, the leather vest creaking under the pressure.

"I was invited. By VP Michael." I wanted to give his last name but I'd never learned it.

"Who?"

I thought for a few moments. "Schnoz. And he's expecting me."

"Is he? How lovely for you." Calhoun didn't move.

I raised my own eyebrows. I'd dealt with belligerent and threatening women in my profession before, but this wasn't my turf. I lifted my chin, pulled out my phone, and opened it up. She smirked at the flip phone as I scrolled through the contacts to find Michael's number.

"You want me to call him to verify? Or maybe you'd prefer me to call Luke? Whichever. Quick click of the key for me." I shrugged to show my nonchalance despite my heart thundering in my chest.

Calhoun lost her smirk and eyed the phone, still

blocking my path. I shrugged again and clicked Michael's name before holding the phone to my ear and meeting Calhoun's gaze.

"Hello."

No matter what I was doing, Michael's deep voice soothed the fear right out of me and calmed me down. "Hey Michael, I have Calhoun here and she's not convinced I'm allowed on site. You wanna give her the four-one-one?"

"If it's necessary."

I nodded and held out the phone to Calhoun with raised eyebrows. "He'll talk to you."

She took the phone while I checked to make sure I had all the things I wanted from the truck, including my purse and coat. I'd already gotten them out, but it gave me something to do while she was getting the third degree.

Finally she handed the phone back. "Guess he wants you to stay. But don't think you have that much freedom. Watch your back, sister."

"Number one: don't call me sister, we don't have that kind of relationship. Number two: everyone watches my back because I have a great ass." I took the phone and strode past her, and I swear I heard her snort with amusement and grumble, "Damn, she *does* have a nice ass."

"Thanks for that, Michael. Is Jeff there with you?"

"No, I believe he's in the infirmary."

"What? Why?" I immediately shifted my path to the clubhouse and increased my speed. "Is he all right?"

"He's fine. That was the only computer available for him to do research."

"Oh." I blew out a relieved breath as I stepped inside the clubhouse. "Good. I'll catch up with him there, then."

"You're coming back to the cabin tonight, though, right?"

I heard the hesitancy in his voice and some of my earlier concern came back.

"Yeah, I planned on it. Are you okay with that?"

"Yes. Text me before you leave the infirmary. I'll have supper waiting."

Relief and warmth filled my chest and I smiled despite my surroundings. "Okay, Michael. That sounds great. I'll talk to you later." I closed the phone and shoved it in my purse, the smile firmly in place until I stepped into the infirmary.

The tableau in front of me made me hold my breath. Panic surged from what it looked like on the outside. Jeff typed feverishly on the computer, sweat sliding down the sides of his face while a broad-shouldered tattooed man with Asian features and a thick beard with silver highlights stood over him. The biker's intense gaze rested on Jeff despite the other man's work on the keyboard.

Two other people worked in the room, both watching the situation at the computer. Both appeared to be of Native American heritage, though one looked like she hailed from the northern nations of Alaska. Both had their hair braided with colorful beads that glowed against their dark tresses, but the Alaskan woman wore a necklace of bear claws around her neck while the other woman wore turquoise jewelry.

Before I could ask what was going on, the man watching Jeff turned his gaze on me, and his eye's glowed green like a cat's when caught in headlights. I swallowed hard and cleared my throat.

"Hey, Jeff. How's it going? Everything okay in here?"

Jeff looked up and his expression mellowed from the high intensity. "Hey, Haley. Yeah, it's good, I've just been dodging tracking bots and malware. The folks on your list really don't want to be researched beyond the surface."

"Ah." I nodded as I moved closer, keeping an eye on the bearded man. "That doesn't surprise me, given the secrets I suspect they're hiding. Everything all right? Did you piss someone off?"

"What?" Jeff raised his eyebrows and shot me a look until I gestured at his tattooed shadow. "Oh, no, this is Samurai. He was in the infirmary when I came in to use the computer. Dislocated his shoulder."

I winced in sympathy. "Ouch. Very nice to meet you, Samurai."

The bearded man nodded. "Nice to meet you, Michael's."

The way he said it suggested a possessive at the end, but I ignored the idea given my surname and smiled before turning back to Jeff.

"So have you found anything interesting?" I grabbed a rolling stool and settled beside the computer desk.

"Oh yeah. Actually, Sam has been really helpful in outfoxing the tracking bots, letting them chase their tails while I work." Jeff shot Samurai a warm look and I blinked. Could Jeff be interested in the tattooed man?

"Whatcha got, Watson?"

"Sherlock never said that." Jeff grimaced.

"I'm a twenty-first century Sherlock. You get what you pay for." I snorted.

"I haven't paid you anything."

"Exactly. So what did you find?"

"Your list was pretty interesting. Most of the names on it were law enforcement of one kind or another—FBI, Marshals, NSA, police, county sheriffs—including people from the judicial branch. Lawyers and judges." Jeff swiveled the monitor toward me. "But there are a few businessmen, some Canadian Mounties, doctors, and governmental solicitors that snuck in there, too. At first glance, none of these people seem to have much in common. They came from different walks of life, different cities and states. None of them went to the same colleges or academies. They seem completely disparate from each other. Except for this."

He pulled up a satellite photo of the Rocky Mountains

west of Boulder, Colorado. A little town sat nestled between the higher peaks of the Rockies with its own airport. Granby Resort Town, or GRT, sat to the south of Lake Granby, a natural reservoir set up to keep the town hydrated and provide hydroelectric power through the Granby Dam.

"What is that and how does it fit with these names?"

"It's a resort town, set up specifically for the wealthy and well-connected to get away without roughing it." Jeff rolled his eyes. "From what I could dig up, every person on your list has either traveled to, paid for gas in, stayed at, or worked at Granby Resort Town since they've gained whatever position they have."

"Wait. Every person on that list shows up at GRT?" I frowned. "Is it a tourist trap?"

"No, as far as I can tell it's swanky as hell and twice as expensive. They have their own airport for glory's sake. And if you zoom in on that lake, I count no less than three marinas with yachts galore."

I rubbed my chin as I stared at the names on the list and the information about GRT. "But some of these people are living on police and county sheriff salaries. Hell, I think that guy there is a public defender. How are they spending time in GRT?"

"I dunno, but I'm not done digging. But one thing's for sure. GRT is the link between all these people, particularly the local ones." Jeff shook his head and frowned. "Even some of the people from out of state and Canada have come here, too." He tapped his chin. "Do you think they have law enforcement seminars or meetings there?"

"That would make more sense, but again, why not do it in Denver? The flights would be cheaper and there are plenty of conference centers there. Why go to GRT?"

"Perhaps they were trying to find a place no one would see them all together." Sam spoke into the frustrated silence and I shot a look at him, my mind turning over that piece of information.

"Look up another name to see if it shows up at GRT. Butler."

"Okay, first name." Jeff began typing.

"No idea, but check around the times when the majority of the names show up at GRT together."

"Let me see what I can come up with."

I sat back and let him work without interrupting, but my mind turned over the information he'd found. My guess was Butler and the Thug-in-Charge were using GRT as their face-to-face meeting space when they needed to get information to a lot of people at once. It was out of the way but still close to Denver, an easy drive or quick flight to the airport. Roughing it without actually roughing it.

Fuckin' glamping.

"I'm not finding anything. There's no Butler at the hotel or resort logs, or residents with that name."

I rubbed my eyes as my stomach growled. "I bet it's an alias to give to the minions." I groaned and stretched my neck. "I'm gonna get something to eat and call it a night. It's been a long day." I nodded at the computer. "Are you gonna keep going or go home?"

Sam stirred from his preternatural stillness. "It is late and starting to snow again. It is better if Jefferson stays off the roads tonight. I will find him a place to sleep."

I blinked and shot Sam a surprised look. "It's starting to snow? It was clear and warm when I got back..." I checked the time. "Forty minutes ago."

"It is better to stay than go." Sam's expression remained stoic but confident.

"Okey dokey." I pulled out the phone and texted Michael that I was on my way. "You do what you need to do but be safe." I gave Jeff a meaningful look and switched my gaze to Sam before bringing it back. "I'm gonna grab some dinner."

"Yeah, that sounds good. My eyes are starting to cross

anyway." Jeff nodded and closed all the programs. "I'm starving."

Supper still hot and waiting for you.

Michael's text warmed me up and made me smile. "Get some food and rest and I'll catch you in the morning if you're still here."

"What about you? Are you heading home?"

I shook my head. "Nope, someone trashed my place, remember? It's better for me to be here, off my personal grid."

"Right, I forgot."

Jeff rose from the chair and stretched, and Sam watched him like a dog watched a delicious treat. I thought about taking Jeff aside and warning him to watch out for Sam, but while the biker wore a hungry expression, I didn't get the sense he meant to hurt Jeff. Good thing because I was too tired to kick anyone's ass physically.

"I'll see you in the morning."

"Good night, Haley." Jeff wrapped me in a hug and for a moment I let someone take the weight I'd been carrying around with me.

"Good night."

I backed out of his arms and left the infirmary before anyone saw the tears in my eyes. Damn, when did I ever get so emotional about the stress of my job? Never, that's when, and it was weird.

I shook off the odd feeling and stepped out of the clubhouse. As Sam had said, fat flakes of snow cascaded down, coating the gravel yard and all the buildings. The air smelled of cold water and I suspected this storm would give us a decent snowfall. I shivered in my light jacket and hurried through the falling fluff to Michael's door.

He opened it before I could knock and just the sight of him made tears come to my eyes again. I tried to say hi but a sob broke loose from my chest as the corners of my mouth turned down.

"Haley, are you all right?"

"Oh glory, Michael." The stress of the day overrode my usual calm and I threw myself into his arms.

"Hey, love, what's going on? I have you. You're safe."

He kicked the door shut behind me and pulled me against his chest, murmuring sweet nonsense as I soaked his shirt with my tears. All my fear, frustration, excitement, and stress emptied themselves into his willing embrace and I relaxed for the first time in days.

Michael held me as I sobbed out the overwhelming emotion that had been building up since I witnessed O'Donnell's murder and he let me use his strength to hold me up. With him, despite his profession, I felt safe and cared for. Yeah, he could be overprotective from time to time, but when I needed it, he was there.

I finally wound down from the initial outburst and pulled back, wiping my eyes on my sleeve.

"Better?" He gave me a half-smile full of compassion and gentleness.

"Yeah, I think so. Thanks." I sniffed and cleared my throat.

"You're welcome, love. Come have something to eat. As my friend Attila says, eating puts everything in perspective."

I snorted. "Attila says that?"

"Well, it comes out more like, 'och, get a wee bit o' haggis into ya and the world willna be so dire,' or some such."

I laughed at his exaggerated Scottish accent. "I'm starving so he might not be wrong." I followed him to the little table outside this kitchenette. "What's on the menu tonight?"

"Homemade mac n' cheese, seared zucchini, and crusty bread with garlic butter."

"Damn." My mouth watered as I washed my hands in the sink. "Not low calorie but sounds divine."

Michael snorted. "I don't know about divine, but Grub doesn't get cooking wrong."

He pulled covers off the plates waiting on the little table and a delicious scents of baked cheese and garlic hit my nose. I moaned with pleasure and slid into one of the chairs.

"Oh, this looks like heaven."

He chuckled and shook his head. "I'll treat you to heaven later. Right now, eat."

****

Michael

I watched Haley eat, only picking at my food as my gut churned with my Mother's directive. I had to choose if I was going to stay with Haley through all her trials and adventures, which bloody well scared me. Or if I was going to walk away.

Just the idea of turning my back on her made my stomach rebel and Grub's wonderful meal threatened to come up. *I got the tattoo. It means she's meant to be mine, doesn't it?* Yeah, probably, but I couldn't keep her in my life if I didn't tell her what and who I was. Voluntarily walking away would do less damage. I'd planned this intimate dinner to tell her my heritage, my connection to the divine, but the moment she threw herself into my arms, crying out her stress and fear, I couldn't bring myself to add to her woes.

She might think dating an angel is brilliant.

True, given her reading proclivities, she might be thrilled with my angelic origins. But she read fiction, and the reality of an angel sitting across from her, making love with her, might be more than she could handle. *Or believe.*

That was the hard part. I liked where we were, the way she wanted me to hold her and comfort her. I liked that she trusted me enough to come back to me. But could she really trust me if I didn't tell her who I was?

Haley sighed and sat back, her plate clean. "Good glory, that was good. Give my compliments to Grub. He's a master."

"I will. He'll be pleased to hear it." I rose and collected the plates. "Tea?"

"Yeah, I could definitely use some tea after today." She sighed and rubbed her face with her hands. "I got a tip that ADA Mitchem was doing something hinky and I followed him."

I damn near dropped the plates in the sink. "You did what?"

"I followed him to an abandoned train yard." She stretched her shoulders and neck, unaware of my horror and disbelief. "He met with a guy named Butler to talk about the murder of ADA O'Donnell and how he needed to fall in line or he could end up the same."

I braced my hands on the counter and tried to breathe through my clenched teeth to calm down my irrational fury.

"The thing is, Butler might have been the one speaking and giving the orders, but one of the thugs they had with them is the real guy in charge. I'd bet my life on it."

Sweet glory, she's already betting her life on this. I tried to calm myself down because the last time I'd told her she couldn't do something, she'd coerced my brother into taking her where she wanted to go. And Mom had reminded her I had to trust her if I wanted her to stay in my life. Trust that she could do her job and ask for help when she needed it. Even if I wanted to tie her down and keep her safe.

I took a deep breath just as the kettle started to whistle and I pulled it off the stove. *Pour the tea and simmer down.* My own pep talk didn't work as well as usual but I managed to bring two mugs and a teapot to the table.

"What will you do now, then?" I hoped my voice

sounded mild despite my urge to shake sense into her. How could she put herself into such danger? Facing danger was my job.

Haley gave me a smug smile. "I got video of the meeting on my phone."

I wanted to throw up. The only way to do that was for her to have gotten close. I gave her a watery smile. "Did you? Can you identify the speakers?"

She nodded. "I already know Mitchem, and Butler is distinct. The hard part will be identifying the Thug-in-Charge. He's big, burly, and dumb-looking, which definitely works to his advantage. He can be at all the meetings and his 'contacts' don't suspect a thing. I bet he sees a lot more than his supplicants suspect."

"But you don't know who he is?"

She shook her head as she sipped her tea. "No. It might take me a while, but I'll figure it out. Even if it takes divine intervention."

I blinked. *Divine intervention.* Mom had come that afternoon to knock some sense into me, and to threaten consequences to my actions like a good parent. The question came down to what I really wanted, and it took me a few moments to realize this was it. I wanted the domesticity of Haley coming home and telling me about her day. She didn't hide it from me even though she knew I didn't want her putting herself in danger. She trusted me enough to share it. I swallowed hard. I had to return that trust if I wanted her to stay with me to have more of these domestic moments.

"Speaking of divine intervention, I need to tell you something."

"Oh yeah?" Then she rolled her eyes. "Yeah, I bet. I should've asked you how things went after I left."

At first, I gaped at her. How did she know the Goddess came to visit? Was it showing on me or something? But then I realized she meant to return the favor of domesticity and wanted to hear about my day. I chuckled uncomfortably.

"My mother stopped by to see me today."

"Your mother? Is she in the club with you and Luke?" Haley's eyes widened and she blushed. "Does she know we had sex the other night?"

"Oh, yeah. That's not a question."

"Oh." She grimaced and rubbed the back of her neck. "I'm kinda glad I wasn't here for your meeting with her, then."

"Yes, that would've been a little awkward, I suppose." Not as awkward as telling Haley my Mother was the Goddess of All. *Which you still haven't done, you blooming twat.* I cleared my throat. "Anyway, she made it clear that I needed to trust you to do your job and take care of yourself even though I'm usually the one going into battle."

Haley smiled. "I like her already."

"Right, well, she thinks pretty highly of you, too." At least the Goddess wasn't opposed to me being with Haley. But I still hadn't figured out how to tell her I was an archangel, with wings and flaming sword. "She wanted me to tell you—"

The ring of my cellphone broke the moment and I recognized Loki's ringtone. What the hell was he calling about at the moment? I was tempted to let it go to voicemail and call him back as soon as I was done explaining things to Haley, but I'd learned long ago ignoring Loki's call often led to rough consequences.

"Excuse me a moment." I grimaced apologetically and opened the phone. "Michael."

"Michael, something has come up and I need you to take care of it, ja?"

"Right. Does this have to be done now or can it wait a bit?" I shot a look at Haley who yawned behind her hand.

"You'll go tomorrow with Scott and Attila. Some of our vendors aren't living up to their ends of our deals, and must be convinced to change their perspectives. I need you to help them understand the error of their ways."

I nodded. Keeping people in line once they'd agreed to work with us was part of my duties. "Right then. When?"

Haley rose and pointed toward the bathroom. "I'm gonna go take a shower and get into bed."

"Haley, wait—"

"You'll leave at first light tomorrow morning." Light amusement laced Loki's voice and a suspicion bloomed in my mind. Was the sodding bastard making sure I couldn't talk to Haley?

She waved at me and disappeared into the bedroom as Loki noticed my silence.

"Michael, are you listening?"

"Yeah, I'm here. Tomorrow at first light. Which vendors are making trouble?"

I only listened with half an ear as Loki rattled on about our suppliers and distributors, but I wanted to go after Haley. I wanted more time to connect with her and tell her who I was. I'd finally made the decision to do it and I wanted the time to follow through.

"Right then. Sounds good. I'll be ready at first light." I knew my voice was curt, but I needed to get off the phone.

"Det er bra. See you in the morning." Why did he sound so damn amused?

I set the phone on the charger and headed for the bathroom when someone knocked on the front door. Who the hell wanted to talk to me now? I reversed direction and opened the door.

"Oh good, you're not busy. Loki's got a wild hair up his ass about this and he needs us to coordinate before we go tomorrow." Scott pushed his way into the living room with Attila right behind him.

"Oy! Now's not a good time. Can't we do this in the morning?"

Attila shook his head as he wrinkled his nose. "No,

Loki wants to do something special with a few of these laddies. Are ye in the habit of wearin' cologne now, Michael?"

"No, why?"

"Yer scent has changed. It's…sweeter almost." The werewolf narrowed his eyes at me. "By the First Canid, you're mated!"

"What?" I gaped at him.

"What?" Scott gaped at me.

"Aye, that's what it is. You've gone and found yourself a lover and by the smell of it, they're a special one indeed. Who is it? That lovely lassie that's been here the last few days?" Attila looked around as if he'd find Haley hiding under a couch cushion.

"You got yourself a long term lover? Male or female? Or someone else?" I had to hand it to Scott. He might have looked like set-in-his-ways biker, but he'd embraced the knowledge of the LGBTQ community.

"Woman, her name is Haley, and yes, she's been here the last few days. In fact, she's here now, so do you think you could come back later to do this?" I gestured at the door, urging them back outside.

Unfortunately, neither seemed inclined to leave.

"Wait, she's here now? I want to meet the woman who snagged my buddy Schnoz's heart. Or is that dick?" Scott moved toward the bedroom but I blocked his path with a growl.

"Don't you have your own woman to love up?" I turned him bodily around.

"Aye, Scott may have his own lassie to shag, but not me. Perhaps she'd like a taste of a wild Scot." Attila made an attempt to head back into the bedroom, but I blocked him as well.

"Either sit your ass down in the front room and tell me why you think we need to work this out now, or get the fuck out." I'd lost all my humor and apparently it made an impression because Attila backed off immediately.

"Okay, okay. Keep your shirt on. Here's what we were thinking of doing." Scott sat down at the table and spread out the plans.

I tried to pay attention and I knew my memory would remind me later, but I really didn't want them to stay any longer than they had to. We went over how we'd approach the vendors and remind them who they worked for, and we ironed out how we'd deal with some of the trickier ones. That would be my job, soothing ruffled feathers.

By the time we'd come to agreements on what we needed to do and who we'd see first, it was close to ten at night, and Haley hadn't come out of the room. I shooed my fellow members out the door with a little more of their ribbing, and locked it behind them. Sighing, I turned out the lights and headed for the room.

I hoped she'd be awake and waiting for me to talk to her, but she'd curled up in the bed and fallen asleep with her tablet beside her. My heart swelled in my chest and I grasped the tablet, moving it to the bedside table where she could find it in the morning. She didn't move, just snuffled a little in her sleep, making me bite my lips to keep from chuckling aloud.

I wanted to wake her and tell her who I was and how much I wanted her in my life. How much I needed her. How much I loved her.

But it was a conversation best held when she was fully awake, and I'd have to wait until I returned from Loki's last minute trip. Both the trip and Scott and Attila's visit had mischievous interference all over them, and there was nothing Loki liked better than to watch people around him squirm in frustration and fear. *Bloody bastard.*

Sighing, I used the bathroom and undressed, sliding into bed with Haley. I'd leave her a note if she didn't wake before I left. But I'd hold her for as long as she'd let me.

CHAPTER FIFTEEN

Haley

I scrubbed my face with my hands and blew out my breath in frustration. It had been three days of non-stop research and staring at screens of information, and I knew I was close to figuring all this mess out, but I wasn't there yet.

I had Tori's list of names, and I'd added ADA Mitchem and the mysterious Mr. Butler, but it still didn't show me what I wanted to know. Other than being lawyers for the City of Denver, they didn't have a lot of connection. And the Thug-in-Charge had remained obscure.

I growled over my tablet and sipped from the latte beside it. I'd finally left the compound that morning and ventured to coffee shop away from my usual haunts. The barista had very kindly decorated with a cream heart, but it didn't cheer me up. I had to figure out this pattern and do it soon before someone recognized me and alerted the powers-that-be.

Michael had been gone damn near three days, though he'd called and texted often when he wasn't "threatening miscreants" or "renegotiating deals." He hadn't offered details and I hadn't asked. I had enough problems with my own puzzle.

Someone had passed the word to the rest of the Concrete Angels' membership that I was Michael's woman and should be treated as the "old lady" of the VP. *I'm about as much "old lady" material as a bundle of sticks is a lovely bouquet in a flower vase.* But I wasn't going to argue with them treating me well. At least I hadn't had to fight for my place.

The best part was I'd made some real friends with some of the women in the club. Apparently my snarky comment about my ass won over Calhoun and the woman had defrosted a little around me. She'd introduced me to Viper, a sharp-featured white woman with raven-black straight hair who reminded me of the lead from a sci-fi TV show with her dry wit and gravelly voice. She loved romance novels as much as I did and we bonded over our favorite series.

The other person I'd connected with was Quan-Yin, the guard at the front gate. She reminded me of a wolf, wise, patient, guarded, mysterious, watchful but playful when the situation required it. I got her to laugh at something I said and it totally transformed her face and showed me the mischievous amusement in her dark eyes. I counted my connection with all three of them to be a victory.

Which is the only victory I got going on right now.

I groaned and brought up the names on Tori's list again, searching for any and all ties between them. Jeff's research on Granby Resort Town had helped a lot. Almost all of the names on the list had either visited in the last three months or had returned there multiple times. I still couldn't find Mr. Butler or the Thug-in-Charge's names, but everyone else lived in GRT.

Wait, no. That's where they were seen together.

I flipped through my screens to see what I'd written

down. It was a little swanky resort town located just south of Lake Granby with its own private airport, which made clandestine meetings between the wealthy very easy. The sheriff in town had been accused of losing evidence and crime coverups, but nothing had come of the allegations. I narrowed my eyes.

"Come on, let's get funky." I dug into the notes I had on the place people like Mitchem and O'Donnell, along with a lot of district court judges, liked to go for weekend jaunts. *Not your usual beer keggers crowd.* No, these were the wheelers-n-dealers setting up contacts.

"Oh my glory, it's a chessboard."

I stared at the ever growing list of names—judges, cops, lawyers, a couple of businessmen, FBI agents, Marshals, Canadian Mounties—that Tori had compiled and Jeff had verified, and the pattern they made. Move one piece and another would take their place to help the whole. All of the pieces spread out like a mosaic to show their bonds like chemistry models and who owned whom. The connections seemed to show this group owning that one, but in reality there was a big fat invisible spider at the center of the web, pulling on all the threads. *The Thug-in-Charge. The head of Backlog? Or just a local boss?*

How the hell had Tori put all this together? *She's a marvel, that's how.* "She's a fuckin' savant at this stuff." She might have been only the paper's layout manager, but the woman had research skills.

And Jeff just added to her baseline.

I swallowed hard as I stared out at the afternoon sky, a light snow swirling past the coffee shop's windows. If anyone found out how much Tori and Jeff knew, how much *I* knew, it'd be lights-out for all of us. With how powerful some of the chess pieces were, it wouldn't take much to make them disappear.

Or me, for that matter.

The weight of the juggernaut of corruption settled onto

my shoulders. How was I going to expose this and not end up dead? I saved everything and closed my tablet, seeking a path through the landmines and pitfalls.

I'm gonna need an alias and a makeover. And help from someone bigger than me in the news scene. I sat back in my chair and considered my options. It was hard to know whom to trust in the news networks. Between selfish glory hounds who'd steal a story just to make themselves look good to those who were on the take from the wealthy corruption dealers, the choices were few and far between.

I'd considered talking to Ryan Sutton, my mentor, but I hadn't wanted to come to him with anything less than proof of a real story. He didn't suffer fools, and that included overeager newbie reporters who wouldn't know a real conspiracy theory if it bit them in the ass. I didn't want to hand him this until I was sure.

I'd hit that point, but I hadn't spoken to Ryan in a while and I didn't know if the news had jaded him enough to let him cut corners of any kind. I couldn't imagine him doing something like that, and he'd been an old pro when he took me under his wing. But it had been years.

I sipped my latte as I tapped my cellphone. *To call or not to call, that is the question.*

I watched the cars outside the coffee shop pass by for a few moments as my phone buzzed in my hand. A couple of black SUVs with tinted windows slid past the front of the coffee shop looking like official FBI type vehicles, but they rolled out of sight and I dismissed them as I opened the phone.

Almost to Fort Collins. Fancy a cuppa joe with me at Black Gold in Fossil Creek?

I couldn't help the giddy smile at Michael's text and the jubilant voice in my head squealing, *He's coming home!* Yeah, I wasn't smitten at all. I thought about the call I had to make.

Yeah, that would be great. I missed you. See you

there in about 35 minutes?

As I waited for Michael's response, Viper, Calhoun and Quan-Yin came into the coffee shop and waved to me. I waved back as they ordered drinks and remembered to stuff my tablet in my bag with my purse and keys. My phone buzzed again just as Viper and Quan-Yin sat down at my table.

Brilliant. I've missed you, too. I have some big news I need to talk to you about when you get here.

I bit my bottom lip and excitement made my stomach flutter. Oh yeah? Me too. I think I've figured out how to break this story. I'll tell you more when I see you.

"What's that smile for, girlfriend?" Viper tilted her head. "Did you get a text from the old man?"

I laughed. The club's referrals to everyone totally didn't fit. Michael wasn't old by any stretch of the imagination. I suspected he was in his late thirties, a little older than me, but nothing incompatible. Despite that, I acted like a teenager with her first crush.

"Can I plead the Fifth? I gotta make a call." I winked at them and took a deep breath before I dialed Ryan Sutton's number. It was an old cellphone number he'd given me years ago, but I hope it still worked.

"Sutton here."

I swallowed hard and took a moment to calm my nerves. "Hey, Ryan. It's Haley Michaels."

"Haley! Wow, blast from the past. How the hell are you?" At least he didn't sound disappointed to hear from me.

"I'm good, well, crazy busy but good. Hey, I wanted to run something past you if you have time. Have you got a minute?"

"Sure." I heard him get up and close a door. "What's going on?"

I grimaced as Calhoun joined us and pinned me with her intense stare. "I got a huge story brewing. I haven't told anyone because I needed to get my facts straight before I came to anyone. But it's big, Ryan. And I suspect Colorado is just the tip of the iceberg." I dropped my voice and covered my mouth with my hand, cupping it around the mouthpiece. "It involves all levels of law enforcement and the judicial system, and murder of the local ADA who wouldn't play ball."

Ryan's voice sharpened. "And you have proof of all this?"

"I definitely have proof of the ADA's murder, and connections to all the rest. But I already have guys after me and I need a signal boost."

"Are you all right?"

"Yeah, I've been laying low and keeping my head down, but I gotta get this to someone I can trust so I'm not the only one who knows. I can't let the story die with me."

There was a short pause. "You've always written fluff pieces, but you never struck me as a person who sensationalized things. Are you sure you want to do this?"

"You're the only one I can trust to do it right and run with it."

"All right, I'll help you, but I need to know more before I'll take over."

"Now, I just need your help getting the story beyond the small papers and stations. I don't want you to get the blowback, but this has to go nationwide." I bit my lip as I glanced out the windows again. The snow seemed to have stopped. "I don't really need you to take over. I need you spread it far and wide and credit a confidential source. This is too big and too entrenched to identify the people who've put this story together."

"Whoa. What have you gotten yourself into, Haley?"

"Nothing you wouldn't have done, but when I first started looking at it, it was one dead FBI agent and a dead US Marshal. Digging proved it was much, much bigger."

"Okay." I heard something going on in the background

and shot a look at Viper who tapped her wrist. "Don't tell me over the phone. I'll text you an email address that is secure where you can send stuff and I'll look it over."

"They're just notes, but the connections are clear." Unease coursed through my veins. "There's something else. There's a guy I'm pretty sure is at the center of this local tangle, but I don't have anything to identify him with. He's hiding in plain sight and is so well disguised, I have no proof of him being the puppet master here. But I'll send you what I've got and we'll talk about it more."

"Good. I'll text you the email. Be safe."

I snorted. "I'm definitely trying."

I ended the call and looked at the time. The conversation had taken fifteen of my thirty-five minutes and I had to get going. The phone buzzed with Ryan's text and I nodded before forwarding it to Jeff, with an additional note of, "Hold onto this for me until I get back."

"All right, I gotta get going to meet Michael."

"See, I told you he's her old man." Viper raised her chin with a smug smile. "Pay up, Calhoun."

"Yeah, yeah, whatever." She flipped Viper a ten spot.

"Did you really bet on whether Michael and I are a committed couple?"

"Damn straight, we did." Viper nodded. "He's never brought anyone back to the compound and he doesn't take advantage of the honeys, ergo..." Viper spread her hands.

I laughed. "Did you just say 'ergo'? Seriously?"

"Just because you don't know how to use the language right, doesn't mean I should stop." She winked as we all gathered our things to leave.

I'd learned earlier that week Viper actually had a Masters in Romantic Literature and had once won a national spelling bea. I had no doubt she knew how to use our language. In fact, if I wrote this news story, I considered using her as an editor.

"You still speak American English, you know."

Calhoun sniffed with perfect disdain though her eyes twinkled with amusement. "And you get the names for things wrong quite often. Like boot and bonnet of the car, a warm jumper, and what we're walking on now is pavement."

"Ha! Boots are for feet, bonnets are for your head, and jumpers are for little kids. And this is the sidewalk." I could tell this was an old argument between them as we strode down the "pavement" toward our vehicles.

"What kind of rubbish is that?" Calhoun glared at Viper. "Your lack of knowledge is appalling."

I was laughing at their antics when the screech of tires made us all look up. The black SUVs with tinted windows I'd seen from the coffee shop skidded to a stop beside us, making us all step back and stop.

"What the fuck?" Viper yelled as men poured out of the closest SUV.

"Holy shit!" They came straight for me and I just had the presence of mind to toss my bag at Viper as Calhoun moved with militaristic precision to intercept the nearest thug. "Oh my glory, let go of me!"

I tried to twist away, but though I ducked one thug, there was another behind me to yank me off my feet. One arm snaked around my waist while the other jerked my head back, his hand sealing my mouth as he hauled me against his chest. He smelled like old tomato sauce and garlic with a hint of oregano and I could taste the grease of the pizza he'd eaten from the hand over my mouth.

Especially when I bit him.

"Mudfucker! The bitch bit me."

He yanked his hand away and cuffed my head, making me see stars.

"Just get her in the truck."

I was shoved into the back of the SUV and had to scramble out of the way as the thug followed me. I kept going, hoping to open the opposite door and launch myself out the other side, but that door opened and another mean-looking brute got in, drawing me up short. He gave me a nasty smile as I found myself sandwiched between two creeps.

I tried to make myself as small as possible. My heart pounded in my chest and tears burned in my eyes. I wasn't sure if it was from the Garlic lump next to me or panic reaching up from my gut.

"All right. We got her. Let's get the fuck out of here."

I wanted to demand who they were and what they wanted with me, but I didn't want to give them my voice. I knew who they were from. Backlog. It looked like my time had just run out.

****

Michael

I settled into a chair around the table near the window of Jitters and checked my phone. No new texts from Haley since the last one that said she'd meet me at the coffee shop twenty-five minutes ago. Apparently she had some news to share. I swallowed hard and tried to let the snowy afternoon calm my nerves.

I have some news to share, too.

At least I'd told her it was big news. I was going to take a chance on her and tell her who I really was. I wasn't supposed to do that. Humans didn't deal well with the Elder Races. They either feared us and tried to kill us— something that rarely worked out for them—or they tried to use us for some sort of inane power-grab. The human intending to grab power usually ended up taking a dirt nap.

But Haley was my true mate, the one who'd won my heart and held it in her hands, and we'd never be truly together if I didn't reveal who I was. Mom had been right. It would be scary to bare this secret to her, but it would be worth it in the long run. The problem was, I still hadn't come up with a good way to say it.

So, right, you know all those stories about the winged beings called angels and one of the most powerful being Archangel Michael? Brilliant, that's me.

Somehow that didn't sound nearly as plausible at the moment in a coffee shop in Fort Collins. And that didn't even begin to cover the frustration of having to wait three extra days to tell her, thanks to Loki. I'd figured out what he'd been up to and remembered what he'd done to both Scott and Karma when they'd found their loved ones.

Just before we'd headed out to ride, I'd pulled Loki aside and looked him dead in the eyes.

"I know what you're doing. You want all this drama for you to watch. But mark my words, Loki. Your own personal drama is coming like a storm just over the horizon, and it'll make our tribulations fade into insignificance."

He'd given me his patented self-assured smile and wished me well on our endeavor. I wanted to kick the living shit out of him, but the knowledge of the upcoming storm of karma took some of the fury away. I was done with his meddling errands and I could focus on Haley.

Despite having made my decision, nervousness ricocheted through me and I checked my phone. Eleven minutes until she'd be there. I rubbed my hands on my jeans and tried to find my smile as the barista brought over two coffees. I suspected it came out more like a grimace. She didn't seem to notice and sauntered away just as my phone rang.

I hoped it would be Haley, but it was Viper's ringtone. I frowned and answered the call.

"Yeah, Viper, what's up?"

"Holy shit, Michael! They just snatched her, right off the street. You gotta get here." She sounded angry and scared, not a good combo in Viper.

"What? Slow down. What are you talking about? Who got snatched?" I was already on my feet and moving toward the door, coffees in hand.

"Haley!"

My gut sank and I went cold all over.

"They just grabbed her and took off in these ugly ass SUVs. I didn't see the tags, but Calhoun might have caught them." Viper's voice was breathless. "Holy shit, we couldn't get to her before they were peeling away. I'm so sorry, Michael."

I tossed the cup in the nearest rubbish bin as I shot past surprised patrons who scrambled out of my way.

"Who, Viper? Who took her?"

"I don't know, dumbass. The SUVs didn't have any biz decals."

I snarled something only my brother Luke would understand and jumped on my bike, connecting my phone to the new Blutooth speaker in my helmet.

"Where were you when they took her?" I started the bike and tore out of the parking lot, leaving spooked pedestrians in my wake.

"South of campus. They took off toward the industrial complexes."

"Fuck!"

"I'm really sorry, Michael. They came outta nowhere."

"Get Torch and Samurai on it, and tell Neo to start tracking the tags when Calhoun remembers them." I sped south through traffic with a sinking feeling. "If it's who I think it is, they're headed to an out of the way spot."

"Who do you think it is?"

I snarled. "Backlog."

"Fuck." I heard her own bike start up. "How the hell do they even know her?"

"She witnessed one of their murders and now they're looking for her. They ransacked her place which is why she was staying with m– us."

If Viper caught my slip, she didn't acknowledge it. "Holy fuck. Why didn't you tell us, Schnoz?"

"I didn't think they'd come for her in broad daylight with you ladies around her."

"Yeah, well, you were wrong about that. Okay, Calhoun said they're heading into the warehouse district off of Saddleback. We're gonna try to slow them down or head them off."

"Right. I'll be there." Damn straight, I'd be there. No one took my woman without severe consequences.

Weaving through traffic, I heard Mom laugh. *Good for you, my Dear One. Find your lady and love her well. I'm very happy for you.*

I swallowed hard and focused on the scents of Haley, sunrise and magic. I didn't need any electronic gadgets to follow her. Her scent flowed down our connection—*We have a connection?*—and led me like a trail of breadcrumbs through the city. I'd come by my roadname honestly and I used my schnoz to find Haley. She was mine and they'd messed with the wrong angel.

CHAPTER SIXTEEN

Haley

I'd seen enough car chases on TV to recognize when I was in one, but they always showed them from the perspective of the good guys. That's not where I was and not how it went. The men around me yelled and pointed while the driver tried to keep up with the SUV in front of us and not hit anything while charging between buildings at top speed.

Then there was the shooting.

Gunfire rattled around as the assholes beside me fired out the windows toward whoever followed behind us. The driver took a turn fast and I was pressed up against a sweaty male body despite my efforts to avoid it.

"Get the fuck away from me, bitch!"

Oh yeah, I so want to be snuggled up to your nasty ass. He tried to shove me away, but the momentum of the vehicle made it impossible. If I'd been more like those TV heroines I could've wrestled with him for the weapon like that assassin with the smart mouth in a red outfit did when stuck in a truck full of bad guys. But I was so out of my element, I just sat there and tried not to get in anyone's way. They were already kidnapping me. I didn't need to get shot too.

The rumble of motorcycles bounced off the warehouses and it took me a few moments to realize the thugs were shooting at members of the Concrete Angels. It would've been exciting to see them come after me if I wasn't in one of the SUVs. *It would make a great story.* Hell yeah, it would. Car chase—*Motorcycle?*—in the middle of southern Fort Collins' warehouse district with speeding SUVs and a fleet of bikes. I bet the photos would've been spectacular.

Get your damn head in the game, Michaels.

Michael. So weird that we shared a name. In all the hoopla, I'd forgotten I was supposed to meet him at Jitters. I shot looks at the men around me and used my hands to grip the seats in front to keep from hitting them. I wanted to lean forward to see what the hell was going on, but the guys kept flailing their arms as they argued and shot out the windows. I turned my body to look through the rear door over a bag of discarded weapons and ammunition, spying a pistol fallen to the side.

Biting my lip, I considered grabbing it and shooting someone, but I had no skill and I didn't even know if it was loaded. I'd only succeed in getting myself dead that much faster. The flash of something out the window made me look up.

And then things got really weird.

Someone ran across the building on the right side of the vehicle, leaping off the three story roof. At first, I thought the guy had a parachute—*is there a paramilitary group after us?*—but then I realized the huge silver-black thing behind him came in two pieces and had a distinct wing shape. *What is this, a Marvel movie?*

Bullets peppered the buildings around us but never hit the winged man. *Winged man? I must be going crazy.* At the last moment, I recognized Michael's face and cut, and all coherent thought left my brain.

Michael has wings. Michael has wings. Michael has wings.

Movement to my left made me shift my attention just as we roared past Torch dismounting his bike. He threw his arms out and changed from a big, burly biker into something a lot more strange. Something long, scaly and iridescent green with purple spines that looked remarkably like a dragon. When it reared back and belched fire from its gaping maw, I shrieked.

The driver jerked the wheel to one side and skidded to a stop just as the SUV in front of us exploded into a ball of fire. The men who'd gotten out of the burning wreckage scattered, firing at the bikers I could just see beyond the flames. I recognized Quan-Yin just before she shifted into a huge lion-dog thing that stood as tall as a horse. The Quan-Yin lion leaped through the flames and landed on the hapless thug with an automatic rifle and tore his head off with a spatter of blood marring her dark chocolate fur.

"Holy fuck! What in the holy hell was that?" At least the thugs around me had started to get a clue that we weren't dealing with run-of-the-mill badasses anymore.

Then Samurai ran between our SUV and the one in front of us, his cut showing the gargoyle before red fir sprouted all over his body and a long tail shot out his ass. It had a white tip at the end and it waved like a banner as he disappeared into the SUV. He returned and turned his glowing golden stare our direction. He looked like a red fox with black ears and legs, but he stood the size of an English mastiff. He advanced on our SUV with a menacing snarl I could feel in my chest.

I sat frozen in place, my breath short enough to hyperventilate. What the fuck was I seeing?

Michael leaping off a building into a hail of bullets with a large pair of silver-black wings to slow his fall—and not getting hit by any of the projectiles.

Torch morphing into an iridescent green dragon with purple and blue spines running down the length of his back and spouting fire at the speeding SUVs.

Quan-Yin and Samurai shifting into fearsome beasts, one lion-like the other wolf-like, and running men down.

Holy shit, holy shit, holy shit!

This couldn't be real. Seriously, it couldn't be real. Hell, I'd been scared of the men who'd grabbed me right off the street in front of Calhoun, Viper, and Quan-Yin. But looking out the windows had been a whole other education in reality. What the hell had happened to the normal world?

The SUV in front of us crackled in flames right there on the street and the men around me shouted expletives. I shrank back against the seat and tried to think small as the Samurai fox headed for the driver's side. They fired their weapons out the front windshield, but the fox only ducked out of sight.

"What the fuck was that?"

"How the fuck should I know? Just keep firing, asshole."

I threw my hands up over my ears as they let loose a barrage of gunfire, squinting against the muzzle flares. Then I saw something that damn near stopped my heart.

Michael landed directly ahead and slammed a huge fucking sword through the hood of the vehicle. The engine stopped dead and steam hissed out from under the shorn metal. His eyes blazed with white light, something I'd expect from Thor, God of Thunder, but that guy didn't exist except in myths and movies.

Except there's a guy named Loki who looks like Thor, and Michael has wings, and Torch is a dragon and...

"Oh, sweet glory..."

I slid lower as one of the big guys pulled up his automatic rifle and pointed it out the destroyed windshield again. "Let's smoke this asshole."

I closed my eyes as he fired straight at the winged

image of Michael. The sound made my ears ring and I screamed as the men roared their belligerent fury at their target. Someone grabbed me by the arm and yanked me out of the SUV. I jerked my eyes open and tried to fight back, but he cuffed me across my ear and the shock stunned me enough to stop resisting. He dragged me to my knees outside of the vehicle and hauled me to my feet.

"Run, bitch, before I kill you right fuckin' here."

I didn't doubt him, but I didn't want to go anywhere. *Is it better to stay here and get roasted by a fucking dragon?* I wasn't sure that was an improvement and I let him tow me a few stumbling steps to an aluminum door. He slammed it open with his shoulder and dragged me into the gloom of a nearby warehouse. It appeared abandoned and smelled like it, too. The metal door slammed shut behind us as we faced a rabbit warren of partitioned rooms resembling cubicles. He wove through them, looking for an open space and I trailed along, still trying to come to grips with what I'd seen.

How the hell had Michael sprouted wings? What made Quan-Yin's skin turn brown and her body shift into a lion-dog? How could Torch just become reptilian? Why did Sam look like a big fucking fox? None of it made sense or could be real. They were supposed to just be bikers, for glory's sake. But Michael's sword had stopped the SUV and Torch had torched the other SUV in front of us.

At last, my personal thug dragged me into the open portion of the warehouse and pulled me across the dirty concrete floor. But I'd had enough and I tore my arm out of his grip.

"No, let me go!" I managed to get free but he swung his rifle toward me and snarled.

"Fine, I'll just kill you right here. They weren't gonna let you live anyway."

What? Who wasn't gonna let me live?

He raised the muzzle and fingered the trigger. I

squeaked and closed my eyes, holding my breath. But a loud thud and a pained grunt hit my ears, and the shots never came.

I peeled my eyes open and looked toward my would-be killer. He was nothing but a crumpled mass at the foot of a very angry, winged-warrior. The winged man—*angel, you moron. He's an angel*—yanked his blade free from the body and turned to face me. I swallowed hard.

Michael as a biker was hot and sexy, powerful in an understated sort of way. I'd always felt protected when around him. This Michael stood taller, broader, with actual fucking wings and glowing white eyes, and I was afraid he'd throw lightning down on me or something. Who the hell was this guy? Apparently I didn't know him at all.

I took a step back and swallowed hard, my hands tightening into fists. Michael's expression softened and he reached out toward me, but I shifted away from his hand. He frowned and dropped his arm.

"Are you all right, Haley?"

No, definitely not all right at all.

I shook my head, studiously ignoring the mass of bloody flesh on the floor a few feet from me. The sounds of gunfire had stopped and an ominous silence gripped the warehouse. I couldn't quite find my voice to express my confusion and shook my head again.

"Talk to me, love. Are you hurt? Did they harm you?"

I shook my head harder. "I told you I saw wings. I told you!"

It was an inane thing to say because it referenced our first meeting, but a deep sense of betrayal sank into my chest and lodged there, making tears overflow my eyes. Anger followed and I raised my gaze to him, my lips peeling back from my teeth in a snarl.

"You lied to me!" My voice thundered across the space between us, ricocheting around the empty warehouse.

Michael's eyes dimmed and his wings drooped a little.

"I never lied to you, Haley—"

"Yes, you did. At the Museum. I said I saw wings and you said they were an illusion. But they weren't. Aren't. You have fucking wings and you lied to me."

I shook my head at my own stupidity. Of course, why I was upset about this instead of the existence of mythical or magical or impossible beings in a stupid biker club didn't make sense either, but I would run with it.

"I didn't know you then."

I barked a laugh. "You didn't know me then? Fabulous. How about when you brought me to your place after my apartment was ransacked? How about when you shared breakfast with me? How about after you *fucked* me? Did you know me enough then?"

"I know this is hard to understand—"

"You don't know shit!" I snarled as I turned away from him and marched through the rabbit warren of cubicles back the way we came. Back to where more mythical creatures roamed the street outside.

I couldn't look at Michael. I wasn't sure I could look at any of them. And I'd left Jeff behind the gates of the menagerie without a clue. I'd trusted these people. They were my friends or so I'd thought.

I managed to find my way back to the door and stepped out into the dim afternoon. What the hell would I do? I couldn't go back to my apartment and I wasn't sure I had a place in the Concrete Angels' compound after their secrets had been exposed. Did I even want to go back there? *Hell, will they let me leave now that I know?*

A rustle of cloth behind me let me know I was no longer alone. I could smell Michael's rosemary bread scent but it didn't bring me the comfort it had before. I stepped aside and turned to keep an eye on him.

"Haley, I'm sorry."

He reached for me but I wrapped my arms tight around myself and hunched my shoulders, shrinking away from him. His hands returned to his sides and his shoulders dropped with them as his face blanched with sorrow. His wings had disappeared, gone to wherever they went when he wasn't showing his divine self.

"Don't touch me."

"I'm sorry, I won't. I just wanted to be sure you aren't hurt."

I shook my head. "No, not physically hurt other than some bruises."

He reacted to my choice of words, grimacing at the nature of my pain. His lips tightened when I mentioned the bruises but he didn't make another move to touch me.

"I can heal them for you. Just a touch of grace and you'll be right as rain."

My eyes burned with tears that I refused to shed despite the anger and betrayal and fear reaction coursing through my body. I clamped my hands on the shoulders of my jacket to keep them from shaking and retreated to stand against the warehouse wall.

"What does that even mean, 'right as rain'? Why is rain right about anything? It's just a friggin' atmospheric phenomenon when clouds get too full of moisture. How does that make it right?"

"It's just an expression, Haley."

"I fucking know that, Michael! I was looking for the etymology of it."

"I know you're angry with me. I know you're hurt. And I know you deserve answers." Michael grimaced. "But we need to get you somewhere safe."

"And where is that? My home was tossed and I was a temporary guest at your cabin. *Your* cabin. I don't have a safe place anymore."

If anything, he appeared more wounded by that than by my initial anger.

"I never meant to make you feel unsafe. But right now the safest place for you is at the compound. We'll get this sorted and decide from there, all right?"

He gestured away from the burning wreckage of the other SUV. I didn't look too closely at the ground, not ready to see bodies of the thugs who'd taken me. I moved woodenly as I passed the vehicle I'd arrived in and suddenly wondered how I'd get back to the compound. I must have stiffened because Michael swung around me and studied my face just before Viper slid between us and wrapped me in a bear hug.

"Oh good glory, I'm so fuckin' happy to see you."

I wrapped my arms around her and let loose my tears. I needed someone to lean on and the one person I'd thought was safe was something else. Sobs galloped out of me, dragging all the emotional stress with them.

"Shh shh, I got you, sweet girl. I got you." Viper kept murmuring gentle nonsense to me as I cried, her arms never wavering from their hold.

After minutes passed, I finally calmed down enough to pull back and wipe my face. She gave me a goofy smile and squeezed my arms.

"Better?"

I shook my head with a grimace. "No, but at least I'm done crying for the moment."

"Good enough. Here's your bag. I made sure everything stayed in it."

I took it and nodded as I threw the strap over my head. "Thanks."

"Let's get you home." She tugged on my arm.

"I don't have a home." I shook my head as I clutched the strap against my chest.

"Oh, that's a load of horseshit." Viper snorted. "Come on. I'll give you a ride back to the compound on my bike. Just some girl time to regroup." She turned to Michael who still hovered nearby. "I'm sure you understand, right, Schnoz?"

Though he glared daggers after us, Viper didn't wait

for his answer and tugged me down the road between warehouses to her bike. She gave me a helmet that looked like an honest to goodness Egyptian pharaoh's headdress. The ridiculous thing sat on my head and draped around my shoulders with a sense of power and protection. I dropped the visor down and I'm sure I looked too cool for my shoes, but I didn't have the energy to pull it off.

Viper started up her bike and we sailed away smoothly like we didn't have a care in the world. But my mind kept turning over what I'd seen and what Michael appeared to be, and the tears threatened again. I swallowed hard a few times and closed my eyes as I gripped Viper's waist on the ride home.

By the time we arrived, I'd felt my phone buzz a couple of times with incoming texts but I couldn't reach it in my back pocket. Viper parked her bike in the Barn and I took off the pharaoh's helmet. Damn, I could get used to wearing that. She smiled and helped me off the bike before leading me to the clubhouse. I didn't see Jeff or Sam or Quan-Yin, but that was probably for the best given how unsettled I was.

"Let's get you something hot to drink and maybe a blanket, and we'll figure this all out. Mmkay?" Viper pushed through the doors like she owned the place and even the Scooters scrambled to get out of her way.

I followed, wishing I had half her assurance, but any confidence I might have gained by wearing the cool helmet died at the feet of the people waiting for me inside the main room. Karma and Chem stood behind the bar where Loki, Neo, Attila, and Michael sat like a tribunal. Other members sat or stood around the common room and none of them looked friendly, either.

I swallowed hard and followed Viper, stopping a little behind her as a shield against the lack of welcoming faces. I didn't know how Michael had managed to beat us back to the compound, but considering I'd seen wings on him, I shouldn't have been too surprised. *There's definitely gotta be something magic going on here. Either that or really good hallucinogenic drugs.* Had someone spiked my coffee?

Viper received a mug of hot brown liquid from Chemistry and pulled me over to an unoccupied armchair near the TV. She sat me down and handed me the cup before she wrapped a fuzzy blanket around my shoulders.

"Now, I want you to sip that slowly. It's Chem's special blend of chocolate meant to soothe heartache and emotional expenses. I'm gonna give you some time to sort through some of your shit alone before we talk about everything that happened, okay?" Viper gave me a searching look, her customary smirk missing. "You're gonna be okay, Haley, I promise. It always works out in the romance novels."

I snorted. "This isn't a romance novel."

She shot a look over her shoulder at where Michael sat. "Of course it is. You just have to have a little faith, right? Drink the chocolate and we'll talk."

I nodded as she patted my shoulder and walked away. I didn't bother looking up at anyone else. The room wasn't silent, but I could feel everyone's rapt attention on me. I sighed as I sat with my head down, my hands wrapped around a mug of hot chocolate. When the hell had I stepped into the Twilight Zone?

Torch turned into a fuckin' dragon. And Quan-yin became a lion dog. And Michael...

I couldn't finish the thought. He'd sprouted silver-black wings, bigger than any bird, even the prehistoric ones. *Who the hell is he?* And who was I to him?

I shot a look toward where he sat in brooding silence, his gaze lasering into me. *Yeah, right back atcha, buddy.* I didn't know what to think or do. I was only human, a trait I'd taken for granted. Sure, I'd made mistakes, that was the nature of being human. But my whole world had tilted upside down and it turned out I might have been the only human in the whole place.

Michael, Quan-Yin, Torch, Sam. Hell, there's even something weird about Attila. And don't get me started on Loki. I sucked in a breath quickly. *What if he's the* real *Loki?*

My heart quailed at the thought. That meant other gods and goddesses might be real. Vampires, werewolves, Frankenstein's Monster. *Holy crap, what if all the stories in the tabloids have a shit-ton more truth to them?*

"Hey, Haley, how are you holding up?" Calhoun settled beside me, biting her bottom lip in concern.

I laughed, sounding suspiciously like a sob. "How am I holding up? Let's see. I was snatched off the street by thugs, engaged in a hardcore car chase and shootout, and then the guy I've been fucking turns out to be an honest-to-whoever angel with a huge fucking sword. How do you think I'm doing?"

"Yeah, I can see how that'd be a lot to take in."

I barked an unhappy laugh. "A lot to take in? Are you fuckin' kidding me? The mythical creatures from fairytales are walking around here and you're acting like it's no big thing. How are you okay with all this?"

Calhoun shrugged. "I dunno. I reckon hanging out with cool people was all good. Yeah, so some of them could bench press a Mack truck, but physical strength doesn't equate scary. Or bad. What's your big problem with them?" She narrowed her eyes. "Is it that the mythical beings are real? Or that you've been lied to all your life about them?"

I opened my mouth to reply but closed it again as I thought about what she'd said. What was I really upset about? Wasn't it cool that I'd being hanging out with angels and dragons? Yeah, it totally threw my world into chaos, but how was that different than usual?

Oh, shit. And all that angel romance I've been reading. Guess Michael did know how hot angels could be. I blushed to the roots of my hair.

"I think it's that everyone I trusted lied to me. They—you didn't trust me with this."

Calhoun nodded. "Yeah, that's bollocks for sure. But to be fair, we've only known you for a week. It's hard to know if you're trustworthy enough for this kind of secret. Especially because you're a reporter."

She had me there. I was a reporter, the most curious human known to mankind next to a scientist, and most reporters would sell their souls for this kind of story. But I'd grown to like these people, even Loki though he scared the living daylights out of me.

I grimaced. "I see your point. If I was such a threat to you all, why did you let me stay? Why did you make me think I was welcome? I could've discovered this at any time."

Calhoun twisted around to look at Michael and I followed her gaze.

"Because I wanted you here despite the risks." Michael moved to stand before me, his expression full of ancient sorrow. "The Elder Races of this world are far safer when humans are ignorant of our existence. But you were more important to me." He nodded to Calhoun who gracefully made her exit with a squeeze to my hand.

"But I'm human, and humans kill or destroy what they don't understand. Right?"

He nodded. "They definitely don't deal well with paradigm shifts." I blushed at his insinuation. No, I hadn't dealt well with this discovery at all.

I sighed and sipped my chocolate. "So what now? What happens to me? I'm only human, after all. Will you kill me to keep your secret?"

Agonized sorrow etched his features as he knelt in front of me. "I'd sooner destroy all the art in the Denver Museum. But some secrets are meant to be kept. The question is, can you keep this one, Haley?"

Yeah, that definitely was the question. I was the kind of person who sought truths and let the world know. It was my job to expose secrets that could hurt people, secrets of crimes, both on-going and past, that caused damage and required change.

Is this really that kind of secret?

I thought over the amazing things I'd seen in the Concrete Angels MC. Quan-Yin's huge lion-dog. Samurai shifting into a big ass fox. Loki's scary otherness. Torch shifting into a sinuous dragon, with huge wings and a barbed tail.

Do you hear yourself? You're really going to believe all this?

Yeah, I was, and I would protect it with everything I had. These people might have been more than human, but they'd still protected and rescued me. I'd spent several days with them and they'd welcomed me, even knowing what I was. They were a family, and I wasn't going to break that trust. They weren't human, but it didn't matter. They were just as valuable to me as Tori, my cousin Jeff, or my parents had been. *And they need to be protected even more than the humans who read the papers.*

I raised my gaze to meet Michael's, nodding slowly. "Yeah, this is my secret to protect. It's my job to expose corruption, not..." I gestured to the people sitting around me.

"We're called the Elder Races, lassie." Attila winked as he sipped a mug of tea.

"Is that because you're old?"

"Och, go on. Weren't ye taught to respect yer elders?"

I laughed. "Yeah, but I don't think you were what they had in mind."

CHAPTER SEVENTEEN

Michael

I'd never felt relief like I did in that moment. Haley's laughter loosened the knot in my chest that had developed the moment she pulled back from me in the warehouse. I'd never felt such loss or fear in all my centuries of life. I'd gone a little overboard when it came to cutting down the thugs who'd kidnapped her, but I'd made the decision about my connection to Haley and they'd attempted to rob me of my choice.

All I wanted to do was swoop her up in my arms and haul her to my cabin where we could make love until the sun rose. Unfortunately, Loki had other ideas.

"Det er bra. This would be a good time to make a contract, ja?"

Oh sweet glory of all. Loki's contracts. To sign one was to give one's life to the club and hope no one found a loophole with which to bleed that life away. I'd seen the contracts Numbers, Scott's woman, and Eric, Karma's man, had had to sign. There was almost always a hidden death clause.

"Contract?" Haley sat up straighter and her expression sharpened. "What kind of contract?"

"A contract to ensure you write what needs to be written about our club, but also keep the secrets that need to be kept." He crossed his arms over his chest and the others around us nodded. I wisely kept my mouth, and my expression, closed, especially when he shot me a narrow look. "It is good to get all the terms down in writing to ensure everyone abides by the rules, ja?"

She narrowed her eyes and tightened her lips. "Including you and the club members?"

Loki smirked as his eyes returned to mine. "Especially me, and ja, the club members too."

Haley nodded slowly. "All right. What are the terms and will they be written down?"

"Ja, written down, witnessed and signed." Loki's smile broadened.

I wanted to tell her she didn't have to do this. That we could still be together even if she didn't sign a contract, but I couldn't gainsay my president in front of the members and my survival, as well as the rest, depended on her not sharing the nature of our club.

And you don't know if she's going to give you a chance after she saw who you are.

Bloody hell, there was that.

But it wasn't the time to pull her aside and ask if we had a chance. And would it even matter? The secret had to be kept whether she chose to continue our relationship or not. I just hoped she wouldn't resent me for it if she chose not.

Neo stepped forward with a tablet and handed it to Haley. She took it and raised her eyebrows.

"Wow, you guys have done this before, huh? You have it all prepared and everything?"

"Yup. Just sign at the bottom." Neo handed her a stylus.

"Oh, no no no. That's not how this works." She took the tablet but refused the stylus. "I'm gonna read this and I'm gonna amend a few things because I'm not crazy or naïve."

I didn't smirk or smile, but satisfaction settled into my gut. She'd thwarted Loki's easiest play. Now the question came if she'd catch all his loopholes. I shot a look at Luke and Attila and raised my eyebrows. Luke shook his head, indicating he didn't know what was in the clauses, while Attila raised a pint glass of beer, toasting either my choice in woman or her intelligence.

Most of the other members went back to their amusements while Haley read the contract, but I kept my attention focused on her, trying to sense what she read in the nuances of her expression. Loki chatted with Karma and Neo, though he kept his voice low as if any sharp noise would give away the pitfalls he'd built into the contract.

"Okay, I have a few changes and demands." She sat up and fixed Loki with a firm look.

He waved his hand regally. "Please share them with us."

"First, if I'm gonna be your freelance press liaison, I get full membership privileges of this club. If I'm supposed to know what I can and cannot tell the press, I can't be going in blind." She never looked away from Loki's gaze but I felt her testing the waters with her statements.

"Agreed." He nodded. "What else?"

"Second, I want my expenses covered. If I'm driving up here all the time, I need fuel and mileage covered for my vehicle. Snacks, too."

A chuckle ran through the members watching the negotiation. It was hard to argue with snacks.

Loki grinned. "Fine." He nodded to Neo. "Anything else?"

"Yeah, I'm my own person. As much as Viper, Calhoun or Quan-Yin. No one's going to treat me like the honeys you have wandering around here. They signed up for that, I haven't. Anyone violates that, I'm gone."

He tilted his head thoughtfully, but smiled. "All right. Have you more demands?"

"Yeah, I get paid. Well enough to take the time away from my regular job. Well enough that if I get fired from my other job, I still can cover my monthly expenses."

"Very well. Is that all?"

"That's all I can think of." She eyed Loki narrowly.

"Det er bra. Here are my additions. You will be required to live on site."

While that made me happier than I expected, Haley frowned.

"But I work in Fort Collins. It's a thirty minute drive on a good day."

"You work for us, now, and you've become an investigative reporter. They travel a lot for work, ja?" Loki tilted his head as his gaze bored into her. "You will remain connected to your office through email, phones, social media, which we will monitor."

"No, my email and phone are to be mine alone. I can't be an effective investigative reporter if my sources don't trust their anonymity." She raised her chin and stared Loki down. I had to hand it to her, she never flinched though I suspected she knew with whom she dealt.

Loki huffed a short laugh with a half-smile and nodded. "Ja, okay, but you will have a club email assigned to you for club business and sensitive information. You will reveal none of our secrets or sensitive information that governs this club as it is considered club business and could endanger the lives of club members if revealed. In particular, that the club members are anything other than human. Failure to keep these secrets will result in immediate and permanent silencing."

I swallowed hard just as Haley met my gaze. "Silencing?"

Loki nodded. "In any way we see fit."

Haley licked her lips and bit the bottom one thoughtfully. "Okay, but I require the freedom to tell family should it impact those relationships."

"You may tell one trusted family member." Loki nodded regally. "Family is important, ja?"

He shot a look at me and I swore he winked, but no one else chuckled so I might have imagined it. But I did let out the breath I hadn't realized I'd been holding.

"Do you agree to these terms?"

We all stared at Haley, who'd grown more and more calculating as the negotiation went on. I suspected she weighed all the variables in an attempt to see all the pitfalls. But when making deals with Loki, no one ever saw the loophole until it'd closed around their neck.

"I agree to these terms." She held out her hand and Loki's grin widened uncomfortably.

"Are you asking me to shake on it?" Laughter rippled through the watching club members as Neo disappeared toward the offices to collect the printed contract and Loki's special pen.

Haley shrugged. "That's one way to seal a deal in front of witnesses."

"Ja, it is one way. But in the Concrete Angels, we sign. In blood."

Haley looked at me. I couldn't read her expression and I desperately wanted to know what she was thinking. Was she debating if I was crazy? Or if I was worth all this trouble? I closed my hands into fists to hide my unease as she shifted her gaze away.

Neo returned with the papers and handed them to Haley. Loki took the pen as we watched her read over the contract carefully. Satisfaction settled into my chest. She was wise to make sure Loki hadn't added anything to the contract on the sly.

When she finished, she again shot a look at me before

she nodded. "The contract looks good. You're serious about the blood?"

"Ja. It is always been this way. Then there is no forging the signature or pretending the agreement is invalid." He held up the pen. "For either of us."

Haley took the pen and considered our president. She nodded slowly then placed the pen on the paper and began to sign. But she hissed as it pricked her finger. Blood flowed from the tip of the pen onto the paper. "Shit, that hurts."

"A little bit of pain for a lot of pleasure, ja?" Loki's gaze slid to mine and I barely managed to keep my expression stoic.

She scowled but signed her name in her own blood on the paper. She handed the pen back to Loki who cleaned it with an alcohol wipe, and then signed his own name. The blood shimmered for a moment before settling into a dark red ink on the page.

"There. It is done. Welcome to the Concrete Angels." He shifted toward his office.

"Hold on a moment. You better scan that puppy and get me a copy. That way we all know where we stand on this." Haley pointed at the paper with her name in blood. "And I want it in full color."

Neo smothered a smile as Loki grimaced and handed him the signed contract. "I'll just get this scanned and emailed."

"You picked a hard woman, Michael." Loki's sapphire blue gaze landed on mine.

I tilted my head, an unusual sense of pride and amusement filling me despite dealing with the God of Mischief. "Not hard, Loki. Wise, aware, and careful. As she should be when dealing with you."

He snorted with grudging admiration and nodded. "Ja, it's true." He clapped his hands and smirked. "Good luck with that."

I ignored the niggling worry his words incited as I caught Viper and Calhoun speaking to Haley. They appeared to be encouraging her and welcoming her to their ranks. Both women were human, but they'd known about the Elder Races of the club since their induction a couple of decades earlier. I hoped they offered her some solace in her choice because I wasn't sure she'd made the best one for her.

After a bit, the last of the club members meandered away to find something else to do. Calhoun and Viper spoke to Haley for a few more moments, offering their congratulations or consolations, I couldn't tell which. But eventually it was just us left in the main room of the clubhouse and I didn't know how to start the conversation again.

"So you're an actual angel." Haley rubbed her hand on her jeans.

"Yes. Well, more than that, really. An archangel. You know, the Archangel Michael? That one."

Her eyes widened and she blinked a couple of times. "Wait, you're *the* Archangel Michael? The one people tell stories about in religious texts?"

I rubbed the back of my neck. "Yeah, that's the one."

She gave a short laugh. "You're not serious."

"Yes, I am."

"Come on, you're pulling my leg." She laughed again.

"No, Haley, I'm not. I'm the Archangel Michael." I didn't smile or tease and she slowly lost her grin.

"Sweet glory."

Now I smirked. "Yeah, you did say that about my loving."

"Shut up."

"Perhaps I need to remind you. In case you've forgotten." I reached out to help her stand. "I'd be happy to give you a refresher course right here and now."

She eyed me with an air of curiosity and amusement.

214

"I really did see wings at the museum, didn't I?"

I nodded as I tugged her with me out of the clubhouse. "I daresay you did, though I'm not certain how. Most humans can't see them at all unless I show them deliberately."

"Maybe I'm just special."

"Oh, there's no question of that." I tucked her against my side and brought her to my cabin. "I'm of a mind to show you just how special you are."

She snorted as I let her inside but she paused in the entry and frowned. "Loki says I have to live here on site, according to the contract. Where will I stay?"

Rather than blurt out the first thing that came to mind, I squared my shoulders and took a deep breath. "I'm hopeful you will stay here, with me."

She set her bag down next to the comfy chair and hung up her jacket in the closet before she met my gaze.

"I read a lot of angel and demon paranormal romance. In some of them the angelic or demonic main character often knows their One-and-Only mate soon after they see them and it becomes a fated mate thing."

I swallowed hard as she stated my own knowledge.

"Does it work that way with you?"

I nodded slowly. "Yes. Would you like some tea?"

She blinked at me then laughed as she strung the security chain on the door. "Yes, I'd like some tea. Tea makes everything better."

"That's right."

She pulled off her shoes and set them beside the door as I put the kettle on to boil. "You know, I just realized I've been drinking more tea than coffee since I met you. Maybe you're rubbing off on me. Or your grace is."

"I'd like to rub a lot more than my grace on you." Maybe the tea could wait. I moved back into the living room to gather her into my arms, but she held up a hand.

"I'm sure you could rub more than your grace on me,

but I'm still trying to get my mind around you being the Archangel Michael. That isn't something I can just take in stride." She moved past me to the kitchenette to set out two mugs. "Tea and talk first, rubbing grace later."

I sighed and tried to rein in my desperate need for her. To help things along, I zapped the kettle with a little extra boost so it would boil faster and soon she poured the water into the mugs. She handed me one as she returned to the living room and we both sat down on the loveseat.

"Okay, I'm trying to understand who you are. Everyone knows what an angel looks like and generally what they're purported to do. The holy books are full of stories of, well, you and your...kind? Siblings? Friends?" She grimaced and sipped her tea a moment, gathering her thoughts. "I guess what it comes down to is why. Why are you here, why with a notorious and not particularly 'good' biker club, and why me?"

I could have answered flippantly, spinning a fun tale to get her to smile, but I recognized I could also lose her in an attempt to deflect her questions. I took a few moments to sort through the answers she needed versus the answers I could give. But she was my One-and-Only, and that gave her privileges beyond the norm.

"You don't ask simple questions, do you?"

"I'm a reporter. Simple questions don't get me the answers I want."

"Oh, I'll give you what you want and more, but first the answers to your questions."

She snorted and shot me a dry look as she sipped her tea. I took my own fortifying sip.

"I'm here to balance the chaotic neutral that is Loki Odinsson. Now that you know who I am, I'm sure you recognize who Luke is. We're the weights on either end of the balance beam resting on Loki's pivot point."

Haley swallowed. "So Loki is *the* Loki from Norse legend?"

I nodded.

"And since you're the Archangel Michael, then Luke is...is..."

"Luke is my older brother, the darkness to my light, balancing out my strengths."

Her eyes widened. "Does he have wings, too? Big, leathery bat wings? And horns and a tail?"

I laughed as I recalled Luke dressing up in a cheesy devil's costume for Samhain.

"No, he's an angel, like me, with a great set of feathered wings. No horns or tail, though I reckon he could wear them for effect. I suspect my brother takes on the appearance each being needs to see when the time comes."

Haley nodded slowly, her thumbs rubbing her mug. "That's why you're both here with the Concrete Angels?"

"Yes. No one is all angelic good." I winked and some of her unease slipped away. "Nor are they all demonic evil. The apparent bad things the club is into are balanced out by the good things they do."

"What good things do they do?"

"Is this an interview, Haley? Do you want a rundown of our charitable donations?"

She grimaced and ducked her head. "No, not really. I'm just trying to figure out how actual angels come to be in a motorcycle club in Fort Collins, Colorado." She frowned. "How does that work, exactly? What about all the people who pray to the Archangel Michael? How do you help them if you're here?"

"How does Santa Claus visit every home at Yule?"

She snorted. "Santa Claus doesn't exist."

"Doesn't he? Yesterday, you might have said the same thing about angels."

Haley opened her mouth but closed it as my words filtered into her understanding.

"What do you really want to know, love?"

"I want to know if this is a big joke. If you're just

messing with me. I know what I saw, but in my world, those sorts of things are products of hallucinogenic drugs and imagination. If you're really the Archangel Michael, you always have to save the world. That's your job, isn't it?" She set her mug down and rose, pacing away from me with her fists tight at her sides. "I want to know if I'm always going to come second to everyone else."

I set my mug beside hers and stood. Then I held my hand out to her. "Come with me, love."

She let out a big sigh and took my hand, but followed me willingly enough into the bedroom. I never thought I'd have to prove my devotion—I was the Archangel Michael, for the Goddess's sake, no one was more devout than me—but Haley was human and had learned angels existed for real. Normal rules no longer applied. We were in new territory and neither of us had any idea of how things were supposed to go.

I drew her to the bed and had her sit down before I shut the door and turned to face her.

"I know you think I'll always be on call, like a doctor or a firefighter, but the magic of prayers and angels doesn't quite work like that." I shrugged out of my cut and tossed it in the closet. "Their prayers are heard and answered, though not always in the way they expect, and I'm rarely required to make a physical appearance."

I removed my shirt next and her gaze riveted to my chest. My cock responded with the kind of salute I'd come to expect when around Haley, and I didn't bother to hide it from her.

"You keep looking at me like that and this explanation will get cut short."

Her gaze jerked to mine. "It's not my fault a hot guy is getting undressed in front of me. What, am I supposed to pretend I'm not interested? Heh, not gonna happen."

I grinned. "I like to hear that."

She snorted. "Doesn't change my interest in your

explanation."

"There's not much else to tell." I shrugged as I unbuttoned my jeans. "When I'm with you, my attention is on you. Only you." I dropped my jeans and let my cock support my statement with emphatic punctuation.

CHAPTER EIGHTEEN

Haley

I'd never get tired of seeing Michael naked. He was perfection in male form. Which made sense given his divine origins. And his cock, standing straight and rigid, only enhanced my natural attraction to him. I wanted to drop to the floor and suck on his impressive flesh, satisfying a need I hadn't known I'd had.

Fortunately, he strode toward me, relieving the need to go to him. But instead of allowing me to do more than take his cock in my hand, he held my shoulders and required me to look up at him.

"I want to make love with you, Haley, because you're the one person I've been looking for in my long life. You asked me earlier how I know and this is how."

He pointed to his left pectoral where a tattoo of a feathered quill stabbed through a heart rested above his nipple. I let my fingers trace the tattoo and he shivered under my touch, his cock flexing in my other hand.

"I only receive tattoos when I've either done something momentous, have accomplished something important for the world, or have encountered someone or something essential for my own growth." He met my gaze without amusement, but serenity filled his eyes. "This represents you, the writer and journalist, who have captured my heart and pinned yourself to it."

I swallowed hard as I traced the lines on his skin with my fingers. "So you didn't get this done?"

He shook his head. "No, it just appeared."

"When?"

"After we had sex the first time, the day after I brought you here."

I stared at the tattoo, studying the elegant swirls of ink marking out the plumed quill and the drop of blood dripping off the barbed end protruding from the stabbed heart. Each line stood out against his skin perfectly in rich detail and the more I looked at them, the more right they felt. I raised my gaze to his again.

"Do you always just accept new ink as a message of importance?" I didn't mean to insert the skepticism into my voice, but I wasn't a journalist for nothing.

He smirked. "Experience in receiving tattoos has taught me a few lessons along the way. And Mom stopped by to remind me of the tattoo's importance."

I swallowed. "Mom?"

"Yes, Mom. You know, the Goddess?"

"*The* Goddess, the deity who watches over everyone. That's your *Mother*?"

He tilted his head as he cupped my face with his hands. "It's a lot to take in, I know, but I'm the Archangel Michael, one of Her sons with a lot of responsibility."

"It sucks being the oldest, doesn't it?" I laughed to keep my nervousness at bay.

I'd fallen in love with an archangel. Probably the most famous archangel, whose mother was the Goddess. Talk about having to make a good impression at Thanksgiving. It wasn't as if I could avoid Her.

"I'm actually not the oldest. Luke's older, but I have

almost as much responsibility as he does." Michael shrugged as if it was the most ordinary thing in the world to talk about archangels and managing miracles.

"Oh, Michael, how is this gonna work? I mean, you're an angel with wings and I'm just a human woman. Are you sure?" I looked into his rich, brown eyes, trying to find understanding as doubts flooded my mind.

"I've never been more sure of anything, Haley." He tugged at my shirt to pull it over my head, exposing my breasts. "I knew you were special the moment I saw you." He set the shirt aside and started on my jeans, his cock bobbing as he worked. "Your kindness, compassion, and love drew me like a moth to a flame. I couldn't look away. I had to learn more about you."

He pushed my jeans and underwear off my hips and drew them away from my feet before standing in front of me. He held my gaze rather than stare at my boobs or my mound, and some of my learned nervousness faded.

"Maybe it was my insatiable curiosity that attracted you." I shivered but I wasn't cold. My pussy flexed with his nearness and arousal flooded my folds.

"You're curiosity isn't the only insatiable thing about you." A sultry smile curled his lips as he leaned forward to kiss my forehead, my cheek, and my neck. "I rarely take advantage of someone's weaknesses, but I cannot resist with you."

He hefted my breasts in his hands, strumming the nipples with his thumbs as he laved my neck and shoulder with his tongue. I closed my eyes and gave myself to his touches, relaxing in the pleasure of his attention. But his hard cock bumped my thigh and reminded me I wanted something more than him pleasuring me.

"I have one request, Michael."

"Anything, love."

He didn't pause in his caresses and he made it difficult to think. But I was determined.

"I want to suck archangel cock before you make love with me."

He pulled back to meet my gaze, his eyebrows raised. "That's not necessary—"

"Oh, but it is." I pushed him toward the bed and made him sit with his legs spread. "I have needs, Michael, and one of them is tasting your cock. I want to feel this hot, hard flesh between my lips. I want to slide my tongue over the head..." I caressed his dick with my fingers to illustrate where I'd put my tongue. "...down the shaft, and over your balls." The shaft flexed in my hand. "I want to take you deep into the back of my throat and swallow you. Think you can handle that?"

I knelt between his legs and looked up at him. He swallowed hard, strain and arousal tightening his features.

"Michael?" I stroked his thighs with feather-light touches, and wondered if his wings would feel the same against my skin. My pussy clenched with arousal at the thought.

"Y-yes, I can handle that."

"Good." I grasped his shaft in one hand and stroked his balls with the other. "Because I'm gonna enjoy this." And I slid the thick head between my lips.

Michael moaned as I licked his cockhead, rubbing my tongue over the edges of the glans. His sweet, spicy flavor hit my taste buds and arousal surged through me. I sipped at the slit in the head, teasing more precum out of him as my fingers caressed his sac.

I'd always liked giving blowjobs to my lovers, but Michael made the experience sublime. He hissed and moaned as I caressed his taut, hard skin, each surge of precum filling my mouth with delicious flavor. I gently raked my teeth over the edge of the glans and he whimpered with pleasure. I held back my grin and licked down the length of his cock.

"Sweet glory, Haley. Your mouth is divine." Michael's

voice had grown rough and he shoved his hands into my hair. "Glory, I could keep my cock in your mouth for hours."

I chuckled and tilted my head, swirling my tongue around his length like an ice cream cone. His fingers tightened in my hair and he thrust his hips, allowing his shaft to slide between my lips. I held the base of his cock with one hand and the other squeezed his scrotum, massaging the balls under the soft skin. Satisfaction filled me. I was giving pleasure to an archangel. Me, an ordinary woman. Excitement built in my chest as I tightened my lips around him.

His moans and thrusts increased in volume and strength, and I reveled in my ability to give him pleasure. I sucked hard on his rigid flesh, savoring the sweet, erotic flavor of his precum in my mouth.

"You have to stop, Haley."

I think I *mmphed* something in surprised outrage because he groaned and petted my head.

"If you keep going like this, I won't be able to hold back."

I snorted. *That's my goal, big boy.* I doubled down on my efforts and renewed my attention on the thick head, rubbing my tongue on the underside. Michael's breath came harder and faster and his hands squeezed into fists in my hair.

"Haley, sweet glory. Haley. Haley!"

His cock stiffened impossibly hard in my mouth and hot, sweet cum slid down my throat. I couldn't get enough and kept sucking on his smooth shaft to get every last drop. He grunted and pumped, holding my head to get the maximum pleasure out of my lips and tongue.

At last he relaxed, dropping onto the bed as his breath sawed in his chest. I pulled off his cock and licked my lips with a satisfied smile. Oh yeah, I'd made him boneless with pleasure and I'd do it again in a heartbeat.

"Are you okay, Michael?"

He lay with his eyes closed as his chest rose and fell with his breath, making the quill stabbed through the heart appear to wave. It took some effort, but he opened his brown eyes and gave me a sultry smirk.

"I'm better than okay, love. But now that you've brought me down with your mighty tongue, I believe I must repay the favor."

He sat up quickly and pulled me on top of him, his hot, hard body cradling my much softer one. He rolled me over until he rested atop me, his groin cradled between my legs, and his cock already hardening again.

"My goodness, you're ready quickly."

"Only for the woman who holds my heart. I will always be ready to pleasure you."

He rubbed his hardening shaft against my mound as he kissed my neck, and my pussy grew wetter than it had been while I sucked him off.

"Oh, I can feel how wet you are on my dick. Do you want me to slide it inside you, Haley?"

"Oh, glory, yes." I grasped his hips and wiggled mine, trying to position the end of his hard dick at my nether lips. "I want your cock so much, Michael."

"Very well, my naughty woman, but we're going to do this slowly and completely. I want you to know who is shagging you slow and deep." He rocked his hips as he continued to kiss down from my collar bones to my breasts. "I'm going to savor your body and the gift of your pleasure as I make love with you, Haley."

The passion and intensity of his words coupled with his kisses on my nipples drove my arousal higher. I gasped as he sucked one taut nub into his mouth and rocked my hips. The tip of his cock dragged between my nether lips, strumming my clit with perfect precision.

"Oh, glory, Michael. I need you so much." It was true. I'd never been so turned on before. "Please make love with me. Please give me your cock."

"Not yet, love. I want to make sure you're good and wet for me." He slid down my body until his shoulders pushed my thighs apart. "I want to taste your lovely quim and savor your cream before I add my own."

Oh, good glory, I'd never thought I'd like a man to talk dirty to me, but every time Michael did, it turned me on more and more. I wriggled my hips in front of his nose and he gave me a dark chuckle.

"My lovely minx, do my naughty words turn you on?"

I whimpered. "Yes."

"Brilliant." He dipped his head and slicked a swath across my nether lips. "I'd love to feast on your hot cream, but I have different plans for you."

He pressed his face to my core and used his thumbs to spread my vulva apart. His tongue painted hot wet lines between my nether lips and delicious sensation flooded through me. I threw back my head and moaned as he sipped on my sensitive flesh with feather-light flicks of his tongue. The teasing caresses made me both want them to go on forever and to immediately become firmer.

"Sweet glory, Michael. I need you. I need your cock inside me."

He hummed against my pussy, amusement and arousal in his tone. "You need my cock, you say? How badly do you need it, Haley? How badly do you want it?"

"I want it so bad. I need you inside me. Please, Michael. Please give me your cock." I'd never begged for a man's dick before in my life, but I'd never wanted anyone's dick as much as I wanted Michael's in that moment.

"Aw, love, when you beg so sweetly, how can I resist?"

He pulled away and crawled back up my body, kissing as he went. When he positioned his cock between my nether lips and met my gaze, he gave me a smile and leaned forward just enough to split my vulva with the smooth head.

"Wait, Michael."

He froze. "What is it, love? Have I hurt you?"

I shook my head and offered him a shy smile. "When you make love with me, show me your wings. I want to see them around us when you fill my pussy."

He tilted his head a moment, considering me with his brown eyes, his lips curled in a half smile. "You mean, like this?"

His wings came into view as he slowly pushed his dick into my tight pussy, and wonder hit my mind. The pleasure of his thick, smooth shaft filling my core mixed with the beauty of those silver-black wings draped around us and I was lost.

"Is this what you wanted, Haley?"

"Glory, you're so beautiful and you feel so good." I wrapped my legs around his thighs and squeezed my inner muscles on his shaft. "You're making all my fantasies come true."

"Oh, yes?" He slowly pulled out and pushed back in with a long smooth glide. "Tell me your fantasies, Haley." His voice sounded even but as I squeezed my pussy again, he groaned and shivered though he didn't change his pace. "Your quim is so hot and tight. But you're not getting out of telling me your fantasies."

"I had a fantasy of being fucked by an angel with his wings around us." My words ended on a moan as he pulled his cock out and stroked my clit. "Oh glory."

He smiled as he thrust in long, measured strokes, filling my pussy completely with his hard flesh. I squeezed him again, but he didn't change his rhythm, inexorably driving my arousal and need higher.

"I'm happy to shag you, love. But I won't be rushed." He grinned as I flexed my inner muscles. "I promised slow and deep, and I always deliver on my promises."

I gasped and whimpered as he made love to me, his arms cradling my head as he stared into my eyes. I couldn't look away, drawn to the love, serenity, and desire in his gaze. My heart opened for the first time since I connected with Jeff, and I realized Michael was as much my One-and-Only as I was his.

"I love you, Michael." I didn't know where the words came from, but I meant them from the bottom of my heart.

"Do you, now?" He lost his smile. "You know that you're my One-and-Only, don't you?"

"Yeah, and you're mine." I squeezed my pussy again and this time he lost his amusement. "I need you, Michael. I need you so much."

"Then you shall have me."

I expected him to thrust into me hard and fast, but he set his jaw and kept up his slow, hypnotic, deep rhythm. My arousal kept building like a tsunami, relentless and powerful. My nipples hardened against his inked chest and I rocked my hips to get more friction on my clit. His eyes blazed with the same light I saw at the warehouse, but instead of being frightening, the light seared me in warmth, comfort, and welcome. I fell into it and into the best orgasm I'd ever experienced.

"Oh, Michael, yeessssss!"

He grunted and stiffened above me as we both toppled over the precipice of ecstasy and flew into the cosmos of pleasure. My heart shot out with my mind and opened in a swirl of brilliant light. For just a moment, I could see the future – a long, strong relationship, with love, friendship, children, and family. We'd grow old together, though how that worked with his angelic disposition I didn't know, and I'd be his forever.

Then everything faded back into the moment and I realized he'd rolled onto his side to keep from crushing me. But his cock remained in my pussy's tight grip and I really didn't mind.

For a few moments we lay together in silence, feeling the love and physical pleasure coursing between us. I could almost sense his satisfaction and contentment with our lovemaking.

Correction: I can actually *feel his satisfaction and contentment.*

It was true. Instead of assuming or inferring Michael's pleasure, it ricocheted through me like an echo of my own – a masculine echo with a decent dose of swaggering pride. An "aw yeah, look at me. I made her happy" sort of emotion.

Holy shit! Amazement and amusement cascaded through me like the fall of multicolored hair, the strands of each intermingling. On the one hand, his satisfaction made me laugh because he wasn't wrong. But on the other, how the hell could I *feel* his emotions?

"That answer is simple, love."

"What? What answer?"

"To your question." He nuzzled my neck below my jaw.

I blinked. "Can you read minds now?"

He snorted softly. "I always could do that if I chose. But now, with you, some of your thoughts are very loud. Or rather, very emphatic. You can feel my emotions because we're bound as fated mates, as I felt the first time I saw you."

"From the first time, at the shelter."

"Yes."

"Even though we never spoke and I didn't see you.

He chuckled. "Yes, even so."

I sighed and laughed a little in disbelief. "I really am living in a paranormal romance novel."

He rumbled another sound of amusement. "Would you wish it any different?"

"Nooooo. I like right where I am."

I wriggled and tightened my pussy muscles around him

again. He groaned and thrust his hips a little in response, and I sighed happily. I could have easily stayed there forever and not thought about the world outside his little cabin. But there were two things I'd have to do once the euphoria wore off.

First, I'd have to get my story straight about Backlog, the Concrete Angels, and the deaths of the federal agents who'd come before.

And second, I'd have to tell Jeff about who Michael and Samurai really were.

"Michael?"

"Hmm, yes love?" He'd snuggled me closer to his chest and draped a wing over me. It was sexy as hell.

"I'll have to tell Jeff who you really are."

Time and sound stopped in that moment. I swore he stopped breathing and the world held completely still.

"You can't, Haley. You signed a contract."

I nodded. "I know. But he's my only family. And he's starting to get interested in Samurai. He needs to know why I'm suddenly going freelance and moving in with you, sequestered from everyone."

"You're not sequestered from everyone. You'll be free to come and go as you please. You must take this seriously, Haley. That contract is inviolable."

I nodded again. "I know, but Loki said I could tell one trusted family member, and that's Jeff. That was in the contract, too."

Michael sighed. "Just remember, you're putting him in danger by telling him. If he chooses to say anything, Loki could take action against him. Think long and hard before you decide to let Jeff in on our secrets." He wrapped his arms tighter around me and nuzzled my neck again. "And no matter what you decide, I will always have your back, even in opposition to Loki."

I raised up on one elbow to look down on him. "Seriously? Didn't you sign some sort of loyalty contract?"

He smiled up at me. "I did. But I had stipulations as well, and one of those was understanding that should I choose someone for my heart, he or she would be my top priority. Even against the club."

My jaw dropped. "Did you know you would meet me when you joined the Concrete Angels?"

"Oh, I had no idea when or where I'd meet the one who filled my heart. But it seemed like a wise precaution when dealing with someone like the Norse god of Mischief."

I laughed at his smug smirk. "You wily angel. You gave yourself an out."

"Bloody right, I did. One has to when one deals with Loki."

"Ain't that the truth." I chuckled as I settled back down into Michael's arms. "And that should tell you all you need to know about the Concrete Angels Motorcycle Club."

"Actually, I need you to know one other thing, Haley."

"What's that?" I opened my eyes and met his gaze.

"That I love you. You have won my heart and that's a feat that rarely happens." He stroked my face with his hand. "I've known love, but nothing like what I feel for you. I didn't think it was possible to feel this much love. But it's clear I can."

I gave him a tremulous smile as he leaned down to brush his lips across mine. "How about I show you what other kinds of love you can feel?"

"Well that sounds like a challenge. What do you have in mind?"

I grinned as I rolled over on top of him, straddling his hardening cock. "You're a biker. How 'bout you give your woman a ride?"

"It would be my absolute pleasure." He slid into my slick sheath balls-deep and sighed. "Let's ride."

"Hell yeah."

CHAPTER NINETEEN

Haley

I parked my Subaru outside the rest stop and waited a few moments as I took a look around. Nothing moved except the grasses in the field beyond the parking area and a pair of abandoned shoes tied by the laces to the cross tree of a sign post. They weren't even a matched pair. Another car sat a few spaces from mine but the driver must have already been in the building.

It's gonna be okay. It had been my mantra for the last month since I'd signed the contract with the Concrete Angels. But it had taken me that long to find the courage to tell my cousin about it.

Jeff hadn't arrived yet and I had to pee, so I pushed out of my car and headed for the doors. The cold wind knifed through my jacket and scarf, and I shivered. It might have been sunny outside, but the heat didn't start until at least April, and we were in the middle of March.

I pushed through the doors and hurried to the bathroom, hoping Jeff wouldn't be long. I should've probably kept him in the dark about the Concrete Angels and just how inhuman they were, but he'd come to know them and trust them, and that was a lot for Jeff.

I finished in the bathroom but stayed in the foyer of the rest stop. I couldn't quite face the wind again. I scanned the parking lot and found Jeff just pulling in, his bright red SUV appearing like brilliant poppy in a sea of brown grass. He'd thought I was nuts to meet at a rest stop, but most folks wouldn't travel at this time of year. *Less likely to be listeners.*

And glory knew, the story I had to tell would recommend me for the Arkham Asylum.

You only end up in Arkham if you're insane.

The definition of insanity was doing the same thing over and over and expecting a different result. But this time, it pertained to something so different, so completely outside mainstream thinking that folks might just come to the same conclusion. I hoped Jeff knew me well enough to know I wouldn't be having him on. Not about this.

I tucked my hands under my armpits as I watched Jeff park. The other people who'd been there when I arrived had returned to their car and drove out ahead of him. The sun glinted off his hood, blinding me for a moment, and I swore I saw a flash of Michael sitting on his bike just at the edge of my view. But I blinked, and when I looked again, only Jeff remained in the parking lot.

You're imagining Michael 'cause you're scared to face Jeff.

Correction, I was scared I'd lose Jeff when I told him about the Concrete Angels.

He pushed into the open foyer and waved, his expression worried. I'd been cryptic when I called him and he probably feared the worst. *He's not wrong.*

"Hey, Jeff. Thanks for coming." He wrapped me in a hug and I closed my eyes, taking what comfort I could.

"Not a problem. What was so urgent that we had to meet at a random rest stop?" He pushed me back and scanned my face.

I was struck at how beautiful he was with clear light-brown eyes, golden brown skin, dark hair and full lips thanks to his mixed race heritage. He stood a good six inches taller than me with a sleek, athletic frame and shoulders slightly broader than mine. We could've been siblings as we shared the same eye shape and wide mouth, and as far as I was concerned, we were.

"I gotta tell you something and you have to hear me out before you label me as crazy or insane or off my rocker, okay?" I led him over to one of the picnic tables they'd installed inside to allow travelers shelter from the wind. I sat down facing the door to keep an eye on people coming in and waited for him to join me.

Jeff raised his eyebrow but settled at the table across from me. "What's going on, Haley? First you want to drive out here to this random rest stop. Does this have to do with the Concrete Angels? You already know I thought you were crazy for spending time with them."

"Yeah, you did until you met Sam and Talon, and now you love them."

Jeff blushed and glanced out the windows at the parking lot. "Love is a strong word."

I opened my mouth to ask more about that, but I was only stalling and pulled my curiosity back under control.

"Okay, this is something so big and so out there that I need you to promise me you'll tell no one. Not even family or lovers."

He snorted. "I don't talk to family since they disowned me and I don't have a lover." But his voice suggested there was a 'yet' at the end of his sentence.

Focus.

"Jeff, I need you to promise you'll tell no one."

He tilted his head and the humor left his face. "Okay, okay. I promise. What is it?"

I gathered my courage with a sigh. How did I present the news that people around us weren't human? Even thinking it made me question my own sanity and I'd *seen* Torch shift into a real, fire-breathing, winged dragon. And Sam had turned into a giant fox.

"Just spit it out, Haley."

"The bikers of the Concrete Angels MC aren't human." I bit my lip after the words came out in a rush.

"What?"

Oh, glory, he's gonna make me say it again.

"They aren't human."

He snorted. "What, are you saying they're aliens?" He smirked, but I shook my head as my heart sank. He wouldn't believe me.

"No, not aliens. Not like from outer space. They're inhuman, other, mythical even."

He looked at me like he was waiting for the other shoe to drop. When I didn't grin or laugh, he frowned.

"You're being serious."

"Yes. Very serious. Why do you think I had you meet me way the hell out here to talk about this?" I threw my hands out. "They're not all human."

"How do you know they're 'not all human'? They told you?"

I shook my head. "They didn't have to. I saw them when they threw off their human disguises."

"Oh, come on, Haley." Jeff rose to his feet and paced to the window. "Human disguises? We aren't in some sci-fi flick or a fantasy story. This is real life. Mythical creatures don't exist."

Little did he know. I didn't say anything. What if I'd made a mistake telling him? I had my reasons for doing so, but if he wouldn't believe me, I'd wasted the effort to bring him into the new world I'd discovered. I rubbed my chin and studied the little flecks in the plastic table.

"Think of it as New Year's Evolution."

"What?" He turned to stare at me.

"New Year's Evolution – a shift in the year matching a

growth in understanding." That sounded wise and pithy, right?

"But it's March, not even close to New Year's."

I shrugged. "The time frame isn't important. This is a new year, a new beginning and a whole new understanding for us. It's evolution of perspective and like it or not, we can't go back to not knowing."

I stopped talking and waited to see what Jeff would say. It was a lot to take in, and it totally destroyed what we thought we knew of the Concrete Angels Biker Club. *Well, normal biker clubs.*

"Why are you telling me this?" He sat back, his mouth drawn tight.

I shrugged, trying to dispel my unease. "I know you liked Samurai and Talon, and they treated you with respect and kindness." I shrugged again. "I wanted you to know what you'd be getting into if you kept up with them. And I didn't want to hide this from you. I, uh, accepted a position as their in-house PR writer."

"You're quitting the Bugle?" He blinked.

"Not exactly. I'm going freelance as an investigative reporter." At least, I would be as soon as I got this conversation over with. "Look, I probably shouldn't have told you about the bikers, but you're my family. The only one I have left that I can trust, and it's a secret I didn't want to carry alone."

Jeff bit his lip and raised his gaze to mine. "You shouldn't have told me. What if I was too scared to accept it?"

"Are you?" My voice sharpened.

He grimaced and gave a one-shouldered shrug, his gaze sliding away. "I don't know. They've been really nice to me, and I do like Sam and Talon. But what you're telling me is so fantastic and out there, y'know? How can you be sure they aren't fucking with you?"

I sighed and glanced out the windows of the rest stop,

glad the cold, windy weather kept most people inside their cars. "I've seen them do their thing, Jeff. I can't tell you everything because it's not my story, but believe me, they're not human. Or at least some of them aren't. Didn't Loki give you the heebie-jeebies?"

Jeff shivered. "Yeah, he's scary."

I didn't tell him the half of it. If he knew the Norse God of Mischief was hanging out in Fort Collins, he might shit himself. Hell, I was still spooked at the idea and he'd made me sign a contract about exposing them. In blood.

"Yeah, so, you gotta keep this to yourself if you want to keep in contact with them and me."

His gaze snapped to mine. "What do you mean 'and you?' Is this now some sort of secret cult?"

In some ways, it kinda was. But only because humans were destructive toward anything different. Hell, we couldn't even handle humans with different skin color, sexual orientation or gender equality without violence. Glory knew what we'd do with other species.

"No, it's about safety. Remember when we were growing up, we always wanted the dragons and unicorns and gryphons to be real?" He nodded. "Surprise, they are real, but they have to hide because humans suck."

"You are human. We both are."

"And I work for the newspaper. I get to see the worst of our species, all for the love of money and power."

"That's because it's all y'all concentrate on." Jeff glared at me. "If it bleeds, it leads, remember?"

I sighed. "Yeah, I do. Better than most. Which is why protecting these people is important to me, and not just because my life's at stake."

"What?" Jeff's eyes widened. "Did they threaten you?"

"No, nothing like that. They made me sign a contract." I didn't tell him the consequence of breaking said contract was probably my death or worse.

He took a breath, but snapped his mouth shut and

narrowed his eyes. "What does your famous gut have to say about this?"

"It says this is the right thing to do. Michael is the love of my life and he's worth this kind of effort." I couldn't get more honest than that.

Of course, I wasn't about to tell Jeff that Michael was the Archangel Michael and his older brother Luke was a far more famous fallen angel folks were meant to revile. *And forget about mentioning Sam's foxy self.* Besides, I liked Luke, and who could say they'd hung out with the Devil and actually had a good time? Jeff would learn who everyone was soon enough. Or I'd have to cut him off to protect everyone, including him.

"I don't know if I can handle this."

I sighed. "What else do you want me to say? They're people, just like humans. They just have some skill sets we don't."

"Like breathing fire?"

I remembered Torch's breath and Michael's flaming sword. "Yeah, like that."

"This is insane, Haley."

"Why? Because they're more effective at hiding who they truly are than everyone else? Hell, I bet they've perpetuated the idea that they're myths just to keep us dumb humans from finding out the truth." I shook my head and let my gaze fall on the day outside. The clouds had rolled in with the wind and hidden the sun.

"Look, Jeff. You're my family and I wanted you to know that I'm going ahead with my relationship with Michael. He's worth every effort on my part, even if he's not human."

"Wait, *Michael's* not human?" Jeff looked like he'd swallowed too much peanut butter. "What is he, then?"

I grimaced. "I had to sign a contract, Jeff, to protect their secrets. I can't tell you if you can't handle this. You're family, but if it's too much, I at least wanted you to know why I'd have to cut you off. It's for your protection as much as for theirs."

Glory, it curdled my stomach to say that. But I'd chosen Michael and Luke, Calhoun, Viper, Attila, Torch, Sam, Talon, Nightingale, hell, even Loki and the Scooters. They'd be my new family and considering how many weren't completely human, that was a powerful family to have.

"You'd really cut me off?" He looked wounded and my heart bled for him, but I nodded.

"Their secrets are that powerful and they're worth it to me to keep them, contract or no." I bit my lip and took a deep breath. "I love you, Jeff, but what's it gonna be?"

This was it. He could choose whatever he wanted, but I'd have to make good on my statement and I really didn't want to lose him. He was just as important to me as Michael and the Concrete Angels. But I'd given my word to keep their secrets and I wouldn't go back on it even if it was inconvenient.

"I can't believe you'd choose them over me, after all we've been through together."

I nodded. "It doesn't have to be that way, you know. All you have to do is keep their secret." I rubbed my chin and took a chance. "And considering how you feel about Sam, I'd think it'd be something you'd choose to do, too."

"What the hell does that mean?"

Jeff's voice sounded a little panicky and I gave him a one-shouldered shrug.

"I'm a reporter, and a pretty damn good one. I notice things. You've opened up and relaxed around him, smiled and laughed more. Don't think I haven't noticed."

"He's a friend."

I nodded again. "I know. Someone you trust and like and respect. The thing is, if you want more time with him, you're going to have to make this decision." I straightened my shoulders. "Think of it this way. You can either get a whole new family of people who might not be what you expect but still accept you as you are. Or you can lose the only family you have left, including Sam and the others. That's what it boils down to."

Jeff didn't say anything and I figured I'd said all I could. It was time to head out. I had other people to disappoint. Of course, they were bad guys and I was looking forward to it, but I couldn't stay there.

"Just think about it and text or call me with your decision." I wanted to give him a hug, but I didn't think he'd welcome the touch, though he'd allow it. "No matter what, I love you. Take care, Jeff."

I gave him a pained smile and walked away. It just about broke my heart. He was the only one who knew my past and cared. We'd shared so much, but the past was only memories and I couldn't live there. I'd made my choice and I wanted Michael as he was, even if it meant losing Jeff.

I took a deep breath and squared my shoulders as I stepped out into the windy, gray day. I would be strong and I could do this. At least, that was what I told myself. *Fake it till you make it.* The words were easier thought than put into practice.

I climbed into my car and wiped my tears away before I started the engine. I was moving into the compound and I needed to pack up the last of my things. My lease ended at the end of the month and I just needed to finish cleaning and turn in the keys.

"It's gonna be okay."

I tried to listen to my famous gut, but my mind got in the way and garbled the message. I backed out of my parking space and headed for the freeway entrance, refusing to look back. This was my decision and I'd made it. Hell, I'd exposed a national shadow group infiltrating law enforcement. I could deal with my cousin taking his time to absorb this information.

I took a deep breath and blew it out. "It's gonna be

okay."

I kept telling myself that all the way back to Fort Collins.

CHAPTER TWENTY

Michael

I told Jeff about the club. I think he's convinced
I'm on drugs or crazy, or both.

Haley's text came in as we cleaned up after the annual
St. Patrick's Day Parade in Fort Collins. We always rode
the parade, our bikes decked out in green streamers and
saddle bags. She'd taken her time to tell her cousin until
after her story on the Assistant District Attorneys
O'Donnell and Mitchem came to light. Her good friend and
mentor Ryan Sutton had helped her break the story, and she
became the hottest investigative reporter in the Rocky
Mountain region.

She'd been so in-demand, she'd had to make a false
profile with a new photo that looked nothing like her, a new
name, Nicole Chatman, and a PO box for an address. Her
email led to a blind and hidden server, her phone number
remained unlisted, and her electronic footprint sat hidden
behind multiple firewalls. I understood little of it except
that it kept her safer than she'd been when only writing
fluff pieces.

She continued to write a few of those under her real

name—art shows, children feeding the ducks at the park, the latest outdoor fashions for the discerning hiker—but overall, her focus remained investigating more of Backlog and where their tendrils led. I worried about her getting caught, but Neo assured me he'd taken extra precautions when it came to her online persona.

What did he say? I tried not to be too nosy, but I was curious at Jeff's reaction. He'd always struck me as rather down-to-earth with everything.

This particular information might be too fantastical.

"Damn, you fuckin' have to see this!" Trigger came running in with a tablet showing the evening news and the story breaking across the airwaves. "That's our girl. Or maybe I should say, Michael's girl, rockin' the world to its core."

"She's not a girl, Trigger. She's all woman." I shot him an enigmatic smile as the others around me raised their green beers. "She also a badass investigative reporter who can find out just about anything."

"Holy shit." Eric gaped as he stared at the tablet, shaking his head. "She totally exposed the corruption in the local FBI and Marshals' offices. You know that's gonna make her a target, right?"

I nodded. "It would, except the woman on the article who did the research was blond and named Nicole Chatman. She has a friend who has contacts at CNN, MSN, CNBC, BBC, ABC, CBS, NBC, and far more acronyms than I can remember." I shot a look toward the current dark big screen against the wall. "Each one has their headline story about the mysterious group infiltrating law enforcement and how the current and former ADAs were part of it. It was brilliant."

Eric sat back in his chair and wrapped his arm around Karma's waist. "This is going to be a total shitstorm." Then he frowned. "Won't they be able to find her?"

I smiled. "No. She technically doesn't exist. She was at

the news conference as a member of the Fort Collins Bugle, but she was just another staff reporter in the crowd . She walked right out the front doors and no one knew she was the one to break the story." I nodded to Gadget. "Thanks for the prosthetics for the online profile. They totally changed her face."

Gadget nodded and raised her glass of port. "Anything for a good cause." The Basque woman winked and sipped.

"Where is Haley now?" Calhoun swiped a corn chip out from under Friar's watchful eyes.

"Oy!" He grabbed his plate and moved it out of her reach.

"You snooze, you lose, Friar." She winked.

I laughed. "Haley's out talking to her cousin about her change in address. They should be along soonly."

"Soonly?" Gopher blinked owlishly. "Who the hell says 'soonly'?"

I shrugged and lifted my green pint. I'd learned the phrase from the woman who held my heart. I just had to convince her that Jeff would come around. Because he would. I could sense that in my gut. Mom had plans for both Jeff and Samurai, but it would be a helluva ride getting to the finish line. Luke and Loki would have a field day.

I hoped Haley would come home soon, but I knew she had to talk to her best friend about the changes to her work environment. Not only did Loki have requirements, but I had a sense that something big was coming. Something big enough for her to need some protection, but not necessarily from Backlog. Unfortunately, the message was frustratingly vague, and I could only give her unclear warnings. I'd sent Torch to follow her at a discreet distance to be sure no one interfered with her errands, but I wouldn't settle until she came home.

He didn't really say anything other than he was amazed I'd cut him off if he couldn't keep the secrets about the Concrete Angels.

I could feel the sadness in her words, but their survival depended on both she and Jeff keeping mum on the distinct inhumanity of the club members.

He'll come around. Just give him time. It's a lot to take in as you well know.

Her text came back faster than I expected.

Yeah, I know. I just don't like being at odds with Jeff. I should be home in 40 mins.

Home. She'd used the word as if she meant to stay. *Glory, I hope so.* She was bound by Loki's contract to reside in the compound, but she still had an apartment in Fort Collins with a few items left in it. She could decide it wasn't worth the trouble to break with her cousin and move in with me.

The unease made me set aside my beer and roll to my feet.

"Where are you going?" Scott raised his eyebrows as Numbers handed him a soft pretzel Grub had just made. "Things are just gettin' started here."

I shook my head. "Got shit to do. Haley will be back soon and I promised her tea."

He narrowed his eyes. "Is that another way of saying sex?"

"Scott!" Numbers thumped him while the others chuckled.

"What? It's a legit question. The Brits have some of the weirdest names for shit. Like "knackered" for tired, and "wheelie bin" for trash can. I was just adding to my translation guide."

I wasn't going to dignify that with a response as I left the clubhouse and headed for my cabin. Haley needed a home, a place where she felt safe and supported, and there were still a couple of things I needed to do to make that a reality.

Years ago when we remodeled this old 1950s era

motel, I'd requested my room have an extra space built into it. Not a full room, but an alcove that could be closed off with a Japanese rice paper screen or folding door. I'd opted for the screen with cherry blossoms painted across the panels. I'd set up a desk, rolling chair, bookshelf and filing cabinet in the space to give Haley her own office. I waited for the big reveal. I hoped it would take away some of the sting about Jeff's lack of enthusiasm.

And tea, too, of course.

The tea was hot and the room was ready by the time she drove into the compound and parked beside Eric's sexy peacock green Chevy Corvette. Nervousness and excitement warred for my attention as I waited for Haley to come to the door. Would she like the gift of her own office space?

I had the door open as soon as she knocked and a big smile of welcome that wilted a little at the look of tired resignation on her face. She carried a bin of cleaning supplies and a broom, and set all of it down with a long sigh.

"Welcome home, love. Would you like some tea?"

She gave a tired laugh. "Yeah, because tea makes everything better, right?"

I nodded thoughtfully as I offered her a mug of Jasmine Phoenix. "That, and good sex, but we can do that after you've rested."

That got a louder, happier laugh out of her. "Oh, well, if you insist." She hung her jacket in the closet and took the mug. "Thank you."

"I know it's been a trying day, but I have a surprise for you whenever you're ready."

She sipped her tea. "A surprise? Please don't let it be like Jeff's reaction. I don't think I can handle that kind of surprise at this point."

"I promise not to take the piss out of you, love. This is a good surprise." I offered her my hand. "Come with me."

"Come with you? Where is there to go?" She followed my lead and stopped at the rice paper screen. "What's this?"

"This is your new office." I folded the screen up and showed her the space.

"Are you kidding me right now? This has been here the whole time and I've never noticed it? How is that possible?" She set her mug down on the bookshelf beside the alcove and stepped into the space. "Wow, it looks a lot like the one at the apartment. When did you do this?"

I shrugged as warm pleasure filled my chest. "While you were cleaning your apartment and packing up. I wanted it to be a surprise for when you fully moved in."

"Wow." She turned around to run her hands over the desk with her new laptop and external hard drive. "It's perfect."

"Neo has made sure there's a dedicated server and IP address so you can connect to the 'net but no one can follow you back to our system." I waved at the little blinking contraption on the shelf. "I don't really know how it works, but Neo assures me it'll do." I rubbed the back of my neck. "Do you like it?"

Haley threw herself into my arms with a huge grin. "I love it. A much better surprise than I had earlier today. Thank you so much, Michael."

"So, this is a good reason to stay, right?

She grinned as she wrapped her arms around my neck. "Yes, it's a great reason to stay, though not the primary one."

"I love you, Haley. Never doubt that."

"I definitely won't. I love you, too. Especially when you fuck me while showing your wings." She shivered with exaggerated pleasure. "That shit is sexy as hell."

"I think you mean sexy as heaven. Hell is my brother's thing." I pulled back and tilted my head with a raised eyebrow. "Unless there's something I should know?"

She laughed. "While a threesome is great in the romance novels, I don't think I want to be that intimate with your brother. I'm all yours, forever."

"Good answer." I dipped my head and took her lips in a deep kiss to put a seal on it. She was definitely mine and I was hers. Forever.

EPILOGUE

Samurai

I always prided myself on being cool, inscrutable, aloof. My Asian ancestry helped with it. Most of the gaijin around me couldn't figure me out, and that was preferable. Kitsune weren't common anymore after the loss of the Japanese dynastic regimes, but we were even less common in the New World, and being alone and aloof helped keep my heart safe.

That crumbled the moment I met Jeff Holliday in Nightingale's infirmary, the aloofness went out the window. Just a few moments talking to him, and I hadn't been able to walk away.

I'm so fucking screwed.

My fellow club members seemed to be finding love and companionship around me like it was all the rage. First Scott with Oriana, then Karma with Eric, and Michael with Haley. Even Attila seemed to be romantically restless.

Things are going south fast.

I'd never felt romantic inclinations for anyone in my long life and I hadn't been about to start.

Until Jeff. Who'd been avoiding the compound for the

last two months.

Haley looked the way I felt; sad, anxious, and out of sorts. Oh, sure, she still got excited when she figured out something new about the Backlog story and she appeared content with Michael's love. Who wouldn't want an archangel's undivided attention? But I could scent her wistfulness and it mirrored my own.

Which is all kinds of wrong.

I tried to throw off my malaise and focus on my jobs of managing the club's strip joints in Fort Collins and Wellington. But whenever I saw a young, hot male dancer, I'd remember Jeff's perfect golden-brown skin and tall, taut athletic body, and my cock would stand up to attention. Unfortunately, some of the dancers thought I was reacting to them, but the moment they offered me their bodies, my dick would wilt.

Not a great way to inspire my employees.

I'd heard Haley's conversation with Jeff about our club's secrets hadn't gone well, but Jeff had given me his cell number while he'd helped her research her story three months ago. I'd told him it was just in case he couldn't get a hold of Haley, he could contact me to get through the gates. But in truth I just wanted his number to text and call him.

And for the first month, it had been great. We'd shared funny memes and small talk, building an unlikely friendship through digital communication.

Then Haley told Jeff he had to choose to keep our secrets or lose her forever.

And he stopped answering my calls or texts.

I'd taken to wandering the edges of the compound, looking outside the walls for something, and I didn't know what I wanted to find. But something was definitely missing.

Yeah, you brainless kit, love, companionship, and intimacy.

I ignored my inner smartass fox and kept up my circuit around the compound in an effort to outrun the truth. I'd never been lonely before. Why the hell was I feeling such a disappointing emotion?

Fortunately, a commotion near the front gate of the compound distracted me from my inner turmoil, and I gratefully turned my attention outward as a familiar figure strode into the yard. I immediately left my perch on the hillside in an effort to meet the man who'd somehow captured all of my attention. But I stopped before I made a spectacle of myself. I thought my heart would explode and tears started in my eyes as Jeff walked into the yard and Haley came to meet him.

I swallowed a growl of envy as I inhaled the scent of him. He reminded me of delicate cherry blossoms of my homeland with the deep strength and depth of the gnarled trees that grew on mountain slopes. He had a thick shell around his tender heart and I couldn't stop the need to figure out the puzzle of him.

I blamed the fox in me.

Jeff hugged his cousin and the scent of her relief matched my own. Haley had broken the news to Jeff that the Concrete Angels weren't all human and he'd have to make the decision to join us in keeping our secrets or let us all go, including her. I'd felt his silence harder than I'd expected for only knowing him a month.

Jeff stood back and kissed Haley on the forehead before his gaze slid away to find mine. Those amber brown eyes, so much like a fox's, hit me like a two-by-four to the chest and I grunted with the physical impact of our connection.

You know what this means.

I ignored the voice and inclined my head deeply to show my love and respect for my beautiful and precious kit.

And he's definitely mine.

I shoved the thought away, because if I acknowledged it, I'd be bound to Jeff forever. Once a kitsune found his favorite, there was no going back. I didn't think Jeff was ready for that. Hell, *I* wasn't ready for that.

I made myself wait for him to approach, hiding behind my perfect, stoic mask.

"Hey, Sam. How's it goin'?" Jeff stood back, dipping his head and looking to the side as if afraid to meet my eyes this close.

"Better. You haven't answered my calls or texts." I couldn't help the censure in my voice. The pain of his silence still stung my heart.

He grimaced and rubbed the back of his neck. "Yeah, I'm sorry about that. I, uh, had a lot to think about."

I tilted my head, but didn't say anything.

He shot a look around at the people still in the yard staring at him. "Could we, uh, go somewhere a little more private to talk, maybe?"

I let him sweat a few more moments before I gave him a sharp nod and turned on my heel and headed back for the hills. To my cabin with the little serenity garden and a sacred cherry tree grown from the seeds of my great grandmother's grove back in Japan. I never brought anyone to my cabin, not even the honeys who stuck around the club specifically for sex. Jeff would be the first. I just hoped my decision wouldn't bite me in the ass.

The End

MY FOREVER COCKY BIKER ENCOUNTER
CONCRETE ANGELS MC, BOOK 1
SNEEK PEEK

Leather, Lies, and Larceny...Forensic Accounting was never so sexy!

Oriana Hunter

I don't trust many people. Most especially, the bikers from the Concrete Angels Motorcycle Club. When I'm abducted by my "best friend" to come work for them as a forensic accountant, I pretty much have zero choice. They're not the typical biker club. And some of their members make my hair stand on end. Hey, I got them to sign a contract, and it comes with dental. All I have to do is find out who's embezzling from them and I can go home. It would go a lot faster if I didn't have a sexy cocky biker hanging around. I have far too many personal demons, and then I start seeing angels. Literally. The question is which folks are more scary, those wearing the Concrete Angels' cuts or the FBI jackets?

Scott Free

Oriana Hunter is the most beautiful and dangerous woman I've ever seen walk through the gates of the Concrete Angels' compound. She's badass, through and through. I don't believe in mates-for-life, but Oriana makes me want to give it a try. But she doesn't trust anyone, me especially, and I can recognize the signs of someone dealing with PTSD from my time in the Army. Turns out, she's a former FBI agent and has major trust issues. Not that I blame her. With Loki at the helm and his habit of making people squirm, I wouldn't trust us either. I know she'll figure out our money leak, and quickly. Which means I'm popping the clutch and going in full throttle to prove I'm not what she thinks. And that she's safer with me.

DUDE WITH A COOL CAR
CONCRETE ANGELS MC, BOOK 2
SNEEK PEEK

Bikers, Badge, and Backlog: Marshal DeVille always gets his man…and his Karma.

Cooper DeVille, US Marshal

Being undercover has its perks. I get to do stuff the day-to-day me would never experience. Like infiltrating the Concrete Angels Motorcycle Club and meeting Karma, the gorgeous Enforcer of the MC. Being handcuffed to her bed is a dream, but that's the problem with undercover work. Everything I'm doing here is only half true. The Concrete Angels—and Karma—are connected to Backlog, a shadow organization infiltrating law enforcement. The Fed undercover here before me was Backlog's bitch, and now he's dead. I have to determine which side of this fight the Concrete Angels are on… before Karma comes to bite me in ways I won't enjoy.

Karma, Concrete Angels' Enforcer

You bet your ass, I'm that karma, the one people pray never catches up to them. But my own karma has found me, seeing as the hunky P.I. who drove into the MC compound with his cool car is my Goddess-chosen true mate. But as my luck—and the Goddess' sense of humor—would have it, Cooper's an undercover US Marshal trying to ferret out our connection to a group called Backlog. Would've been nice to know before I took him to bed and discovered he's the best damn submissive this Madam could want, because I don't deal well with liars. And no one's happy when Karma's pissed. But Backlog has Cooper in its sights, and to survive… my mate might just have to die.

OTHER BOOKS BY SIOBHAN MUIR

Her Devoted Vampire
Queen Bitch of the Callowwood Pack
Second Chance Succubus
Darwin's Evolution
Wildfire's Heart

Bad Boys of Beta Squad Series
Bronco's Rough Ride
The Navy's Ghost
Rimshot's Hard Target
Bam-Bam's Inked Hart
Deli's Take Out

Cloudburst Colorado Series
A Hell Hound's Fire
The Beltane Witch
Christmas I.C.E. Magic
Cloudburst Ice Magic
Cloudburst Coffee & Spa
Courting the Dragon Widow

Concrete Angels MC Series
My Forever Cocky Biker Encounter
Dude With a Cool Car
Angel Ink

Rifts Series
Take the Reins
A Centaur's Solstice Wish

In Death's Shadow

The Ivory Road
A Walk in the Sand
Outback Dreams

Triple Star Ranch Series
Rope a Falling Star
Star Light, Star Bright
Star Spangled Banner

Warbler Peninsula Series
Order of the Dragon
The Valkyrie's Sword
Burning Yuletide

Coming Soon
The Concrete Angel (Concrete Angels MC novella)
A Dance Between Worlds (The Ivory Road Serial #3)
The Samhain Soldier (Cloudburst Colorado #7)